THE DELPHI TECHNIQUE

JC RYAN

BOOKS

By JC Ryan

Rex Dalton K9 Thrillers

The Fulcrum

The Power of Three

Unchained

Sideswiped

The Inca Con

The French Girl

Duty of Care

Donna Teresa

Under the Pope's Windows

The Shanghai Strain

The Delphi Technique

Holes in the Wall

The Abyss

Unearthed

Remorseless

The Message

Dedicated to my good friend Mitch Pender, a military dog trainer, for giving me the idea for this series and guiding me through the intricate and amazing capabilities and psychology of those majestic four-legged soldiers.

Mitch has a lifetime of experience and an exceptional depth of knowledge as a military dog handler and trainer.

Vinci Books

vinci-books.com

Published by Vinci Books Ltd in 2025

1

We see people in the Middle East begin to have dreams of a new Ottoman Empire where everyone will be subjected to some of what we've seen happen in those countries where we helped bring about an Arab Spring that's turned into a Winter Nightmare.

—Louie Gohmert

About The Delphi Technique

Rex, Catia, and Digger are on Rhodes Island, Greece, when an assassin kills two people right in front of their eyes.

They jump into action to help. The assassin flees, but Rex and Digger give chase, and when they catch up with her, she commits suicide.

Back at their hotel, while busy reporting the incident to John Brandt, three masked men storm into their room with guns blazing.

The trio is drawn into a CIA operation to uncover the identity and whereabouts of a terrorist mastermind about to unleash death and destruction across Europe.

Chapter One

A BRUSH PASS

Rhodes City, Rhodes Island, Greece

Day 1

It was Digger's curiosity that inadvertently hauled Rex Dalton and his wife, Catia, out of their Greek Island holiday back into the world of covert operations.

Usually, when the Daltons, both history enthusiasts, went exploring, they preferred to do it on their own, avoiding organized excursions where they had to adhere to strict timelines, predetermined routes, and often unknowledgeable guides. However, this morning after breakfast, when they visited their hotel's information desk to collect information about the Palace of the Grand Master, the lady, speaking perfect Italian, changed their minds. "The guide today is Liza, the most knowledgeable and friendliest you'd encounter anywhere on this island. She'll show you every nook and cranny of that palace, and she won't rush through it. She also speaks five languages: Italian, Greek, English, French, and German."

On the bus on the way from their hotel to the palace, Liza, a petite, good-looking, middle-aged, friendly woman with dark brown hair, told the group, "Rhodes Island is the largest of the Dodecanese islands of Greece." She spoke perfect English with a strong pronunciation of the r, characteristic of the Irish brogue. "Although Dodecanese means twelve islands, there are one hundred and eight islands; only twenty-six are inhabited.

"Rhodes city is the historical capital of the Dodecanese islands. It was once the home of one of the Seven Wonders of the Ancient World, the Colossus of Rhodes. It was a bronze and iron statue, thirty-two meters, about one-hundred and five feet tall. It was erected in honor of the sun god, Helios, for helping them fend off the ruler of Cyprus, who besieged Rhodes in 305 BC.

"It's believed that Rhode Island, in the United States, was named after this island."

She only had to use three of her five languages; English, Italian, and Greek, to inform her audience of twenty-one, excluding Digger. He was seated between Rex and Catia, staring at Liza as if he understood every word she was saying, irrespective of what language she spoke.

When they arrived at the palace, Liza handed out a set of wireless earphones to each member of the group. Then tested that they could all hear her before leading them to the entrance of the Gothic-style building where she stopped to give them a quick overview.

"The Palace of the Grand Master is also known as the Kastello. It was the ancient bastion of the Knights of Rhodes. That's the name given to the Knights Hospitaller, a

2

medieval Catholic military order, after they occupied the Island of Rhodes and established their headquarters here.

"The original palace was constructed in the late 7th century as a Byzantine fortress. After the Knights Hospitaller came to Rhodes in 1309, they converted the fortress into their administrative center and the palace of their Grand Master. The palace was damaged in the earthquake of 1481 and repaired soon afterward, and that's the palace you see here today.

"Italy occupied the island since 1912 and repurposed the palace into this ersatz medieval style. Since the Italians rebuilt it, it served as a holiday residence for the Italian king, Victor Emmanuel III. In 1937, Benito Mussolini, the Fascist dictator from Italy, whose name can still be seen on the large plaque there at the entrance, transformed it into a summer residence for his high-ranking military officers and himself. After the war, it was converted into a museum."

Rex, Catia, and Digger were standing at the back of the semicircle of tourists listening intently to Liza when Rex became aware that Digger wasn't paying attention to Liza anymore.

Digger had a 'Service Dog' sticker attached to his harness. Rex had the necessary paperwork to back it up. But the big black Dutch Shepherd wasn't a service dog. It was the ruse Rex had used ever since inheriting the dog from his friend, Trevor Madigan, a former SAS operative from Australia, who'd been killed in an ambush in Afghanistan in 2014. Digger, an Australian military dog, had been his companion since Trevor asked Rex to take care of him with his dying breath. Rex, mortally scared of dogs since he'd been attacked by one as a small child, had agreed.

And since Rex was a man of his word, he and Digger worked through their issues, and they'd become inseparable mates. Digger had acknowledged him as the alpha in their pack and accepted Catia into the pack from the moment he met her. Digger was Rex's 'best man' at their wedding; he brought the wedding rings in on a dainty white satin cushion balanced on his nose.

Although Rex never learned to give Digger proper commands, like military dog handlers do, over the years, working as a team on many missions, they had developed a unique communications system. Some of Rex's colleagues believed that the two indeed spoke a language that only they understood. However, the truth was, it was always Rex who had learned to be very attentive to Digger's behavior as he was doing now.

Digger had gotten up from where he was sitting between him and Catia and moved forward a few paces. He was staring raptly at someone or something to Catia's left. His ears were pitched forward, and his nose was wiggling a little. Rex could see he wasn't alerting to danger, but something must have stirred his senses and curiosity.

Rex followed the line of Digger's gaze, and about four paces away he found the object of interest; a man, about five foot ten, dressed in faded black Levi's jeans and matching Levi's jacket, dark blue t-shirt, and black sneakers. The olive-skinned man, by Rex's estimates, in his late forties, had a smooth-shaven face, dark hair, prominent cheekbones, and dark-brown eyes, lending him an air of intellect. The man carried a small black nylon shoulder bag, about six by twelve inches, hanging off his right shoulder. Although at first glance, his posture suggested he was relaxed, it was his head moving slowly from side to side, his darting eyes, and the biting of his lower lip that were tell-tales of anxiety.

Rex was a highly-skilled former black operations operator with, among many other specialist aptitudes, exceptional spycraft skills. He removed his earphones, put his arm around Catia, pulled her close to him, and whispered in her ear, "The man to your left with the black shoulder bag. He's on edge about something."

"How do you—," she started, turned her head slowly, and looked at the man. After a few seconds, she nodded. Catia was a former Mossad agent, skilled in street craft, surveillance, counter-surveillance, hand-to-hand combat, and use of weapons. "What's making him nervous? He's not behaving like he's a fanatic about to launch an attack," Catia whispered.

"No, he's not aggressive. Digger would've warned us. I think he's looking for someone."

"Questions?" Liza asked in three different languages.

A few paces ahead of the Daltons was an old man with a black fedora hat and full-face silver beard, hornbill glasses with thick lenses, in a wheelchair pushed by a young woman with dark hair in her mid-thirties, dressed in dark slacks, sneakers, and sunglasses. Probably his daughter or his caretaker. The old man asked a question which Rex couldn't hear.

But Liza's reply he heard. "Yes, that's correct. Archaeologists found evidence that this was the exact spot where the ancient temple of the Sun-god Helios once stood and, in all likelihood, this is also the spot where the Colossus of Rhodes stood."

The old man asked another inaudible question. Liza replied, "Yes, in 1522, the island became part of the Ottoman Empire, and they used it as a command center."

The old man smiled and thanked her.

"Any other questions?" Liza asked. When there were none, she said, "Please follow me."

The group followed her through the arched entrance and ended in the quad. Other groups varying in number from fifteen to twenty-five were already inside.

While Rex and Catia surreptitiously kept Digger's man in sight, they saw him opening the shoulder bag. They were ready to spring into action if a knife, gun, or bomb trigger came out of the bag—but he only retrieved a pair of sunglasses and a light-blue bucket hat with London printed in black on the front and donned them. He moved the black nylon shoulder bag to his left shoulder.

"Ahh… signaling someone," Rex muttered.

"Ten o'clock. The blond man with the Roma cap," Catia whispered.

Rex spotted a Caucasian male among a group leaving the palace heading toward them. He was in his mid to late forties, blond hair, about six feet tall, blue jeans, black t-shirt, and blue denim jacket. On his head was a black baseball cap with Roma embroidered in gold on the front. A black nylon shoulder bag identical to London's was draped over his left shoulder.

They saw London making eye contact with Roma, and the very slight, almost imperceptible, nod from Roma.

Roma and London were a few seconds and about ten to twelve steps away from making what was known in the lexicon of covert operators as a 'brush pass.' A technique typically used in a crowded public area, where operatives pass information to each other. In a properly executed brush pass, they won't even stop walking; at most, they'd bump into one another. A common method of exchanging the information was for both to carry identical objects, such as a newspaper, briefcase, magazine, or, as in this case, black nylon shoulder bags, containing the information.

Then they saw Roma come to a sudden stop and twist

around. A tall woman with a shock of shoulder-length raven-black hair, large sunglasses, dressed in dark blue jeans with a white blouse and zipped up jean jacket, bumped into him. She apologized, took a step to the side, and kept on walking straight toward London, who stood about five paces away from Rex and Catia.

Roma had turned back to start walking again, but he took only one step, grabbed his heart with both hands, and dropped to his knees without making a sound, then slowly tipped forward on his face.

In different languages, people had started screaming, "Heart attack!" "Is there a doctor here?" "Get an ambulance!"

By now, the tall woman was next to London. She stopped and turned to look back at Roma, then slowly turned sideways, looked at London, and said something to him. He turned to face her looking surprised, raised his sunglasses, and smiled. The woman put her arms around his neck, and he put his arms around her in an embrace.

Digger started growling, and that was when Rex saw the stiletto in her right hand. Rex pulled the quick-release string on Digger's leash and started toward London and the woman, but he was too late. The stiletto had plunged into London's heart.

London screamed and dropped to his knees; his hand clasped over his chest.

The woman tried to rip the shoulder bag off London's shoulder, but couldn't get it off; his arm was inside the loop of the strap. The woman saw Rex and Digger coming, turned, and ran toward the exit, the stiletto still in her hand.

London toppled forward onto the gray tiles of the court-yard floor.

"Digger, follow! Don't attack! Catia, help him," he pointed to London. "I'm going after the woman."

As Rex set out after the woman, she was already more than fifteen paces away. Mass hysteria erupted as people started yelling, "Terrorists!" "Attack!" "Hide!"

Digger was about three yards behind her, barking and yelping. Rex was worried that the woman, no doubt a professional killer, would hurt Digger with that stiletto if he came too close to her. But Digger must've understood the command not to attack as he kept his distance.

As she exited the palace gate at full speed, she turned left and headed for the nearby copse of trees.

Rex was closing in on her quickly. He was about seven yards away from her when she stopped and turned to face him and Digger with the stiletto in her left hand, swinging it in a wide defensive arc in front of her.

Rex didn't slow down. Digger had stopped out of her reach but kept on growling and snarling.

With her right hand, she reached inside her denim jacket.

A gun!

Rex raced past Digger.

When the woman's right hand reappeared, there was a .22 Beretta pistol in it, and she was about to turn it on Rex. He was three steps away from her; he had the momentum, he leaped into the air and kicked her in the solar plexus with both feet. The force of the kick body-slammed her into the tree behind her with a grunting thud. Her sunglasses and the stiletto were gone. She had light-gray eyes, the eeriest, most lifeless eyes he'd ever seen. *Contact lenses.* She was shocked and bewildered and looked as if she was going to lose consciousness. The gun was still in her right hand, which was crossed over her breasts.

Digger was next to him.

"Stand down, Digger!" Rex got up and took a step forward to disarm her. He was reaching for the gun when her hand twisted slightly, pointing the gun up at her face, and she pulled the trigger. The bullet went through the bottom of her chin, straight through her mouth into her brain. Her body fell sideways.

"Damn!"

Rex didn't touch her or the gun. Below her mane of black hair, he noticed a patch of blonde hair—she'd been wearing a wig. He took his satellite phone out and snapped a few photos. Then he removed the wig and took a few more.

He looked around; there was no one outside who could've seen what just happened. He wasn't sure if that was necessarily a good thing. He'd have to tell the police what happened, and a corroborating eyewitness would've been very helpful. Even so, the absence of onlookers gave him the opportunity to search the body for identification quickly. But the search confirmed Rex's suspicion that the woman was a professional when it only produced two hundred euros in cash, which he left in the jacket pocket where he found it, and an iPhone which was switched off.

He had a decision to make; take the phone or leave it? *Why would you want to do that? What are you going to do with the phone? This is not your case. Yes, but she killed at least one person and was about to kill me.* His thoughts were interrupted by Digger's yelp—a sign that he was distressed. He patted Digger's back, "Don't worry, it's over, buddy, you can relax now." He clipped the leash on. He stood, looked at the phone, which he still had in his hand, and shoved it into a side pocket of his cargo pants. "Let's go and check on Catia."

When they arrived back in the courtyard, Digger snarled and growled a path through the crowd for him and Rex, sat down next to Catia, and started nosing her while making soft whining noises to comfort her.

Catia was sitting on the ground. London's upper body was resting on her lap. Her hands and face and clothes were covered in his blood. He was dead. She put her arm around Digger's neck and whispered, "Thanks, Digger. I'm okay."

Rex moved London's body off her lap and laid him gently on the tile floor. Then he stood and pulled Catia up into an embrace and whispered, "It's over. The police should be here soon."

"Thank you. I'm okay now." She looked in the direction where Roma had gone down. Another crowd had gathered there. "Let's see if we can help."

It didn't take long to find out that Roma was dead. There was no blood.

"A massive heart attack, I suspect," said a paramedic from England.

Rex and Catia agreed but didn't tell him what they thought caused it.

Three people dead in less than three minutes was more than enough to ruin everyone's day, if not their entire holiday. Within minutes the palace had been shut down. No one could come in or go out. The police were on their way.

All but a few had their cellphones out, taking photos and videos, making calls and sending text messages. Rex and Catia made no calls and sent no text messages. Still, as inconspicuously as possible, under the pretext of typing messages, they both took photos of Roma and London and tried to capture as many of the other faces in the courtyard as they could on video.

"Let's find a quiet place," Catia said after a few minutes. "I have to tell you something."

With all the people still milling around in anguish and uncertainty, many of the benches beneath the arcades of the quad were empty. As they made their way to an empty bench, they passed within two paces of the old man in the wheelchair and his minder. The old man was staring quietly and impassively at them as they passed. Rex couldn't help but wonder what was going through the old man's mind, he must have been in shock. The woman with him nodded at them but didn't say anything.

They picked an isolated bench and sat down with Digger between them. Catia noticed Digger's intent stare at the old man and the woman who were now about fifteen yards away. She reached out and scratched Digger's back, "Don't worry, Digger, they'll be okay now." She turned to Rex. "It never ceases to amaze me how sensitive he is to people's emotions."

"It's mindboggling isn't it," Rex said.

"Okay," Catia said, "here's what I want to tell you. In the few seconds, while the man I tried to help was still conscious, he asked me to take a USB flash drive out of his shoulder bag and give it to the CIA man..."

"CIA man?"

"Yes, apparently the blond man with the Roma cap was CIA. I didn't want to rummage through his bag in full view of everyone, so I just shoved his bag into mine. I hope in the turmoil no one noticed."

Rex nodded slowly. "Maybe no one did, unless there were backups as there often are when a brush pass takes place. Still, with two calamities happening in such quick succession, a watcher would've had to keep an eye specifically on you all the time to notice what you did."

"What about the woman you went after?"

"Dead...."

"Did you..."

"No, she preferred to send a .22 bullet into her brain rather than being captured."

"A zealot," Catia murmured.

"Yeah, something like that."

"I saw them hugging, they must have known each other," Catia said.

"Yes, it certainly looked that way."

Catia opened her shoulder bag, and under the charade of searching for something, she unzipped London's bag. Inside was a packet of chewing gum, a small tin with breath mints, a small pack of man-tissues, an iPhone, and a metallic-red thirty-two gigabyte USB flash drive. She took the iPhone and flash drive out and placed them in one of the pouches inside her bag.

Rex caught a glimpse of the phone as Catia transferred it. It looked the same as the one he took from the dead woman. He told Catia about it.

"Okay, I think we should try to get the man's bag back to him," Rex said. He took his bomber jacket off, emptied all the pockets, and pointed in London's direction. "Let's cover him with this."

Catia nodded, took the jacket from Rex, and folded it over the same arm as she had her shoulder bag. They walked over to the body, where she placed the jacket over the dead man's face. London's shoulder bag, minus the flash drive and iPhone, was back with his body.

Back on the bench, Rex said, "So, if we were to believe that the blond guy was indeed CIA, I guess your guy was his informant, and the woman was here to prevent the exchange from happening. I suspect she gave the CIA guy a 'heart attack' with some kind of rapid-action lethal injection."

Catia nodded slowly. "And thus, we find ourselves in the middle of a real spy drama with a poisoned syringe, a secret message, and dead agents."

"Damn. Didn't they get the memo that we don't do this shit anymore?" Rex said.

Catia smiled. "Apparently not. But first things first, how do you want to handle the police?"

"I suggest we tell them the truth... but only about the parts they *need* to know. As far as I'm concerned, what they *need* to know only starts with the moment the people started yelling about a heart attack. What they don't *need* to know is about the flash drive, the iPhones, and what the man with the London hat told you.

"And, of course, they don't need to know what we think happened here?"

"Agreed," said Rex just when the police sirens were heard.

The first police cars arrive, and blazing over the flashing lights, there's a loud siren sound. As soon as the police swarm in and the ambulance arrives, I know what I'm on. Within the first 60 hours all the casualties...

The police had already made their move to work as before. We still feared for what the people who came in here had seen, they were being held up by a few who know them well. Then, very soon, a hundred people might be sacrificed.

Nothing was mentioned and they worked around by long distance transfer. Now, at the brink of an instant, I would come face to face in a few...

Chapter Two

Rhodes City, Rhodes Island, Greece

Day 1

The first police vehicle arrived with blaring sirens and flashing lights. During the next fifteen minutes, five more police vehicles and two ambulances arrived with equal clamor. Half an hour later, two homicide detectives arrived in an unmarked car without sirens or flashing lights.

The police had an unenviable task ahead of them to sieve the chaff from the wheat—the people who saw what happened versus those who believed they saw what happened. There were about a hundred people in the courtyard.

Factors such as poor eyesight and stress would account for some dubious testimony. However, the bulk of the misconception would come from a phenomenon known as 'eyewitnesses talk.' Witnesses would discuss what they saw with each other after the event—the courtyard was abuzz with people talking to each other. The process of 'co-witness conformity' was well and truly in progress, which meant the witnesses would include things in their statements that they hadn't seen at all but heard from others, making them believe that's what they actually saw.

The reality was, bar any covert watchers, Rex, Catia, and Digger were likely the only ones there who had actually seen what had happened and understood how it all fit together.

They knew it was important to get in touch with the CIA without delay—the man with the Roma cap could indeed have been a CIA agent, and the USB flash drive could contain time-critical information. But they also knew the police were going to take many hours to question them all and take their statements.

"Maybe I can get us fast-tracked," Catia said.

Rex smiled; he knew what she was up to. She was a spectacularly beautiful woman. At five foot nine, she was tall for a woman, her eyes were the color of the Mediterranean, blue at times and aquamarine at others, they changed with her mood and what she wore. She had shoulder-length waves of stunning auburn hair, flawless creamy skin, a scattering of light freckles across her nose attesting to the natural red in her hair, and a near-constant dazzling smile that lit up her face.

A few minutes later, with Rex and Digger by her side and Liza as translator, Catia had little trouble convincing the officer in charge to listen to her and her husband before anyone else. In Italian, with Liza translating into Greek, she told him about her role in the events.

"Did the man say anything to you? Did he know who stabbed him and why?"

Catia shook her head. "Unfortunately, not. He tried to talk, but I couldn't make out what he was saying. He quickly lost consciousness. But my husband followed the woman who killed him."

The officer turned to Rex. "What happened?"

"I saw her stabbing the man with a stiletto. I moved to stop her, but she saw me and fled. I chased after her with my dog. Under the trees outside, she stopped when we closed in on her. She pulled a gun, and I kicked her in the stomach. She fell against the tree. She was dazed but still conscious. When I tried to take the gun away from her, she turned the gun on herself and pulled the trigger. She's dead."

The officer was shocked to find out there was another body that they didn't even know about. He immediately dispatched one of his subordinates to have a look. The man was back a few minutes later and confirmed there was indeed a dead woman with blonde hair under the tree with a gun in her hand, as Rex had told them.

The officer seemed to be a pragmatic man. He had two ostensibly reliable eyewitnesses who were both right there in the thick of things when two of the three died—they had to be heard first. He instructed one of his officers to take their statements right away. Their accounts would probably give him a good baseline to measure the reliability of the testimony of the others.

An hour later, when the Daltons were allowed to leave after giving their contact details to the police, they had another problem to deal with; the press had set up camp outside the main gate.

The Daltons, having no doubt that their faces had been captured on the smartphones of many of their fellow tourists, had no desire to also have their faces splashed on TV and other media across the globe as well. No doubt eventually, their faces captured on the smartphones would make it to the mainstream media, but that would take time, which was what they wanted right now—time to get a message to the CIA.

Catia spoke to Liza and explained that she and her husband were very camera-shy. Liza said she understood and guided them to a back door from where they could reach a nearby street and call a taxi. They thanked her, gave her a hundred-euro tip, and told her if circumstances permit, they'd very much like to come back at some stage and finish the tour of the palace under her guidance.

The entire time, while they were giving their statements and now as they were leaving the palace, they'd kept an eye out for any watchers but didn't spot any. However, they knew it meant just that—they haven't spotted anyone raising their suspicions. A professional would've blended into the crowd, and they'd be none the wiser.

On the way out, they passed the old man in the wheel-chair and the woman again. The old man's head was bowed as if he was asleep or resting. The woman was typing on her cellphone, she looked up, and they nodded to each other in a goodbye gesture.

Back at their hotel, Rex took his satellite phone out, activated the scanning app, and checked the room for bugs. It was a routine he and Catia always followed wherever they went. The room was still bug-free.

Catia had the flash drive out, and they were contemplating plugging it into her laptop to have a look at the contents. But then she shook her head. "Rather not. We don't want to take the chance of accidentally activating a self-destruct routine."

"Agreed. Let the IT gurus handle it." Rex took his secured satphone out and pushed the speed-dial number for John Brandt.

Chapter Three

WE'VE GOT A SITUATION

Satellite phone call

Day 1

John Brandt, the Old Man, as most of his underlings called him, was the CEO of Crisis Response Consultancy, CRC, an Arizona-based private military contractor specializing in black operations on behalf of their clients such as the CIA and other US security agencies.

Brandt was a former warrior of the Cold War era, an experienced spook with more missions under his belt than he cared to remember. After retiring from the CIA, he'd formed CRC. He might have been too old, according to the federal government, to be useful as a field agent. But he was not too old to train his own team to do what the 'new' CIA was expected to do but couldn't because of the interference of politicians.

Rex was a former CRC agent. According to Brandt, "The best damn agent I ever had."

Although for outsiders who didn't know better, it might have appeared that the relationship between the two of them was strained, they loved and respected each other as a father and son would.

"Dalton, this better be good, or your ass is going to decorate one of the fenceposts at HQ. Have you any idea what time it is?" Brandt answered the phone.

"I know exactly what time it is. It's 4:00 a.m. in Arizona, and I can't believe you're still abed... unless Madame Proll is with you."

Rex was referring to Christelle Proll, one of the deputy directors of the DGSE, the French equivalent of the American CIA. She and Brandt had met and worked on a few joint missions in their younger days during the Cold War. Back then, there was a romantic spark between them, but the Atlantic Ocean and work had put an end to it. They caught up again in 2015 when they had to work together on Operation Badr to prevent a group of fanatics from starting Armageddon. The old flame was rekindled, and less than a year later, they were engaged. Christelle had retired two months ago. They were in the process of finalizing their wedding plans.

Brandt ignored the innuendo. "Where the hell are you?"

"Rhodes Island."

"What... you're in America?"

"Rhodes Island, Greece, you old coot, not Rhode Island America."

"Ah, and I guess now you're going to cry on my shoulder because Catia has come to her senses, realized what a jackass you are, and dumped you. Well..."

"John, shake your head so that your ears can slap you awake, we've got a situation here."

"A situation... Of course, what else. Wherever you go, situations are sure to arise. What's it this time?"

Rex had put his satellite phone on speaker, and within a few minutes, he and Catia gave Brandt a summary version of what had happened at the Palace of the Grand Master.

"You're right, a situation indeed," Brandt said. "I'll get hold of Martin Richardson and call back ASAP."

Chapter Four

IT'S A MESS

Satellite phone calls

Day 1

It was 7:15 a.m. in Washington, D.C., when Brandt called Martin Richardson, deputy director in charge of CIA operations. Richardson was a few years younger than Brandt. They were good friends.

Richardson looked at the caller ID and his stomach roiled. "I'm listening, John."

"One of my agents, ah… make that former agent…"

Brandt was stammering about Rex's status as an agent of CRC because he had indeed officially departed from CRC a few years before. However, since formalizing his resignation, Rex had been drawn back into a succession of CRC operations following so short on the heels of each other he might as well still have been in their fulltime employment.

"Who's the agent?"

"Rex Dalton. His wife, Catia, is with him. You met them. Remember?"

"How can I forget? The man who told the President of the United States to give him his number as he was too busy to talk to him and would call him back when he had time."

Richardson was referring to an operation in Hong Kong and China about six months before when it was discovered that the Chinese President at the time was about to unleash a lethal virus into the world. Rex, Catia, and Digger played a significant role in the operation to avert a global disaster.

Brandt smiled. "That's the one. So, Rex and Catia are vacationing on Rhodes Island, Greece. They were present when someone who could've been an agent of yours was killed a few hours ago."

"Continue," Richardson said quietly.

Brandt relayed the rest of the information and forwarded the photos of the dead men and woman to Richardson's cellphone.

"I'll talk to our COS in Athens and get back to you," Richardson said.

COS was the acronym used for the Chief of Station, the person in charge of CIA operations in any country where the CIA had an official presence.

Forty minutes later, Brandt's secured mobile phone rang.

"We're in a quandary, John," Richardson started without preamble. "It's all over the news in Greece. No names have been released yet. Fortunately, the Daltons' report and photos helped the COS to make identifications of the two men. The blond man in the pictures was one of our field agents: an experienced operator and handler of the man who got stabbed. They were going to have a brush pass. The woman is still unidentified. Our facial recognition experts are checking our databases as we speak."

"Damn." Brandt sighed.

"We expect that flash drive to contain vital information about a group of terrorist masterminds who had thus far managed to fly under our radar mainly because they haven't made their debut on the death and destruction stage yet. But we suspect they have intentions to do so very soon— with a coming out that's going to stun the world."

"Just what we need," Brandt muttered, "another horde of fanatical malcontents who heard God's voice telling them it's their destiny to start the apocalypse."

Richardson smiled. "Well, I have just heard God's voice telling me that we need to have a look at the contents of that flash drive immediately."

"I'll get my IT guys to get in touch with yours right away," Brandt said.

"One more thing. We, the COS and I, would like to have a video conference with the Daltons as quickly as possible. We'll also have to make arrangements to get those phones to our COS in Athens."

"I'll call you when we're ready," said Brandt and ended the call.

Chapter Five

Video conference

Day 1

Using his secured satellite phone to connect to the CRC operations room and setting it up as a hotspot for his laptop, Rex was able to connect to the secured video conference. Brandt; Chris McArdle, CRC's second in command; and CRC's IT guru, Greg Wade, were waiting for him and Catia.

Greg Wade was the team leader of CRC's small but highly skilled group of IT specialists. They were computer hackers, among the best in the business. With a few keystrokes, they could create havoc, blackout a city, take control of their traffic lights, enter government and corporate databases, access the bank records of any individual and organization, break through firewalls, break encryption, and much more.

"Rex, according to Martin Richardson, your and Catia's presence of body and mind today might have snatched victory from the jaws of defeat," Brandt started. "The blond guy was indeed CIA. He was the handler of the other guy who was killed. They're still trying to identify the woman. They expect that the flash drive will contain crucial information about a newly discovered terror group."

"As if the world has a shortage of psychotic maniacs," Rex mumbled.

"My sentiments exactly," Brandt said. "Richardson and his COS in Athens want to talk to you and Catia. They are waiting for us to dial them in on the conference."

"Give me a second," Rex said, muted the microphone, and said to Catia, "I have a feeling we're going to be drawn into a CIA mission. You okay with that?"

"I can't see how we can stay out of it. My only request is that any information relevant to the security of Israel will be shared with Yaron."

Yaron Aderet was the head of the Mossad's largest department, Collections, tasked with all the many aspects of conducting espionage overseas. He was an old friend of John Brandt and well acquainted with Martin Richardson. Aderet took Catia under his wings a few years ago when her handler suffered a stroke and had to go on early retirement during Operation Badr. Aderet took an instant liking to Catia as if she was his daughter. And he was the man who led Catia down the aisle when she and Rex got married.

Rex unmuted the microphone and said, "We're good with that on one condition; whatever information relevant to the security of Israel coming out of this will be shared with Yaron."

"I'm happy with that, but Martin has the final say. I'll let him know. Now, before we get them on the line, Greg will talk you through the steps to get the contents of that flash drive transferred."

Greg asked Rex to plug the flash drive into the USB port of his laptop and then used an app on his computer to make a remote connection to Rex's laptop. It took him only a few minutes to establish that the flash drive was not 'boobytrapped' and transferred its entire contents to the CRC secured servers. He disconnected the remote session and left the operations room to contact the CIA's IT team to transfer the files to their servers.

Brandt dialed Richardson, who was in his office by now and already had the COS in Athens online. He told Richardson about the request to share information with the Mossad.

Richardson said, "Of course, we have a deal; it goes without saying. We always share with the Israelis and vice versa."

"Good. Hang on, I'll dial them in now."

Video conference

Day 1

After the greetings, Richardson introduced Rex and Catia to Ethan Thomson, the COS in Athens. Brandt explained that Rex and Catia were married, and Catia's relationship with Yaron Aderet and the Mossad.

Digger was not introduced; he was too busy with his

kong to be distracted by a matter as trivial as a video conference. The kong was an odd-shaped toy, part cylinder, part cone, with indentations that made it look like a hard-plastic snowman, with a hole running through it from top to bottom. It was always a joy to see how Digger would lose all dog-dignity as he went into frenzied ecstasy when he saw the kong. It was a special treat, especially when Rex or Catia had stuffed it for him with some delicacy such as dried meat or what Catia called Digger's gelato—peanut butter.

Before the start of the meeting, Richardson had briefed Thomson about CRC, their security clearances, their impeccable track record as a CIA subcontractor, and the need to secure their services for this mission.

First, the CIA men wanted a detailed firsthand account from Rex and Catia. With questions and answers, it took them a little over an hour before it was Thomson's turn to tell them about the CIA operation.

"The name of our agent was Reece Cole, forty-five, wife and two minor children," Thomson started. "We lost a good man today... He's the one who recruited and handled the informant, Nassor Almasi."

"*Professor* Nassor Almasi?" Brandt interjected.

"Yes. You know him?"

"Never met him but read a bit about him. Fancied himself as a moderate, a self-described Islamic reformer— the Martin Luther of Islam. I can't say exactly why, but I took some of those accolades with a pinch of salt."

"That's the one. Egyptian by birth and passport, English by upbringing and education, a popular lecturer of Middle Eastern matters at universities across Western Europe and America. He was about to finish a one-year stint as a visiting lecturer at the University of Athens.

"Ostensibly a man of peace and moderation. On the

lecture circuit, in convention halls, on TV, in newspaper editorials, peace conferences, wherever he had an audience, he had no hesitation proclaiming his Arab heritage yet was never afraid to lay the blame for the dysfunction of the Islamic nations of the world at their own doorstep. He lamented their despotism, failure to educate their people, oppression of their women, and their propensity to blame all their miseries on the Americans and Jews. Although a devoted Muslim, he made no secret of his deep resentment of religious belligerence, including Islamic militancy."

"Sounds like a man who would've made many friends and many more enemies," McArdle commented.

"Indeed," Thomson said. "His backers think of him as the face of progress; his detractors tend to use words such as heretic, blasphemy, apostasy, and such when his name comes up."

Before Thomson could continue, Rex said, "I'm interested to know how you were able to recruit such a devoted pacifist to work for the CIA? And while you're at it, why his fanatical enemies, of which there couldn't have been an insignificant number, had not killed him long before today?"

Thomson blinked. Undoubtedly impressed with Rex's insight, he looked at Richardson, who nodded slightly.

"To answer that," Richardson said, "we'll have to tell you a bit more about Almasi. He caused quite a ruckus and more than a few red faces here at Langley when we heard rumors that he was a jihadi talent scout for Middle Eastern terrorist groups. On the topic of the misfortunes of Muslim countries, lecture halls, peace conferences, and the like never have a shortage of extremist talent. The rumors were that he never did the recruitment himself; he merely identified the candidates and passed on the names."

"My skepticism about the man was not entirely out of place then?" Brandt murmured.

"Let's reserve judgment on that until we've seen what's on that flash drive," Richardson said.

Brandt frowned.

Richardson continued, "When hearing about his extracurricular activities, we decided the professor was worthy of considerably more of our attention. We put him under electronic surveillance. But the relationship was a one-sided affair. We listened to his phone calls, read his text messages and emails, and monitored his internet activities, but the professor gave us nothing in return.

"Then, just when we were ready to let it go, we heard a rumor about an exclusive elite think tank of Muslim literati. And guess what..."

"You didn't know about them either," Brandt said.

"Right. We wondered if Professor Almasi could perhaps be connected to this Islamic brain trust. We gave him more of our attention by placing him under physical surveillance as well. But before we could find out, the attaché of commerce, known among us as our undercover CIA agent in Athens, Reece Cole, had an interesting conversation with Professor Almasi during a cocktail party at the British embassy a few weeks ago. The Professor seemed to have become disenchanted with his fellow Arabs for their unwillingness to find peaceful solutions for their woes.

"Cole was convinced that Almasi knew he was a CIA officer and believed Almasi was 'begging' him for a secret meeting."

In the spy business, there were four methods to infiltrate the enemy camp: First, the most common method in the computer age, tapping into the target's electronic communications such as telephones, email, and internet activities. In

Almasi's case, it had been done but didn't deliver actionable information.

Second, sending in an undercover agent. It was a long and cumbersome, not to mention risky, process, but not applicable to Almasi's case.

Third, the most popular method before the dawn of the Internet and mobile phones, recruit someone on the inside. The motives for an insider to turn allegiance varied; some did it for money, some did it for reasons of conscience or disillusion, and some were blackmailed into it. The latter made possible by the discovery of a vulnerability, often of a sexual or financial nature, which could be exploited. But, because the recruit was coerced into departing information out of fear rather than voluntarily, it was a method also to be used with extreme care.

Fourth, the walk-in, the weirdest of all methods. Someone from the enemy side arrives unexpectedly and unannounced to offer their services, usually for some form of compensation. It was a method always to be treated with extreme suspicion because of the distinct possibility that the defector could be a 'plant' by the other side.

"It turned out that Cole was right. Almasi wanted to talk to him. He was a walk-in as we call them.

"Pretending to be a freelance journalist with connections to a well-known international current affairs magazine, Cole set up a private face-to-face interview with Professor Almasi in his hotel room in Rome, where the latter was one of the speakers at a symposium about the Muslim refugee crisis in Italy.

"They had fifteen minutes. Cole recorded the meeting without Almasi's knowledge."

"Before you play the recording," said Rex, "how did you come by the information about Almasi's secret activities?"

"Our Israeli friends," said Richardson. "They didn't have much more than what we told you. Understandably, they wouldn't tell us who their informant was. Let's see what's on that flash drive and decide if we have to get in touch with Yaron Aderet to get more information."

Thomson now played the recording for them.

32

Chapter Six

IT HAS TO BE STOPPED

Video conference

Day 1

"Professor, thank you for taking the time to talk to me. Due to the time constraints, shall we get to the point immediately?"

"Agreed."

"Professor, at the party in Athens a week ago, I got the distinct impression you had something you want to tell me?"

"Yes, I have something to tell you. It's about a new threat from a radical Muslim fanatic. I use the singular because I suspect the mastermind is acting alone. But don't be fooled by that. When you understand how this person is operating, you'll know how serious this is."

"Why are you telling me this?"

"Because it has to be stopped. People like me; moderates and reformers, have been making steady progress at ushering Islam into the twenty-first century. It's not easy. To westerners, it might seem that we're making no progress, but they're wrong. Change and modernization are swear words to Islamic hardliners. It takes time to make changes and it must be done at the microscopic level. Think about how long it took for the Saudi's to eventually allow women, in 2017, to drive a car in public."

"Professor, excuse me, but we know you're not exactly the peace-loving Muslim intellectual you've been portraying to the world."

"What do you mean by that?"

"We've been watching you closely, and we know, for instance, that you've been a talent scout for jihadi candidates. Why should I believe a word of what you're telling me now?"

"If you had been watching me as closely as you said, you would know that not a single one of those 'jihadi candidates' as you call them had ever picked up a gun, set off a bomb, or exploded a suicide vest. Every single one of the six I've recruited over the years had completed post-graduate degrees. Every single one of them had joined my cause for change and transformation of Islam. I have many enemies, Mr. Cole; you should be more discerning when you listen to them talking about me. Just like spy agencies across the world, they, too, understand the art of misdirection and misinformation."

Thomson paused the recording and said, "Cole was an experienced agent with extensive training in the perception of body language. He told me he had been watching Almasi closely while he was talking, looking for micro-expressions of deception. He found none. But he had to put Almasi through the wringer to make sure he was not leading him down the garden path." Thomson pushed the play button.

"I'll take your word for it—for now," Cole said. "We also know that you're involved in some secret collective of Muslim intellectuals."

"Yes, I am, and that's why I wanted to meet with you."

"To me, it sounds as if you're about to propose something akin to a Cold War defection. What's your motivation, and what's your price?"

"Yes, that's what I'm about to offer you. I'm doing it for one reason and one only, and that's to prevent some lunatic from causing my people irreparable harm, like Osama bin Laden and others of his ilk did with their thoughtless acts of violence. Psychopaths who brought us nothing but pain and suffering. I'm not about to betray my people. I'm offering to help you find the person who's about to cause my people more immeasurable pain and misery."

Cole said, "Professor, I see you're skirting around the issue of the price, but be that as it may, I'm interested. However, for me and my superiors to take you seriously, you'll have to provide a lot more information—accurate and specific information, not conjecture and vagaries. We'll need verifiable and actionable information. The usual process is that the informant comes across to us with high-value information. We analyze and verify the information and then decide whether to proceed or not."

"I understand the process and accept it. However, I'd be remiss if I don't tell you that we might not have much time to prevent the first attack from happening."

"When?"

"I honestly don't know. I suspect no more than a month, probably less, could be days even."

"We've got three minutes left before I have to be out of here, and I haven't heard your offer as yet."

"I'll have a comprehensive report ready for you two days from now when I'll be back in Athens."

"Good. Make sure your report contains verifiable details, which would, among others, include names, addresses, places, dates, and suchlike."

"I'll give you what I have. And I'm hopeful that you'll see that I'm not playing games, Mr. Cole. How do I contact you?"

"You don't. I'll contact you."

"How?"

"You'll know when I do. Now, listen carefully, it's important. Take this USB flash drive. There are five steps: One, shut your computer down. Make one hundred percent sure it's not connected to the Internet or any network whatsoever. Two, plug this drive into the USB drive of your computer and then boot it up. Check again that it's not connected to the Internet or a network. Three, browse to the USB drive and click on the Microsoft Word icon. Four, type your report. And I'll remind you once again about being honest and thorough. Five, when you're done, click the button marked 'Encrypt' in the top right-hand corner, the document will close by itself after the encryption routine has completed. The document won't be visible on the drive after that. Six, take the flash drive out and restart your computer. Understood?"

"I got it."

"Great. See you in a few days."

The recording ended, and Brandt said, "I take it the professor's report is on that flash drive Catia acquired?"

"Yes," Thomson said.

"I expect the report to be ready momentarily," Richardson said.

"While we wait for that, I'd like to point out a potential problem," Rex said.

"What?" Richardson asked.

"That woman who killed them didn't only know the brush pass was about to take place, she also knew both participants. She and Almasi knew each other, and she must have known who Cole was. She came there prepared, knowing they would be there at that specific time and that they were going to have a brush pass. She clearly knew Cole was the more dangerous of the two; hence, she got rid of him first. How did she know?"

Before anyone could respond, Richardson's desk phone started ringing. He held up his hand for everyone to stop talking and answered. It was the manager of the IT team who told him that the documents stored on Almasi's flash drive had been decrypted and were available on Richardson's computer. "Thanks, Ben. Now get some sleep."

At that same moment, in the Daltons' hotel room in Rhodes City, Digger stirred. Since emptying the kong of the peanut butter, he had been lying on the couch by the door, sleeping, but now he was sitting up, staring at the double door, growling softly, ears pitched forward, and the hair on his neck raised.

Chapter Seven

SPEED, SURPRISE, AND VIOLENCE OF ACTION

Rhodes City, Rhode Island, Greece

Thursday, June 22, 2017

Their hotel suite was a large ground floor unit with a separate lounge and bathroom area and a private terrace overlooking Lindos harbor. The entrance to the unit was through a double door from the terrace. For the video conference, Rex and Catia had switched the air conditioning on, locked the door, closed all windows, and drawn all curtains.

Rex and Catia glanced at each other. Hotel staff, police, or...

Digger was telling them, someone, it could be more than one, was approaching their suite. His body language: the raised hair on his back and neck, the low growling and snarling, spelled potential danger. There was no time to think or analyze; whoever it was, was only a few steps away from the door.

Rex whispered to Catia, "Type in the chatbox to John that we've got unexpected visitors. I'll get the door."

Catia nodded and started typing while Rex moved to the door quickly and quietly.

Rex was on the right of the door, on the left side of anyone entering, his back was against the wall. Digger was still on the couch. If the visitors had evil intent, the Daltons, without weapons, no escape route, and out of time, were in a precarious situation.

If you can't be safe, be lethal. Speed, surprise, and violence of action. The mantras John Brandt drilled into Rex during his training at CRC.

The concern on the faces of all but John Brandt was unmistakable. They got Catia's message and stopped talking. And when the line from the Daltons' side went dead without warning immediately after her message, they all took it as a bad sign. It could've been the line that dropped out, but they couldn't shake the feeling that it was something more ominous.

Brandt broke the silence. His words were not addressed to the others; they were directed at an audience who would never hear him. "If you didn't go there in peace, you're about to enter through the gates of hell."

McArdle knew what Brandt was talking about; Richardson and Thomson's knitted brows indicated they didn't.

Brandt didn't even notice; he was staring at his watch as though he was keeping the time, which was precisely what he was doing. He mumbled, "Two, maybe three hostiles. Rex, Catia, and Digger. Three to five seconds tops." *If you can't be safe, be lethal. Speed, surprise, and violence of action.* It was as if Brandt was remotely directing the outcome of whatever was happening almost seven thousand miles away.

"Who are you talking to, John?" Richardson asked.

"Huh?"

"Who're you talking to?"

"The Daltons' visitors. If they're bad guys, they'll all either be dead or seriously injured by now."

"You've got a lot of confidence in them."

"I do."

Catia had barely finished typing the message when their question of friend or foe was answered; the double door crashed open. Two men with ski masks covering their faces charged through the door. A third, also with a ski mask, was one pace behind them. Each of them had a silenced .22 Beretta pistol in hand. The Italian-made gun had almost no recoil, and the noise it made, when fitted with a silencer, was about the same level as a pellet gun—the handgun of choice for many a professional assassin.

As the door shattered, Catia flipped the table over and dropped to the floor behind it. The laptop, mobile phones, coffee mugs, and plates with snacks shattered on the tile floor. The first two gunmen storming through the door started shooting at Catia, but the solid three-inch oak tabletop was enough to stop the small caliber bullets. They kept on shooting and moving forward without looking back, neither left nor right.

Rex waited for a split second to let the first two enter the room before slamming the door into the third man just when he stepped over the threshold. The solid wood frame hit him squarely in the face. He staggered back with arms raised in protection. Rex jumped forward, grabbed his hand, and twisted the gun out of it, breaking the man's trigger finger in the process. Before he could make a sound, Rex shot him in the face with his own gun, twice. Rex pivoted around just in time to see Digger taking down the man on the right shooting at Catia.

Rex shifted his focus to the man on the left and double-tapped him in the back of the head. The man was about two steps away from Catia when he collapsed to the floor like a sack of potatoes. The man's body hadn't reached the floor by the time the sights of Rex's gun was trained on the last gunman. He was on his face on the floor; Digger was on his back with his teeth sunk into the man's neck. His gun lay on the floor, out of reach.

"Digger, stand down!" Rex ordered. But Digger wouldn't let go. Rex stepped up, pushed his gun against the side of the man's head, and said, "Thanks, buddy, I've got him covered. You can stand down now."

Very reluctantly, Digger let go and stood back, still snarling and growling.

Catia was standing next to Rex now.

For good measure, Rex kicked the man in the side and turned him on his back with his foot. The man's throat had been ripped open, and blood was gushing out. His face was covered in blood, gargling sounds escaped from his mouth, and his eyes were tilting in their sockets—he was in the throes of death.

Rex stood back and kicked the man in the side again. "I wanted to talk to you, asshole. But that's what you get for attacking the female of our pack."

Catia had turned away and went to close the doors. "We have to get out of here immediately."

"And off this island," Rex added. He dragged the man who he killed with his own gun into the room. Catia closed the door. Rex went and picked the laptop and mobile phone up from the floor. The laptop showed no signs of life, a sturdy rubber casing protected the mobile phone, and a small green light indicated that it might have survived the fall.

Chapter Eight

CAN YOU GET MY AGENTS OUT?

Rhodes City, Rhode Island, Greece

Thursday, June 22, 2017

Within two minutes, Rex and Catia had gone through the room, bundled their belongings into their backpacks, and relieved the dead men of their guns and mobile phones. Two of them had Samsung phones, and one had an iPhone, which Rex noted were the same as the models Almasi and the female assassin had. The phones were switched off. None of the assailants had any form of identification on them. Rex removed their ski masks, and Catia snapped photos of their faces on her phone. They shouldered their backpacks, closed the double doors behind them, and walked, as if in no hurry, across their private terrace to their rental car.

As far as they could tell, the attackers had no backup.

They were relieved to see no signs that the hotel staff or guests were aware of what had just happened.

As Rex maneuvered the car out of the parking space, Catia said, "How did they know where to find us?"

"The police know," Rex said.

"And Liza… and the taxi driver who brought us here," Catia said.

"And everyone who was on the tour bus this morning when they picked us up," Rex said.

"Too many," Catia said.

Rhodes Island was over five-hundred and forty square miles. It had more than one hundred and fifteen thousand permanent inhabitants and, this time of year, many thousands of visitors. Rex and Catia would be able to hide, but when the horrific mess in their hotel room was discovered, the island would be too small for them. The hotel staff would not turn up until ten o'clock the next morning, but their assailants would've been acting under orders from someone who would very soon be wondering what happened to the three assassins. The police would lockdown the island.

Rex and Catia agreed they probably had two to three hours before it would become challenging, if not impossible, to leave the island unnoticed.

Rex was heading toward Diagoras International Airport, located on the West side of the island about eight miles southwest of the city. It was a bustling airport with daily international and domestic flights. They agreed to take the first flight out, even if it meant they landed in Moscow.

The roads were busy, making it challenging to detect followers. Rex had to make a few SDRs, surveillance detection runs, a spycraft tactic used by field agents to flush out followers. Performing an SDR in their situation with no backup teams meant Rex had to make sudden turns without indicating, pulling off the road a few times, and making U-turns to go back along the same route.

About five minutes after getting into the car, Catia called John Brandt and put the phone on speaker when he answered.

Brandt let out a long sigh of relief and put his phone on speaker as well. Catia gave them a condensed version of what happened since the line went dead. "Three armed, masked men broke down the door to our room. They're all dead. We're unharmed. We're on our way to the airport to get off the island on the first flight out. As soon as the bodies are discovered, all hell is going to break loose, and the police will put the island in lockdown..."

Brandt interrupted. "Ethan, can you get my agents out? Human and canine."

When Brandt and Digger met for the first time, the relationship started off on the wrong foot. Brandt thought it was stupid for one of his agents to go around with a 'damn dog.' Digger was offended, and so was Rex. But over time, as Rex and Brandt sorted out their differences, so did Digger and Brandt. When Brandt had learned what a pivotal role Digger played in rescuing him when he got abducted, Brandt started looking at Digger with different eyes. He had come to realize that Digger was an extraordinary dog. These days, he and Digger liked each other very much, and Brandt regarded him as one of his agents.

Brandt massaged his temples as if trying to get rid of a headache, retrieved a white plastic bottle from his pocket, took out one tablet and swallowed it with water, and mumbled, "damn headache couldn't wait until I'm done."

Thomson was on the phone. A few seconds later, he

said, "Joanne, I need a charter flight out of Rhodes in the next ten to fifteen minutes. Yes, I'm serious. Athens. I don't care, offer them double the normal rate, more if necessary, just get me that flight. Three. Two humans and a dog. Yes, the dog will pay full fare. Thanks, I'm waiting for your call."

Thomson explained that Joanne Sanders was part of the Athens embassy staff, among other duties also responsible for all travel and accommodation arrangements. She had an outgoing personality and a vast network of contacts at major airlines and private air charter companies across Greece and other countries in the region. If there were anybody who could pull a white rabbit out of the hat now, it was Joanne.

While waiting for Joanne to call back, Catia told them that she had photos of the attackers as well as their mobile phones. She sent the photos to them while still talking.

Thomson's phone rang eight minutes later, just when the Daltons drove into the public parking at Diagoras Airport. It was Joanne. She had a plane ready for them.

Twenty minutes after that, the wheels of the twin-engine, turbocharged Beechcraft Baron 58 TC left the runway and headed for Athens, two hundred and forty miles away. They would arrive in Athens in a little over an hour.

In silence and covertly, Rex studied the controls of the airplane and the pilot's actions to assure himself he could take over and fly it if the situation called for it. All CRC field operators were trained to fly various fixed- and rotary-wing aircraft. Although he hadn't flown any aircraft for quite some time, he was confident he could do it, telling himself it's like riding a bicycle; once you've mastered it, you never unlearn it.

The pilot was a friendly and loquacious Greek woman

in her mid-forties. She told them that she had been flying charters around the islands for more than a decade and loved it. But with her broken English, which was the only other language she spoke besides Greek, the conversation soon dried up. Rex and Catia didn't want to talk about the events of the day in front of her, in any language. They spent most of the flight looking out the windows at the Greek Islands and the Aegean Sea while replaying the events of the day in their minds, looking for answers to the many questions they had.

Digger had a window seat but got bored soon after take-off, yawned loudly with a curling tongue, and went to sleep.

Chapter Nine

LEAVING ATHENS

Athens, Greece

Day 1

Shortly after getting Thomson's confirmation that the Daltons were in the air en route to Athens, Brandt called Declan Spencer, the captain of the *TOMATS*, at anchor in Athens Marina in the Port of Piraeus, to arrange with him to pick them up at the private airstrip.

The *TOMATS*, the name derived from the first letters of Ernest Hemingway's classic short novel, *The Old Man and the Sea*, was a luxury superyacht that Rex had appropriated from a Saudi Arabian prince Mutaib bin Faisal bin Saud, an international black-market arms dealer and human trafficker.

For more than a year after acquiring the yacht, Rex had no idea what to do with it. But then John Brandt was kidnapped, and Rex was instrumental in rescuing him. The two of them landed in the hospital together, and while laid up, Rex and Brandt reached an agreement about the disposition of the yacht. He'd signed it over to CRC and agreed that the Old Man would instruct his lawyers to erase the yacht's history, rename it, and hide its new owner's name through an untraceable maze of dummy corporations. Rex and Digger would have a permanent home on the yacht for the token amount of one dollar per year for life. This agreement was extended to include Catia when she and Rex got married.

The *TOMATS* had three decks, was equipped for ocean travel with ultra-modern stabilization technology, advanced communications equipment, a helipad, and every nod to comfort that one could imagine. It had a range of six-thousand nautical miles, a top speed of seventeen knots, and a cruise speed of fifteen. It was powered by two Caterpillar diesel engines producing close to five-thousand horsepower.

Apart from the very comfortable lodgings for the seventeen crew members, including the captain, there were accommodations for fourteen guests in seven luxurious staterooms. There was a hot tub, sauna, Turkish bath, infinity pool, gym, dining room, and several lounges. One of the lounges had been repurposed to house the sophisticated electronics gear and computer equipment that could be concealed when necessary. Another was turned into a secured communications room. Inside the latter was, among others, an impenetrable encrypted satellite video system, the latest technology in communications.

Brandt also had no idea what to do with the yacht but then remembered Declan Spencer. He and John Brandt were bosom friends, born in the same year, in the same hospital, lived in the same neighborhood, grew up together, went to the same school, same university, and joined the

Navy SEALS at the same time. John was recruited into the CIA. Spencer retired as a Commander at the age of sixty-five. Both lost their wives. John's wife, a fellow CIA field agent, had been killed in an operation gone wrong. A heart attack claimed Spencer's wife.

Spencer always had one dream for his retirement—to be the captain of his own yacht and sail the world. Brandt had contacted Spencer to offer him the captaincy of the yacht; he had also asked for his advice and assistance to get the yacht transferred to CRC's untraceable dummy corporation. Brandt wasn't sure at the time how CRC could put the yacht to good use. Spencer came up with the idea. He contacted a few US Special Forces commanding officers, former colleagues, and told them about the exceptional holiday deal for their operators where they could spend some of their R&R on a luxury yacht, free of charge, food and accommodation included, but not alcoholic drinks.

Spencer had a long waiting list of very keen operatives who wanted to spend time on a luxury yacht, even if it meant they had to attend to menial chores. The fact that they could bring a wife or girlfriend with them as long as they performed crew duties made it even more appealing. Even the chefs were military personnel.

Rex, Catia, and Digger had arrived in Athens onboard the *TOMATS* a week before. The day after, they flew out to Rhodes Island for a few days of exploring.

Now, there were four Delta Force operators with wives and girlfriends on board who joined the crew in Rome for two weeks of R&R. In Athens, three Navy SEALS with wives joined them the day after the *TOMATS* arrived. With Spencer and his first mate, the crew now numbered sixteen and three guests—Rex, Catia, and Digger.

Since the launching of the *TOMATS* under its current

name, about two years before, the yacht had served as CRC's mobile mission control center for several major missions around Europe and the last one, six months ago, in Hong Kong.

When the charter plane touched down at the private airstrip on the outskirts of Athens, Spencer and Thomson were there to meet them. With the suspicion that there could be a mole in their midst, Thomson had decided not to trust the collection of the mobile phones and flash drive to anyone else. It was also an opportunity for him to meet the Daltons in person.

After meeting Thomson and handing the devices over to him, he left. Spencer drove them in a rental car to the *TOMATS* in the Port of Piraeus. They stepped aboard less than two hours after leaving Rhodes Island.

Spencer had called the crew back from shore leave. The *TOMATS* was stocked up, fueled up, and ready to go. It was shortly after 4:00 p.m. when the *TOMATS* raised anchor and set course for the Port of Valletta, the capital of Malta, five-hundred and sixty-five nautical miles away. The weather forecast was excellent, and if it held, at the cruise speed of fifteen nautical miles per hour, they would be at sea for about thirty-eight hours.

As they left the Port of Piraeus, they were relieved that no one had tried to stop them so far, and far as they could tell from watching the news, the scene in their room at the hotel on Rhodes Island had not been discovered yet. But it was just a matter of time. At the very latest it was going to be found the next morning around 10:00 a.m. when the cleaning staff turned up.

Chapter Ten

THE DELPHI TECHNIQUE

Video conference

Day 1

Back in their stateroom, the Daltons unpacked and had a quick shower before joining Spencer for dinner. They told him all about their eventful day. As with previous missions, Spencer was going to be responsible for the mission support of Rex and his team.

After dinner, they went to the comms room, where they restarted the secured video conference, which was interrupted by the attack on them earlier. Brandt and McArdle were at CRC HQ in Arizona, Richardson in his office in Langley, and Ethan Thomson in his office in Athens. Before the meeting, Brandt had briefed Thomson about the *TOMATS* and her crew and the role they had played in past missions. Richardson already knew all about the *TOMATS* since the Hong Kong operation.

Rex and Catia gave them a detailed account of the attack by the three men earlier, which wasn't much more than what Catia gave them in summary while she and Rex were on their way to the airport on Rhodes Island. They still had no idea who the men were and how they knew where to find them.

But there was little doubt; the men were after that flash drive from Almasi's bag and maybe his iPhone. And that meant someone else knew they had it, and the only way someone could know was if they had one or more watchers at the Palace of the Grand Master that morning. The answers could be in Almasi's report and on the phones the Daltons had collected or on the photos and videos Rex and Catia captured.

Thomson told them that the phones were in the overnight diplomatic bag and should be arriving in D.C. the next day.

Diplomatic bags or diplomatic pouches as they were also called were not necessarily a bag or pouch; it could be a cardboard box, a briefcase, a duffel bag, a large suitcase, a crate, or even a shipping container. Diplomatic bags were used by countries' diplomatic missions to carry official correspondence or other items between their embassies or consulates and their home governments. As long as the containers were marked as such, they had diplomatic immunity from search or seizure, as stipulated in article 27 of the 1961 Vienna Convention on Diplomatic Relations. The containers may only contain items intended for official use and were often escorted by a diplomatic courier, who had diplomatic immunity from arrest and detention.

Everyone but Rex, Catia, and Spencer had time to read Almasi's report, now displaying on their TV screens, prior to the meeting.

It started with the confirmation of the existence of the group of Muslim intellectuals. The Professor had never met any of them, but he stated that he had a good idea who they were. He would supply the names provided they could come to an arrangement about his protection and remuneration.

Brandt was massaging his neck. "So much for noble intentions," he growled as he took a tablet out of the white plastic bottle on the table in front of him and downed it with water.

Rex couldn't help but note that it was the second time in less than twenty-four hours he saw the Old Man taking pain killers. The only time he saw Brandt taking pain medication was when he was in the hospital after his abduction. Maybe it was the stress of wedding planning combined with a new terror threat.

Almasi stated that not all the members of the brains trust were Arab, or Muslim, for that matter. The group had no name, but for purposes of the report, Almasi called them the Delphi Group.

Spencer sighed. "Here we go. The high priestess of the Temple of Apollo, aka the Oracle of Delphi, prophesied a couple thousand years ago that Islam would rise to world power in the twenty-first century AD. And this group is going to make sure the prophecy is fulfilled. Is that it?"

"Keep your opinion 'til you've finished reading," Brandt snapped.

Spencer nodded and continued reading.

Almasi was talking about the Delphi technique. A problem-solving and decision-making methodology to get the opinions of experts about a given issue, find out to what extent they agreed or disagreed, and achieve a consensus opinion. The Delphi technique was usually conducted through questionnaires. Where focus groups intentionally use group dynamics to generate debate on a topic, the success of the Delphi technique depended on the fact that the participants remained anonymous to each other throughout the entire process so they couldn't influence each other, even after the study.

The participants were given a questionnaire which they would answer, including the reasons for their answers. A facilitator would collate and summarize the answers and send it out again for the experts to revise their earlier answers, considering the replies given by the others. The process would be repeated until the range of answers decreased and converged toward consensus and the best solution.

All of them were familiar with the technique, knew what it entailed, and had used it on occasion in one form or another. But it was the first time they had encountered a terrorist group using it.

"It's a powerful method, but the quality of the output depends very much on the expertise of the participants. GIGO – garbage in garbage out," Richardson said.

Unfortunately, as for who the other experts were, Almasi remained evasive, telling them only that the other experts were scholars of international politics and relations, global security, historians, and students of military history.

He said he had no idea how long the group existed; he only became involved about a year ago. At first, the questions were benign; what would Europe have looked like today if Napoleon won the Battle of Waterloo? What if Hitler won WWII? What was the global economic, political, and social impact of the 911 attacks in the USA?

Then, according to Almasi, about three months ago they received a document providing the background details of how the 2004 Madrid train bombings known in Spain as 11-M impacted Spain's national politics.

The attack happened three days before Spain's general elections. The explosions killed one hundred and ninety-three people and injured more than two thousand. It was the deadliest terrorist attack in the history of Spain and the deadliest in Europe since the 1988 bombing of Pan Am Flight 103 over Lockerbie, Scotland.

Euskadi Ta Askatasuna, ETA, a Basque separatist terrorist organization, and al-Qaeda were the first suspects. But none of it was ever proven. Over the years, people were brought before courts, charged, and found guilty just to have their convictions overturned and set free. To this day, the culprits have not been identified.

The attacks led to the defeat of José María Aznar's ruling *Partido Popular*, Popular Party, in the general election three days later, handing the reins of government over to the Socialist Party, PSOE and led to Spain's subsequent withdrawal from the coalition with the USA and others fighting in the Iraq war. Before the attack, the incumbent Popular Party led the polls by five percent. But the Socialist Party, PSOE, ended up winning the election by five percent. An estimated one million voters had switched their vote to the Socialist Party because of the bombings. More than one-point-seven million citizens were influenced to vote who did not plan to vote, and three hundred thousand were discouraged from voting.

Rex couldn't suppress the emotions welling up in him when he read that. It was the attack in which his parents and two younger siblings were killed. That was the incident that changed his life, and instead of setting out on a career in the diplomatic service as he had planned, he had set out on a path of revenge, becoming a lethal assassin and black ops specialist.

Almasi reported that they were asked to study the 11-M attacks and give their opinions about why no other terrorist attack since then had the same impact.

The questions Almasi and his mysterious colleagues had to address were spine-chilling. They were asked to analyze the terrorist attacks of the past three decades. What did they do right? What did they do wrong? What did they achieve?

According to Almasi, from the follow-up questions and summaries, it was apparent that the secret panel thought that existing terror groups were idiots by sending in single suicide bombers or a few gunmen to shoot up people in the streets or driving trucks into crowds. All they were achieving was to strengthen the resolve of their enemies. According to the think tank, what was needed was a series of attacks of epical proportions. The attacks had to rapidly follow each other. That, they thought, would demoralize the enemy and paralyze them with fear.

The Professor stated that this was when he realized he was not contributing to an innocent scientific analysis of terrorism but the evil plans of a psychopathic malcontent. Almasi said he then also started suspecting that the mastermind could be a radical Muslim fanatic. He said that he remained in the group only to find out more about the people behind it. He was convinced that the mastermind was working on a plan to launch a series of attacks similar to 11-M. Strikes that would keep the architects anonymous but change the world. And he believed he had to do everything in his power to thwart the plan.

"Hmm, I find *that* hard to believe, professor," said Rex. "I would've liked to have a chat with you about some of that."

Being an academic and self-acclaimed reformer, Professor Almasi couldn't help but throw in some of his opinions about the reasons for the sad state of affairs in the Arab world. "The Arabs were once world leaders in the fields of mathematics and geometry. Today, more than fifty percent of them are illiterate, the majority of them women. Millions are not receiving any formal education at all.

"One out of every five people in Arab countries lives on less than two dollars a day, despite the massive income from oil collected by their rulers.

"How did it come to this? Corruption and radicalism. Stop those, and the Arab world would prosper. The money that the dictators stole from their citizens to fund their luxurious lifestyles and their offshore bank accounts in Switzerland and the Bahamas has to come back to the people. Stop pumping money into terrorism and use it to educate and modernize.

"The clerics misinterpret the Holy Koran; they pick verses that suit their goals and quote them out of context, and thus they mislead their followers. They hate everyone who is not of the true faith; they call them the 'kufar,' unbelievers. They take the face of Islam and present it to the world contorted with fury and hatred.

"They have to be stopped because they are leading Islam into a long dark tunnel with no light at the end."

"No surprises there," Spencer mumbled. As a former Navy SEAL commander, he had extensive knowledge of the Arab world and their social deprivation.

The next set of questions required Almasi and the others to identify high-value targets. In other words, targets, when attacked, would change the hearts and minds of the populace, scare them, and leave them feeling desperate and hopeless. For each target, they had to provide an in-depth motivation of why it was selected and how an attack on it would contribute to the goals.

Although Almasi said he had no idea what the priority was, the latest list he saw contained the following targets: Jerusalem, Rome, Berlin, Lisbon, Vienna, Madrid, Paris, Athens, Brussels, Amsterdam, London, Copenhagen, and Stockholm.

"No American cities. Thirteen cities, all except Jerusalem, in the European Union," Rex noted. "I guess Rome includes the Vatican. And of course, no Islamic terror target list would be complete without Jerusalem."

"Yep," Brandt said. "Jerusalem and the Vatican, the two targets Islamists have been drooling about for decades. But as you've said, they certainly have the hots for the major players in the European Union."

Almasi explained that every interaction between him and the facilitator had been through the Darknet. An encrypted network built on top of the existing Internet, which could only be accessed with specific software and protocols, thus providing total anonymity to the users. He stated that he had made copies of all the questionnaires and documents and would hand those over as soon as he had reached an agreement with the CIA.

Rex looked at Thomson and said, "Ethan, is there a way we can get into..."

Thomson shook his head. "I already sent two agents; they were too late. Almasi's apartment had been ransacked. No computer, no paper, no mail, no telephone, even the rubbish bin was cleaned out."

"Damn."

Almasi also said that he had a suspicion who the master-mind was but again would only divulge the information after an agreement was in place. The only hint he gave was that the person's pseudonym was Dragut.

"That doesn't help a whole lot does it," said Spencer. "What's the origin of the name, is there any significance to it?"

Everyone went quiet; slowly, all eyes turned to Rex and Catia, the resident history aficionados. Catia shrugged, "I've heard the name. If I'm not mistaken, he was a famous Turkish naval commander a few hundred years ago. But that's the extent of my knowledge." She looked at Rex.

He smiled and said, "I might be able to save you all a Google search. I came across his name a week or so ago when reading about some of the history of Greece and Turkey. He was born near Bodrum in Turkey. His native name was Turgut Reis, and his nickname was Dragut. Reis means captain in Turkish. He was a close friend of the legendary pirate and later admiral of the Ottoman Navy, Barbarossa. Dragut later became a naval commander and governor. He had many accolades bestowed upon him, such as the greatest pirate warrior of all time, the uncrowned king of the Mediterranean, and, the most exciting of them all, the Drawn Sword of Islam."

Rex smiled. "Those were the days, it seems, when it was a prerequisite for Ottoman naval commanders and governors to have completed a pirate apprenticeship before ascending to such a powerful position.

"Dragut was killed in 1565, during the siege of Malta. So, another accolade is, he was also the man who *almost* conquered Malta."

Richardson and Thomson were shaking their heads when Rex finished; it was their first encounter with Rex's eidetic memory.

"So, what I'm hearing is that this Dragut character was once the terror of the Mediterranean?" Richardson asked.

"Yes, in the very same waters we're sailing in right now," Rex said.

"It's good we don't believe in ghosts," said Spencer.

They turned their attention back to Almasi's report. The frustration was that the report said a lot, and it said nothing. Should they believe it? They decided it could be a fatal mistake if they didn't. But with the lack of specifics, where to begin? Where did Almasi hear the name Dragut? Who was the woman who killed him, and what was their relationship?

Rex verbalized what was on everyone's mind. "So, in summary, we've got a dead professor warning us about impending attacks on major cities in the EU and Israel led by someone fancying himself as the reincarnation of a notorious Turkish naval commander, advised by a group of anonymous intellectuals. Almasi, why did you have to do something so stupid as getting yourself killed?"

"Yep, and the professor's death wish was that we should stop this guy." Spencer was shaking his head.

It was 10:00 p.m. local time on the *TOMATS* when the conference call ended. They went to bed, wholly unaware of the evil that was about to hatch one thousand two hundred miles to the north of their location.

Chapter Eleven

THE DEBUT

The Netherlands

The Netherland's General Intelligence and Security Service AIVD (Algemene Inlichtingen- en Veiligheidsdienst) esti-mated that the country was home to approximately 500 jihadists and several thousand sympathizers. AIVD was tasked with domestic, foreign, and signals intelligence and protecting national security. The Military Intelligence and Security Service (MIVD) focused on international threats, specifically military and government-sponsored threats such as espionage.

"The attraction of jihadist ideology remains and is, therefore, a threat for the longer term," an AIVD statement said. "The threat of attacks is still unabated, despite ISIS losing its caliphate in Syria. The organization has trans-formed itself into an underground movement that is preparing for a resurrection to re-establish the dream of the caliphate. The threat against the West, and therefore also the Netherlands, seems to have become a structural part of

European society."

A study showed that many young Muslims experienced alienation. They felt disconnected from their immigrant parents and Dutch society. They felt deprived—the sense that despite their efforts, they received fewer opportunities than native Dutch people of the same generation. Therefore, they instead identified with radical and orthodox Islamic groups and the global Muslim community who offered them clear answers and a firm sense of belonging.

Even so, the Netherlands, in comparison to other European nations, had seen only minimal terrorist activities, nothing on the scale of France, Germany, and the UK. Over a period of 14 years, they had three noteworthy terrorism incidents: on November 2, 2004, Theo van Gogh, the Dutch filmmaker and political activist, was assassinated by Mohammed Bouyeri, a second-generation Moroccan-Dutchman, Islamist and member of the Hofstad Network. On February 27, 2016, five men attacked a mosque full of visitors in Enschede with molotov cocktails. On August 31, 2018, a man randomly attacked two people in Amsterdam Central station with a bladed weapon. The attacker, a 19-year-old from Afghanistan, told the police he was aggrieved at the Netherlands for insulting Islam.

Over the years, the Netherlands' security and law enforcement agencies also foiled several terror plots.

Notwithstanding, the AIVD didn't have a good track record as an efficient intelligence service. It seemed as if they had been spending much of their time wiping the egg off their faces caused by embarrassing incidents such as the Dutch businessman, Frans van Anraat, who was arrested and convicted for war crimes for selling raw materials for the production of chemical weapons to Iraq during the reign of Saddam Hussein, who turned out to be an AIVD informer enjoying their protection.

Another disaster was when they let Abdul Qadeer Khan go free after he stole Dutch nuclear knowledge and provided it to Pakistan to produce its atomic bomb.

They were accused of negligence when not having focused on and gathering enough intelligence on political violence or environmental groups, particularly following the murder of Pim Fortuyn by an environmental radical.

They lost a laptop and a floppy disk containing classified information from one of their regional AIVD offices. The disk was found by a staff member of a car rental agency and given to Dutch crime-journalist Peter R. de Vries. The information on the disk revealed that the service had been collecting information about the Dutch politician, Pim Fortuyn, and members of his party, as well as left-wing activists. Among other things, the documents accused Pim Fortuyn of having sex with underage Moroccan boys.

Amsterdam | Rotterdam | The Hague | Utrecht

Day 2

They were home-grown, all twelve of them, eight men and four women. Children and grandchildren of immigrants, Turks, Arabs, and Africans by origin, Islam by faith, politically disillusioned.

They didn't know each other at all and would never meet. They didn't know that they were part of a larger plot. Therefore, they had no way of knowing that they had received their instructions from the same person via the instant messaging app Ricochet that used Tor's onion services, the Darknet's communication protocol enabling true peer-to-peer messaging that was anonymized, encrypted, and directly sent to the recipient, with no intermediary server that might log conversations.

They were assigned three to a city: Amsterdam, Rotterdam, The Hague, and Utrecht, the nation's four major cities. Each of them received different targets. They had no idea that others received similar instructions but for different targets, but the date and time were the same for all twelve.

They were armed with fold-stock PK-10s, the Pakistani reverse-engineered version of the AK-47, CZ-75 pistols of Czech manufacture, and explosive vests packed with two kilograms of the home-made, highly volatile explosive, Triacetone triperoxide (TATP), synthesized from acetone, a nail polish remover, and hydrogen peroxide.

Their instructions were clear and straightforward; "you are not suicide bombers you're soldiers of Allah. You're on the battlefront to kill infidels, and you keep on killing until you have no ammunition left. Then you detonate your vest. If the police confront you, you shoot until you have no bullets, and then you detonate. There is no distinction between man, woman, and child—they're infidels, all of them have to die."

It was Friday, sunset was at 10:07 p.m. They arrived by Uber, and the attacks started at precisely 10:15 p.m. The restaurants and theaters were packed, the streets crowded, targets abounded. It was all over by 10:25 p.m. Four-hundred and sixty dead, including the assailants, more than eight hundred wounded and injured. It was the deadliest terror attack in Europe's history. The second most lethal attack was the 21 December 21, 1988, Pan Am Flight 103 bombing killing two hundred and seventy people, known as the Lockerbie bombing. The third most lethal was the March 11, 2004, Madrid train bombings in Spain known as M-11.

It was only by morning when the extent of the tragedy became clear. Many of the dead still lay where they had fallen. Some were still sitting in the seats where they died. Streets were blocked, and businesses were closed, the King, the Prime Minister, and members of parliament visited the scenes.

The party-political rumblings started the Saturday morning but remained somewhat subdued throughout the weekend as a respectful sign of grief.

The economic impact started on Monday at 9:00 a.m. when Amsterdam's stock exchange didn't open. The Amsterdam Stock Exchange, considered to be the oldest modern securities market in the world, had merged with the Brussels- and Paris Stock Exchange in 2000 to form Euronext.

The political blame-game started in all earnest on Monday morning when parliament was in session. The floodgates opened, and the finger-pointing began. How could this happen in a country with some of the strictest gun laws in the world? How could the terrorists acquire combat assault weapons without the knowledge of our security agencies? What had the Prime Minister and his intelligence chiefs been doing? How could they have been so fast asleep at the wheel that they couldn't detect and prevent an attack like this?

Dutch gun laws were quite strict as could be expected when gun ownership was seen not as a right, but a privilege. Hunting and target shooting as a sport were the only two legitimate reasons for owning a gun. But while that was true, it was also true that in Amsterdam, the nation's capital, gun smuggling was as rife as the drug trade.

One politician berated the leftwing media, "This is what happens when healthy public debate is choked and substituted by memes, and the mindless liberal media defines the terms of allowable conversations we're supposed to have."

By Monday, the speculation about who did it was also rampant, but the political grandstanding was still in full swing, and it took them a few more days to realize that no one had claimed responsibility. Someone must have planned it, funded it, and coordinated it, but the architect preferred to remain quiet. No threats, no demands, only silence.

Jihadist websites had posted the usual triumphant comments. And when the names of the 'heroic' martyrs were published, it was not only the Dutch intelligence services who felt an ice-cold shiver ravaging their bodies, the western intelligence community felt it too. Their greatest fear had become a reality; home-grown lone-wolves— twelve of them. Not a single one of them had ever come to their attention before the attack.

Chapter Twelve

MOBILIZING THE TEAM

Video conference

Day 2

It was Friday 11:20 p.m. in the Netherlands and on the *TOMATS* when Richardson summoned them to an urgent meeting.

"An hour ago, the Netherlands came under attack," Richardson started. "The attacks were launched simultaneously in Amsterdam, Rotterdam, The Hague, and Utrecht, the country's four major cities. The death toll already stands at three-hundred and fifty and rising. More than six-hundred wounded and injured and rising. This attack is the worst of its kind in European history. The number of casualties has already surpassed the Lockerbie and M-11 bombings." He continued for a few more minutes, passing on everything he got from the COS in The Hague.

"Anyone claimed responsibility?" Brandt asked in a soft voice, clearly nursing another headache.

Richardson shook his head. "Not even a squeak."

"Any ideas, speculation, guesses, chatter?" Spencer asked.

"The usual suspects, Al Qaeda, ISIS, etcetera. But they themselves have not uttered a single word. And we know those outfits would never pass an opportunity like this to trumpet 'victory.'"

"The last time we saw a synchronized attack like this on several targets was Nine Eleven," Rex said.

Everyone nodded.

Richardson looked at his laptop screen. "Apologies, I've got our COS in The Hague on an open chat, he's updating me in real-time. The poor man is getting inundated with calls and emails, not only from security agencies in the US but from all over the world. I probably don't have to speculate too much about why they're not calling AIVD and MIVD."

"Well, besides the fact that they'd be having more than just their hands full at the moment, I suspect they were also totally blindsided by the attacks. We know they're not the sharpest tool in the west's intelligence agencies shed," Brandt said.

"You're probably right about that, John," Rex said, "but the US agencies are not faring much better, are they?"

"Meaning?" Thomson asked.

"Between the CIA, NSI, NSA, and all the other acronymed agencies, America has the largest, most sophisticated intelligence apparatus on the planet. We have the most advanced equipment and technology. We have eyes and ears on more than ninety percent of all intelligence generated on the planet through overt and covert means in any given twenty-four-hour period. Yet, here we are, staring at each other, wondering what has happened. Billions of dollars spent on building an intelligence infrastructure of industrial proportions, and we can't even make an educated guess of who did it."

"Touché," Richardson said.

"Martin, I hope I'm wrong, but I can't shake the feeling that this was Dragut's coming-out performance," Brandt said. "The Delphi group, as Almasi called them, flexing their muscles. No claim of responsibility, a massive strike that would trigger a massive shift in the hearts and minds of the Dutch people and scare them and their government witless. All the things that Dragut's scholarly consultants advised him to do—if Almasi were to be believed. All of that plus the fact that Amsterdam is one of the cities on the list that Almasi gave us."

A contemplative silence followed. Rex broke it after a long while. "It sounds like it's time to mobilize the team. Even if we're wrong about this attack, we still have to investigate the allegations made by Professor Almasi. Right?"

"Without doubt," Thomson said. "And I have the dreadful feeling that John is right, this was Dragut's coming out."

Richardson agreed.

Brandt looked at Rex and asked, "Your usual team?"

"Yes. Josh and Marissa to the *TOMATS*; Rehka at HQ with Greg."

"Okay, Martin, I suggest we take a break to let the troops know to pack and get to their stations," Brandt said as he unscrewed the top of the white plastic bottle.

Brandt tracked Josh and Marissa down first. Josh Farley was a pleasant-faced, All-American type with blond hair who stood two inches over six feet. Not movie-star handsome, and he looked slightly older than he was. Brandt always told Spencer that Farley was one of his agents whom he judged to be nearly as good as Rex Dalton. Rex had trained Josh himself in hand-to-hand combat and street craft and, in Rex's words, was "one tough, lean, mean bastard."

Between the two of them, they had more than just a few war stories to tell and the battle scars to show for it. They trusted one another without reservations.

Marissa and Josh were married. She looked quite a bit younger than she was, making it appear as if she and Josh were of the same age. Brandt described Marissa as the best of CRC's handful of female agents. And she was beautiful —shoulder-length, raven hair and azure eyes suggested French heritage, and her forty-something years gave her an alluring mantle of maturity. She was almost ten years older than Josh, but one would have to see her birth certificate to know that.

She was an expert social media analyst and spy and, if necessary, could give good account of herself in a fight. She also spoke two languages besides English; Arabic, and French, the latter she had spoken along with English since her childhood thanks to her French father.

Rehka answered Rex's call on the third ring. Rehka Gyan was Rex's technology expert, virtual assistant, researcher, and friend, the daughter of a friend from Bilaspur, India. Rex and Rehka had met when he and Digger liberated her and six other women from the Saudi Arabian prince from whom Rex had confiscated the yacht now known as the *TOMATS*. Mutaib bin Faisal bin Saud, an international black-market arms dealer and human trafficker, a scumbag whom Rex had killed.

With a master's degree in computer science, Rehka had exceptional skills in programming and online research. If anyone anywhere left a digital footprint, be it on social media, email, or online searches, she could track that person down. She had enough black hat and gray hat skills to operate anonymously on the Darknet and get unfettered access to some of the most secure private, government, and law enforcement databases across the globe without leaving so much as a hint that she had been there. And since she had met CRC's IT guru, Greg Wade, and worked with him and his team on missions, her knowledge and skills had gone from strength to strength. And everyone knew about the blossoming romance between her and Greg.

After dispatching the Farleys to Malta, Brandt spent a few moments in thought about the 'usual team' as he called them earlier. There was nothing ordinary about them; they were exceptional, the best. This team had saved the world from major catastrophes in the past, and he had no hesitation; if it came to it, this was the team that would do it again.

His thoughts turned to Rex Dalton, more than ten years ago, when he arrived at CRC. After the M-11 terrorist attack on the Madrid train station in 2004 killed Rex's parents and two younger siblings, the peaceful young man who'd looked forward to a career in the US Foreign Service was emotionally damaged. He'd transformed into a brooding, angry man who'd joined the Marines to avenge his losses. From there, he was recruited into Delta Force and trained as a Special Forces operator. Then he was recruited into Brandt's black ops outfit, CRC, where he was trained to become one of the world's most lethal assassins—a capacity in which he rained terror, destruction, and death on the enemies of the US.

Rex was a skilled sniper who could take a target out at eight-hundred yards to a mile. He could kill with a long gun, short gun, or no gun. He was lethal with edged weapons, explosives, poisons, or no weapon at all. Targets could be taken out from a mile away or die with Dalton's breath in their face.

To that was added intensive spycraft training. He learned how to develop legends, his covers when he was on the move in other countries. He learned about infiltration, explosives, and sabotage. He had been drilled in finding and using safe houses, transmitting secured messages, recruitment of informants, disguises, digital communications, signals, and caches.

And to crown it all, Rex was a polyglot. Brandt had lost count of how many languages he spoke, seven, it could be more, the latest one he mastered was Hebrew. He had an almost supernatural ability to learn new languages, and a mysterious quirk was that he adopted the accents of his language instructors. Therefore, the only language he spoke with a strange accent was Hebrew because Catia spoke it with an Italian accent.

Rex and Catia met in 2010 when she provided him with part of his European tradecraft training. At the end of Rex's training in Rome, he and Catia, although they didn't say so, both knew much more than a tutor-student relationship had developed between them. But they also knew the rules, no fraternizing between agents and handlers. It could get both killed.

They saw each other again in 2011 when she provided him with support for a mission in Naples. After that, it took four years before they saw each other again and realized the spark was still there. They got married in May 2016.

Catia, an Italian Jew, was an only child. Terrorists had also killed her parents. In their case, it was a lone assassin, working for the Jihad Council, the military wing of Hezbollah, who had poisoned them while they were on holiday in the Caribbean, though the official version was they drowned while on a boat trip. It had happened in 2005, the year after Rex's family was killed.

Catia was twenty-two years old at the time. The first thing she did after getting over the initial shock of her parents' deaths was to contact her father's chief of station in the Rome office. She'd told him that she knew her dad was a Mossad spy, and she wanted to take her father's place. She wanted to stop terrorists—any terrorists. It took a lot of talking from her and a lot of dissuasion by the station chief, but she got it her way in the end.

Rather than placing her in the embassy, the Mossad trained her as a mission support specialist—a *sayan*, the Hebrew word for helper.

During the mission to recover the stolen Jewish libraries, more than a year ago, Brandt, who was almost seventy, tried to persuade Rex to take over as CEO of CRC. It came as a total surprise to both Rex and Catia. At the time, Rex didn't accept or decline the offer, and they agreed to postpone the discussion until after Catia's Ph.D. graduation ceremony. After the ceremony, they indeed had another conversation about it, but Rex had kicked the can down the road, telling Brandt he needed more time to think about it.

I'm getting married soon. I'll have to bring the topic up with him again. Maybe, I can persuade him to stand in for me while I'm on honeymoon? Introduce him to my job gradually. Brandt grinned at the thought.

Brandt couldn't help but smile when he thought about Digger. They didn't have a good start, but nowadays, he could not imagine a CRC mission without the big black dog.

Digger was born, bred, and trained at a military base not far from Brisbane, Australia. In Australia, the troops were called 'diggers,' and although way back, it could have been a derogatory term, it wasn't anymore. The Aussies loved and respected their diggers just as much as the Americans loved and respected their soldiers. Even the Australian Prime Minister used the term diggers when they referred to the Australian troops. The name originated from WW1 with the trench warfare—the Aussies, because of their skills as miners, were the ones who designed and dug those trenches.

Dutch Shepherds were known for their affectionate, obedient, reliable, loyal, alert, and trainable temperaments. They are great guard and watchdogs. They are also smart and energetic, loyal and protective, love children and get along with other animals. "Even with an old fart like me," Brandt chuckled to himself.

Just then, Rex, Catia, and Digger appeared on Brandt's screen.

"Laughing all by yourself, John? That begs for an explanation," Catia said with a big smile.

"I'm still sane, I hope. I was just thinking about Digger and me. How our relationship has changed. These days I know I can relax when I know he's with the team. It's like having adult supervision when the children are out playing."

Catia and Rex laughed. "I like your analogy," Catia said. "It's true, he's kept us out of serious trouble, at least on the three missions I've been on. Not to mention how he saved us yesterday on Rhodes Island."

"And saved my ass when he sniffed me out among thousands of shipping containers where my abductors were trying to hide me," Brandt added.

Digger must have figured out the conversation was about him. He sat there, swiveling his head back and forth between Catia and Brandt as if he understood what they were saying.

But Digger lost all interest in the conversation when Rex took the kong out. When he caught sight of it, he yelped and ran straight to Rex, dropped down on his belly and looked up at Rex in anticipation with his tail wagging vigorously. Rex gave the toy to him and said, "There you go, buddy. Catia has put your favorite in it, gelato." Digger wasn't listening anymore; he was too busy trying to get to the peanut butter on the inside.

Chapter Thirteen

SECURED BY ENCRYPTION

Video conference

Day 3

It was 2:15 a.m. on the *TOMATS* when the video conference resumed. Thomson was going to join a bit later as he had an urgent meeting with the ambassador. Richardson started with an update of the latest news from the Netherlands. Not unsurprising, the casualty count was still increasing; they expected that it would continue to do so over the next few days. As could be expected, the President of the United States and other heads of state around the world had contacted the Dutch Prime Minister to offer condolences and assistance. Still, no one had claimed responsibility, but if Brandt's theory were correct that the attack was indeed the work of the Delphi Group, no one *would* claim responsibility.

Brandt confirmed that Josh and Marissa were soon to be

on their way to Valetta. Rex told them Rehka would be boarding a plane for D.C. within the next two hours.

Richardson told them that he expected the Netherlands would soon ask for help from the intelligence agencies of the Five Eyes countries and perhaps Israel as well. Five Eyes or FVEY was formed in 1941 between the US, UK, Australia, Canada, and New Zealand to share SIGINT (signals intelligence) and HUMINT (human intelligence). It was inconceivable that the combined intelligence-gathering efforts of those countries would have missed all of the electronic communications that the attackers and their masters must have used to plan and execute the attacks. Yet, it seemed that was exactly what happened.

When Thomson joined, he confirmed that the cellphones and flash drive were in the hands of the IT experts at Langley.

He also reported that he had briefed the US ambassador to Greece earlier about the situation so that he, in turn, could inform the Greek Prime Minister. According to Thomson, as relayed to him by the ambassador during his first meeting, the Prime Minister was not well-pleased to learn about the killings on Greek soil and insisted on a full investigation. However, the Prime Minister's tune had changed during the follow-up meeting when the ambassador told him that the events in Greece could be related to the tragedy in the Netherlands. From that point onward, the Prime Minister had offered full cooperation. He promised to issue an order that the Daltons were not to be arrested. Nevertheless, he had requested to be kept up to date about the progress on the search for the mastermind, Dragut. The ambassador had agreed to the request on condition that the details given to the Prime Minister would remain secret for now.

When Thomson finished his report, they returned to their discussions. They agreed, for now, there was no role they could play in the investigations in the Netherlands. All they could do was wait and see how the situation unfolded and if intelligence surfaced that might be relevant to Operation Dragut. They were still holding out hope that the CIA's IT experts might retrieve useful information from the cellphones.

They returned to the most pressing question, where to begin to unravel the Delphi Group?

But before they could make much progress, Richardson's phone rang. It was the head of the IT division telling him that she was ready to report about the cellphones. He invited her to join him in his office to inform everyone.

Video conference

Day 3

Sally Adams was in her mid-forties, dressed in a charcoal pantsuit with a white blouse. She was tall for a woman, an inch shy of six feet, and almost anorexically thin. Short dark hair, brown eyes, and thin lips lent her a don't-mess-with-me expression.

Rex thought she looked exactly the type of person required to keep a bunch of free-thinking computer gurus in check. He was not mistaken, although her underlings liked her, they knew which lines not to cross.

After the introductions, Richardson nodded for her to give her report.

"The two Samsung phones are stock standard. One can buy them anywhere. There's nothing special about their firmware configuration. However, both phones had the Signal app installed. Are you familiar with Signal?"

The blank looks on the faces of half her audience answered her question.

"For those of you who know, please bear with me. Signal is an encryption app for smartphones and desktop computers. People who are concerned about privacy love the messaging app. It's open-source, in other words, free, and it's easy to install and use. Signal's main appeal to the security and privacy-conscious is the fact that the provider doesn't log the metadata of who is talking to whom and guarantees when users are both using the Signal app, they can be assured of rock-solid end-to-end encryption. That means only the person who receives the message can see who sent it to them. Even if a Signal message is intercepted in transit, the interceptor cannot see who sent it or who received it. The provider doesn't capture or store any of the messages. Security researchers keep a careful watch on it, auditing and probing it to make sure it remains secure. One of the app's biggest champions is Edward Snowden."

Sally smiled briefly and said, "After all of that, what I am here to tell you is, although we were able to get into the phones easily and look at the information on them, we were unable to access the Signal app's data on any of them."

"Mhh, not what we were hoping to hear," Richardson said.

"Any way of breaking the encryption?" Brandt asked.

"It's possible but would take time. A week or so, I'd say. We do have access to all other data on the phones. Maybe there's something useful there."

"We'll study it when you give it to us, but I suspect what we want to know is on that Signal app," Richardson said.

"I thought with the computing power the CIA and other security agencies have at their disposal, breaking encryptions would be a quick and easy job," Brandt said.

Sally was shaking her head. "Until a decade or so ago, cryptography was almost the exclusive domain of academics and intelligence services. There were only a few cypherpunk enthusiasts trying to break the monopoly. Today, encryption is everywhere; it's easier to use than ever before. In short, the cypherpunks won. The ubiquitous use of encryption is here to stay, no amount of warning and expression of concern about its contribution to escape surveillance by the FBI and other security and law enforcement agencies has been able to change that.

"Secure communications are the new default. Where unencrypted internet-connected apps were like a window without curtains, now, with easy access to encryption apps, the curtains are being drawn to cover the windows."

Rex grinned. "So that verse in Mathew five in the Bible that says, 'The meek shall inherit the earth,' was a typo or back then probably a scripto, should have read, 'the geek shall inherit the earth?'"

When the laughter finally subsided, Sally, still smiling, said, "You've just made my day. My team is going to love that one."

Brandt said, "I get the feeling what you told us about the Samsungs was the good news, right?"

Sally nodded. "Unfortunately, yes. The three iPhones are K iPhones. They are produced by a company, KryptAll, who has designed a special version of the iPhone exclusively for security. They've changed the phone's firmware and added its own VoIP, voice over IP, applications to ensure that all phone calls are fully encrypted. Not even KryptAll themselves can decrypt the conversations. Needless to say, neither can law enforcement agencies. The phones are expensive, but not excessively so. They sell for around four and a half thousand these days.

"The phones are popular with military personnel, politicians, and businesspeople."

"No doubt with terrorists and criminals as well," Brandt growled.

Sally nodded. "KryptAll converted it from a standard phone into a mobile broadband satellite communicator, capable of receiving signals anywhere on the planet. The owner of a K iPhone can call anyone on any phone in the world but has been designed only to accept incoming calls from other devices encrypted by KryptAll. The calls cannot be tapped or tracked. Not even KryptAll knows the details of the calls.

"Here's what they say, 'KryptAll provides VoIP audio calls that are secured by encryption. KryptAll is a zero-knowledge system as calls are not stored on the server network and calling records are not generated. The KryptAll phone can make calls; however, it cannot receive KryptAll calls unless it is from another KryptAll phone. We do not have a history or copies of calls exchanged by anybody on the system. We do not have the decryption keys; thus, we cannot intercept any of the calls sent through KryptAll. KryptAll does not assign or control the IP address.'

"I know this is probably not what you wanted to hear, but the bottom line is we got into the phones, there's no information about the voice calls made on them. And not even KryptAll can help us get it. There's a lot more technical detail I can give you if you want to hear it?"

Richardson looked around at everyone; they were all shaking their heads. "Thanks, Sally, seems as if everyone is okay for now."

Spencer said, "I guess I could ask our IT experts, but while we have you here, I might as well ask you. It's about secured emails."

"Sure."

"A few years ago when it was discovered that a former Director of the CIA and his mistress were using a shared Gmail account to write some of their personal messages as draft emails, which they left in the draft folder to keep their communications private, the method was touted as secure. Is that the case? Are they secure?"

Sally shook her head. "Not at all. It may sound like a smart idea until one understands that emails in a shared draft folder are no safer than transmitting them. Al Qaeda terrorists used the method years ago. It allowed them to exchange information without sending traceable emails. But the unsent emails are still stored in the cloud just like any regular email, and service providers can be compelled to provide copies. And keep in mind, the service providers keep even the deleted files."

Chapter Fourteen

NOW WE'RE GOING SOMEWHERE

Video conference

Day 3

When Richardson's office door closed behind Sally Adams, they found themselves staring at each other with a what-now look on their faces.

"This is not your garden variety terrorist. Nothing like we've ever encountered before," Brandt said. "This terrorist is bent on security and anonymity, and he's better and more sophisticated than we've ever seen. He's outsmarted us and our much-acclaimed technology."

"I agree," Richardson said. "To plan, coordinate, and execute an attack such as this without so much as a single intercepted electronic signal is mindboggling and scary."

"We can't ignore the possibility of a slip-up," Thomson said. "There could have been intercepts that have not been recognized as terrorist chatter at the time. The problem we have now is to find them."

In the aftermath of Nine Eleven, the original sixteen intelligence-gathering agencies of the USA had swelled to over a thousand. More than a decade and a half later, close to one million Americans had top-secret clearance. More than one thousand one hundred government agencies and close to two thousand private contractor companies were working on top-secret projects related to counterterrorism and homeland security at over ten thousand locations across the country. Never again should critical information be allowed to slip through the cracks because it was not shared. But eighteen years later, despite the incredible amounts of money pumped into it, the situation was much the same as on September 11, 2001. The intelligence machine that was created was colossal and complex. More than fifty thousand top-secret reports were created annually, far too many to read, let alone to analyze or collate. So, the bulk of them were simply filed.

"I'm wondering if there could be physical evidence in The Netherlands that would help us establish a connection to what happened in Greece and the Delphi outfit? Such as the cellphones and computers of the twelve martyrs," Rex said.

Richardson was already typing a message to the COS in The Hague. "Done," he said when finished typing. "I guess it'll take a while before we get an answer."

"There's another thing we haven't considered yet," Rex said. "Why did Almasi carry one of these super secure iPhones?"

Everyone was staring at Rex; it was an important question.

"Are you thinking Almasi had been sent to deceive us?" Thomson asked.

"We have to consider it a possibility," Rex said.

"But why did they kill him then?" Catia asked.

Rex shrugged. "Maybe he worked for them but genuinely had a change of heart as he told agent Cole; they found out about it and had him killed."

"The fact is he had one of those K iPhones. Those are not standard issue for university professors," Brandt said.

Richardson nodded. "It certainly puts his report in a different light, doesn't it?"

They were somewhat surprised when the COS in The Hague came back half an hour later. According to forensics experts, from the bits and pieces of the attackers they had seen so far, there were no cellphones. Seven of the twelve had been identified. AIVD agents had raided their homes, but no cellphones or laptops or computers or tablet PCs were found. So far, not a single piece of evidence linking them to extremism had been found. Not even from their traumatized families who had no idea what their sons and daughters were up to.

Catia said, "We know that the jihadists look after their own. If someone volunteers for martyrdom, they'll sometimes pay the martyr's family substantial amounts of money. That's what Hezbollah does in Israel. It might be worth keeping a close watch on the families to see if there is a money trail to follow."

"That's something we should be able to do without asking for the consent of the Dutch government," Richardson said and started typing to the COS.

"Another thing we can do without their consent is to dig into their and their families' social media lives," Catia said.

"Absolutely," Richardson said. "I keep forgetting that

John and I are of a bygone era when we had to open people's letters with steam to learn about their personal lives. Now everyone lives out loud, telling the world what they have done, are doing right now, going to do next, and prove it all with photos and videos. Online followers and likes are more important than friends of the flesh-and-blood kind."

Rex smiled wryly. "Yeah, I'm sure if Descartes were alive today, he would have changed his famous words, 'I think therefore I am,' to 'I'm on Facebook therefore I am.'"

"Rehka is our resident social media expert," Brandt said when they all stopped laughing. "We'll get her onto it the moment she arrives."

"Good. I'll send you the contact details of our team leader of the social media analyst group to work with her," said Richardson.

They threw more ideas around for the next hour or so and agreed that it was time to take what they had to the Director of the CIA so he could inform the Director of National Intelligence, the President, and others. Of course, the information they had was not sufficient. Still, the list of targets provided by Almasi had to be passed on immediately so that the countries involved could take steps to increase security.

Until they could dig up more intel, they were in the maddening position where they had to wait for the lunatics to strike again, knowing the enemy was watching and waiting for the right time to kill again. If nothing else, the Delphi Group, after the resounding success in The Netherlands, would be euphoric. They were sure of a couple things; another attack was as assured as sunrise and sunset, and people were going to die—many of them.

The only question was which target and when.

Spencer said, "So, apart from intel out of The Netherlands which may or may not provide us with leads to follow, we've got nothing else?"

Richardson was looking at his laptop screen and held his hand up. "There might be more. I've just received an email from the facial recognition team. They have identified the three men who attacked Rex and Catia at their hotel on Rhodes Island. The EYP, the Greek National Intelligence Service, was quite helpful since their Prime Minister had a word with them, and identified the men as known members of the Greek mafia who we know often collaborates with the Sicilian Mafia, Camorra, Albanian, Bulgarian, and the Russian mafia. Ethan, will you follow up with the EYP to see if we can get more details out of them?"

"Will do," Thomson said.

Richardson continued. "The female assassin was not in our databases, neither in those of Greece, but the Friends over at the Firm have something for us."

There was a very close and amicable working relationship between the British Secret Intelligence Service (SIS), commonly known as MI6, who called their counterparts in the CIA 'the Cousins' and the CIA 'the Company'; the Americans called them 'the Friends' and MI6 'the Firm.'

"They're saying she was a British citizen. They have a file for her and are happy to show and tell as soon as we can get the necessary authorization."

"Great. Now we're getting somewhere," Rex said.

Richardson muted his microphone and called Myles Stevens, his counterpart at MI6 in London. Five minutes later, he unmuted the microphone and said, "All set. He'll be coming online in the next hour and a half."

Chapter Fifteen

TALKING TO A FRIEND

Video conference

Day 3

Myles Stevens was a tall man in his mid-fifties, gray hair, a sturdy jaw, and nondescript eyes behind gold wire-framed glasses. Even though it was 3:00 a.m. in London, Stevens cut a striking figure of a stately English gentleman, dressed in a charcoal-gray pinstriped suit, white shirt, and maroon tie.

With the introductions out of the way, Richardson started by explaining to Stevens that there could be a connection between the assassin and the mastermind behind the attacks in The Netherlands.

"I'll not be entirely surprised. Her name was Destiny Parker. A British citizen by birth. She's from a well-to-do family. Her father was in the diplomatic service, an ambassador when he retired.

"Ms. Parker had only one sibling, a brother, Tony, two years her senior.

"She attended Oxford University, where she attained an honor's degree in political science. It was while she was at Oxford that she came to MI5's attention because of her association with some unsavory characters of the Russian mafia and former KGB agents. She was not shy to make her political views known, that's to say she seldom missed the anti."

"Anti?" asked Brandt.

"Yes, anti-government, anti-fossil fuel, anti-nuclear power, anti-police, anti-politicians, anti-air pollution, anti-religion, anti-Israel, anti-America, you name it, she was against it. In short, she was a protest-attending, sex-positive, anti-racist, intersectional feminist who drank ethically sourced oat milk and had read everything published by Audre Lorde, twice. MI5 thought it was only a matter of time before she would be entangled with a terrorist group.

"But she was also a paradox. In her final year, she had a steady boyfriend who was a Muslim, Ushan Ozmert. That had the analysts over at MI5 frowning. A woman so independent, progressive, worldly, areligious, vocal, and opinionated, in love with a Muslim was a bit hard to fathom. But the relationship only lasted until the end of the academic year when Ozmert disappeared. Ms. Parker left the country a few months after graduation and never returned. That's when MI5 handed her file to us and made her our responsibility because she lived outside their jurisdiction.

"That was a quarter of a century ago. She was forty-seven when she died."

"Let me guess," said Richardson, "for the past twenty-five years, she had gotten herself involved with radicals of all stripes?"

"One would've thought so, but she seems to have had a change of heart, and instead of protesting about her peeves, she decided to rather take her frustrations out on people by killing them very quietly. She became an assassin, as Rex and Catia observed two days ago. Until we got your report about the killings on Rhodes Island, we were unable to verify that she was indeed a professional killer. Some of the European security agencies got information to that effect and contacted us a few times over the years. So, from the rumors section of her file, that's to say, unsubstantiated information, she later became involved with Islamic extremists and used the nom de guerre Wanderer, an apparent reference to the Brazilian Wandering Spider, the world's deadliest spider. She had a tattoo of one between her shoulder blades.

"Neither we nor any of the other agencies were able to apprehend her for questioning. After receiving the pictures Rex took and our computers finding a seventy percent match, we contacted the authorities in Greece. We supplied them with her fingerprints, and they matched them within a few hours. They've also sent us pictures of the spider tattoo on her back.

"That's what we have on her. Would you like a copy of the file?" Stevens said as he took his glasses off.

"Yes, please," said Richardson and Brandt in chorus.

"Good. I will send it as soon as we're finished."

There was a pensive silence before Rex said, "Mr. Stevens, that boyfriend, Ushan Ozmert, do you have more information about him?"

"Myles, please."

Rex nodded.

"Only a few lines. He was never on our or MI5's watch lists. His name came up only because of his relationship with Ms. Parker. It says here he was a Muslim. He was from Feres, a small town in the northeast of Greece. He studied biochemistry and was a brilliant scholar. So much so, a large Swiss pharmaceutical company headhunted him during his final year."

"Will it be possible to talk to Ms. Parker's friends and family?" Rex asked. "I understand after all this time they won't remember much, but for now, we've got nothing else to go on. She could've contacted some of them over the years."

"I see no problem with that," Stevens said. "I will assign a couple of my officers to conduct the interviews and send you the information."

Brandt caught Richardson's eye and said, "I'd like Rex and Catia to be present."

"Myles?" Richardson asked.

"You're welcome. I'll brief the two officers to get the contact details, make the necessary appointments, and accompany you to the meetings. Let me know when you will be arriving in London."

"Thank you, Myles," Rex said.

It was 5:00 a.m. on the *TOMATS*. They were about six hours away from Valletta.

An hour later, thanks to Joanne Sanders, Rex, Catia, and Digger were booked on a Ryanair flight to London.

Chapter Sixteen

MEETING THE FRIENDS

Valletta, Malta

Day 4

Rex and Catia had no time for their favorite hobby, visiting historical sites. For now, they had to be content to do their viewing of the city of Valletta through the windows of the taxi taking them to the airport.

Throughout history, the Maltese archipelago had always been of strategic importance to those who controlled the Mediterranean. The island-state located in the Mediterranean Sea, south of Sicily, consisted of three islands: Malta, Gozo, and Comino. Malta, the administrative and commercial heart of the Islands, was the largest of the three islands.

The capital of Malta was Valletta, known as the Fortress City, or *Citta' Umilissima*, a city built by gentlemen for gentlemen. The city was named after its founder, Jean Parisot de la Valette, the Grand Master of the Order of St. John. Construction of the city started in 1566 and was completed only fifteen years later. A remarkable feat when one looked at the impressive bastions, forts, and cathedral, and remembered the entire city was built by hand.

London, England

Day 4

After the Daltons cleared customs at Heathrow, they saw a man whose face matched the picture Rex had received on his cellphone from Stevens.

As they approached him, Catia whispered under her breath, "He looks nothing like James Bond."

Rex had to fight hard to suppress the urge to laugh. "Shhh, he might hear you."

The man introduced himself as Julian Gray; the name also accorded with Rex's information. Julian was a friendly, stocky, balding, middle-aged man in a gray suit, light blue shirt, and dark blue tie.

Rex introduced himself and Catia before it was show-time for Digger. He sat down on Rex's right and waited. When Rex said, "And this is Digger," Digger duly extended his right paw. Julian looked at Rex, a little nervous. Rex smiled. "It's okay, he likes you."

Julian bent down, hesitantly, shook Digger's paw, and said, "Delighted to make your acquaintance, Digger."

Digger smiled, but Julian probably would not have recognized it as a smile.

He guided them to a TX$ model black cab or Hackney Carriage as Londoners called their black taxis, which were as iconic as Buckingham Palace, Big Ben, or London Bridge. Reportedly, the TX$ model had starred in over five-hundred movies, including the classics such as Doctor Who, James Bond, and Sherlock Holmes. What Rex and Catia would only learn later was that the cab they were in was one of many owned and operated by MI6 and MI5.

MI6 headquarters at Vauxhall Cross was located at 85 Albert Embankment in Vauxhall, in the southwestern part of central London, on the bank of the River Thames beside Vauxhall Bridge. Julian took them to a small meeting room where they were introduced to the second MI6 officer assigned to their mission, Brooke Palmer. She was in her mid-forties, of medium height, a bit overweight, short dark hair, blue eyes, dressed in a dark pants suit.

Julian did the introductions but forgot about Digger. The latter reminded him with a soft yelp to mind his manners. Brooke, clearly a dog-lover, enjoyed the moment much more than her colleague did at the airport earlier.

Brooke offered them tea and cookies. Although Rex and Catia were devoted coffee drinkers, they accepted the offer because they thought if they asked for coffee, their hosts might serve them the instant version, which Rex and Catia had long ago vowed to drink only in a life-threatening emergency, such as dying from thirst.

Digger was happy with a few pieces of jerky from a plastic container in Catia's handbag.

Julian and Brooke had been briefed by Myles Stevens. They had contacted Destiny Parker's parents and set up a meeting early the next morning. Her brother, Tony, they would see in the early afternoon, and a friend, Emily Hobson, the late afternoon. There were others that they could contact, but none of them had been so close to Destiny as to remember her well enough to be of much help. Brooke, who made the appointments, told the interviewees that she and Julian worked for MI6, Rex and Catia worked for the FBI, their interest in the case was because of an American citizen that was also killed during the incident on Rhodes Island.

It took them the rest of the afternoon to review all the information and make sure the MI6 agents understood how important it was to follow every possible lead, which could get them to Dragut.

When they got to the discussions about the information they were hoping to get from the interviewees, Julian asked, "Who's going to do the talking?"

Rex smiled. "I think it's best if you take the lead. I'm sure British citizens would appreciate being questioned by someone speaking the Queen's English rather than trying to figure out the accent of someone from the colonies speaking a dialect of English."

The MI6 officers had a good chuckle at Rex's wisecrack.

Catia said, "Okay, so what we want to know is everything they can remember about Destiny. Why did she leave Europe? Did she ever come back? When did they last see her? Did she ever contact them?"

"In essence, we're trying to find out who she worked for when she died. And where we can find her employer," Rex added.

"Also, the boyfriend," Catia said. "From what we've read, this Ozmert guy seems totally out of place as the lover of a free-spirited girl like Destiny. So, did they know him? What was he like? What were his political views? How serious was the relationship? Why did they break up?"

Chapter Seventeen

MEETING THE FAMILY

Hertfordshire, England

Day 5

Mr. and Mrs. Parker were in their late and mid-seventies. They lived on a large estate in a small castle in the countryside close to Hertfordshire, about an hour out of the city. They were blue blood and patriotic.

They had no problem allowing Digger into their castle and were thrilled when he greeted them with a paw-shake. They had a little Fox Terrier who yapped at Digger a few times but made himself scarce when Digger growled softly at him as if to say, "Yeah, I heard you, but I'm working here, so take a hike."

The Parkers were in mourning about their daughter's death. Through the course of the conversation it became evident that the Parkers had, in fact, been mourning their daughter for much longer than just the past few days.

Rex and Catia had to look sincere with their commiseration. They couldn't tell the grieving old couple they were there when she died and knew exactly how it happened, let alone tell them their daughter was a professional killer who had killed two people and then committed suicide. Her parents believed she was killed in the crossfire during a gunfight among Greek gangsters.

Although they loved their daughter, they were not ignorant of the unwise decisions she'd made in her life. On the one hand, they blamed themselves for not being good parents. On the other, they claimed to have brought her up in a Christian home with Christian values. Even after twenty-five years, they were still heartbroken that their daughter had turned her back on her family, heritage, country, and religion.

They were still bitter about the time she announced she was going to marry a Greek. Not that they had an issue with Greeks, after all Prince Philip was born in Greece. But they had drawn the line at a Greek Muslim. Especially so when Destiny announced she was going to become a Muslim so she could marry said Greek Muslim, Ushan Ozmert.

"But," said Mr. Parker, "Ozmert disappeared, without any warning. Destiny was devastated. Secretly, we were overjoyed and hoped she would come to her senses. However, not three months later, she left home and country, and we never heard from her again.

"For twenty-five years, to us, it was as if she was already dead." He took his handkerchief out, removed his glasses, and wiped the tears from his eyes before he continued. "Though we love her, we're not as proud of our daughter as we would've liked to be."

Brooke's final question was if they knew any of Destiny's friends that could be contacted.

"Two that we've met," Mrs. Parker said. "One died in that terrible terrorist attack a few years ago when a crazy Muslim drove a car into a crowd of people in London, Finsbury Park I think it was. The other was Emily Hobson. She lives in London, I believe. We haven't seen her since Destiny left."

In the car on the way back to London, the four agreed that the Parkers' sorrow was genuine, so was their statement that they had no contact with their daughter since she had left the country.

London, England

Day 5

Tony Parker was fifty, married with two children, a successful entrepreneur, a big-name venture capitalist with vast interests in telecommunications, television, and real estate. He made his first million before he was twenty-five and reached the ten million mark by the age of thirty. His net worth was rumored to be somewhere north of five hundred million pounds.

He was freakishly tall, probably an inch or two over seven feet. He was skinny, just like his sister. He had graying dark hair and brown eyes. He was dressed informally in jeans, t-shirt, and suede jacket. Apart from his height and lean body, he didn't look anything like his sister.

During the introductions, it didn't escape Rex or Catia that Digger wasn't up to his usual antics of insisting on being introduced as well. He just stood between Rex and Catia, staring at Tony.

Tony's feelings about his late sister were not very different from his parents.

"Yes, it's very sad. But you have to understand that we've been grieving for her for the past twenty-five years. Her death only brought back memories that I had locked up in the archives at the very back of my mind a long time ago.

"It might sound heartless, it's not, it's heartbreaking. Destiny thought her future was not with her own people and country. She made her choices. We tried to dissuade her but to no avail. I haven't seen or heard from her in twenty-five years. She broke contact. I respected her wishes and never tried to restore contact."

"Did you know Ushan Ozmert?" Brooke asked.

"Yes. I met him a few times."

"He was a Muslim?"

"Yes."

"Did you have a problem with him dating your sister?" Julian asked.

"Because he was a Muslim?"

"Yes, or any other reason."

"No, on both counts. He was a very nice guy, highly intelligent. Besides, even if I had a legitimate problem, Destiny would not have listened to me. She never listened to good advice. My parents didn't approve of the relationship, but they didn't even bother to talk to her about it because they knew it would only alienate her more."

"How did you feel when she became a Muslim?"

"It didn't bother me. I'm an atheist, so whatever religion makes one happy is fine by me."

"Why did they break up?"

"He went home to Greece for the summer holidays after

finishing university, before he had to start work at Roche in Switzerland. He stayed in contact with her while he was there in Greece on holiday. A few weeks later, he left for Switzerland to start his job with Roche. But he never turned up there."

"Any idea as to what happened to him?" Julian asked.

"The last time I saw and spoke to my sister, twenty-five years ago, she hadn't had contact with him for over three months. She tried to find him. She started in his hometown in Greece, where she talked to his family, but they had no idea what happened to him. For months, she followed every breadcrumb until she landed in Naples, where she was told Ushan had been killed by a Camorra hit squad and his body dumped in the deep sea. That's when Destiny accepted Ushan was dead."

I'm wondering why your parents didn't tell us any of this? Rex thought.

"Was there any reason why the Camorra would have wanted to kill him?" Julian asked.

"None that I know of."

"How did she take it?" Brooke asked.

"She was depressed for a day or so. That's how she was. Friends and relationships and even her family didn't mean much to her. Then she said she was leaving the UK and we should expect her when we see her again and not ever try to find her. That's it, just like that, and she was gone. She was twenty-two years old."

"You never heard anything from her or about her again?" Julian asked.

"Not directly from her, but over the years, a few friends and acquaintances told us they saw her in various places across Europe, even in Moscow once. All of them had the same experience, though; she didn't know who they were.

So, it's difficult to say if there was something wrong with her memory or if she was just herself, Destiny, the crusader for whatever anti-establishment cause she believed in at the time and wanted nothing to do with anyone from her past."

"Do you know any of her close friends?" Brooke asked.

"Uhh... not that I can... wait, there was a girl. What was her name? Uhh... Emma, no, Emily, yes, Emily, it was. Can't remember her surname, though."

On the way to meet with Emily Hobson, the four agreed that Tony Parker appeared to be believable. Though, it was a bit surprising to hear about Ozmert's death while the parents didn't mention it. But then it appeared the parents were in a much deeper state of shock than Tony. It was also of interest that neither MI5 nor MI6 had anything on record about Ozmert's death. But then neither of the agencies were watching him closely.

Rex and Catia didn't make any mention of Digger's refusal to be introduced to Tony—they couldn't figure out why. Maybe Tony was afraid of dogs or someone who preferred cats, or he could've been irritated because of the interruption of his busy schedule, or he was nervous. It must have been daunting to be questioned by four law enforcement officers accompanied by a big black dog.

Chapter Eighteen

THEY KNEW HIS NAME

London, England

Day 5

Emily Hobson was a biochemist, the CEO and majority shareholder of a highly successful pharmaceutical company in London. According to the MI6 file, she had turned forty-eight the month before. She was of above-average height, in good shape, had medium length blond hair which she kept in a ponytail, and green eyes. She had on a sienna colored business suit with a black blouse and a string of white pearls around her neck. She was married and had three children.

She had what Rex thought to be a stern facial expression and an almost abrupt demeanor about her. The fleeting look of panic she gave Digger when they entered her office didn't escape Rex's notice. And it was probably the reason Digger wasn't interested in being formally introduced to her either.

She's afraid of dogs. Rex surmised in silence.

She asked them to take a seat and didn't offer them anything to drink. "Before we start, I have a question for you," she said. "What were the circumstances of her death? I've only heard she was shot to death."

Emily looked unemotional. But then she didn't strike any of her interviewers as a person who wore her emotions on her sleeves.

Brooke replied, "We don't know much more. The Greek authorities are still investigating. We only know she was killed in a shooting incident on Rhodes Island, Greece, and we received a request to help identify her and help with their investigation."

"Let me guess, MI5 or MI6 found the match for you? She had been on their watch list since her university days."

"Yes, they did, with the cooperation of the Greek police who were able to match her fingerprints with what MI5 had on file," Brooke replied. There was no reason to lie about it.

"How can I be of assistance with your investigation?"

"Tell us about your relationship with her."

In a clinical manner, Emily recounted the history of her relationship with Destiny Parker. They met at university and became friends.

"Destiny," Emily said, "was an activist for anyone with a cause that was anti-establishment. In short, she was a rebel against society. She despised the stiff upper lip society in which she grew up. And that, according to her, was the reason for leaving the country after finishing university. I still remember her words, 'The problem with this country is there are too many Brits in it.'"

"Did you stay in touch after she left?" Julian asked.

Emily hesitated for a second or two and said, "Yes, we did, but you're not allowed to tell her family about it, understood? She made me swear that I'd never tell her family. Even though she's dead, I still want to honor our agreement."

Julian nodded. "When was the last contact?"

"About a month ago. She insisted that we never communicated via email or phone. Instead, we used chat programs. Lately, we'd been using Signal, the secured, end-to-end encrypted online chat application. I don't know why she insisted on using it, our conversations were benign. But then, Destiny had always been paranoid about privacy."

"Do you know where she lived all these years?"

"She never gave me an address. She didn't stay in one place. She lived all over Western and Eastern Europe, also Asia, and the Americas. When I spoke to her a month ago, she was in The Netherlands."

A distant alarm bell sounded in Rex's head.

"Did she have other close friends?" Julian asked.

"None as close as we were, at least not that I know of."

"Do you know her brother?" Brooke asked.

"Tony. Yes, I've met him once or twice way back when Destiny was still living in the UK. The two of them never had a good relationship."

"Did you know Ushan Ozmert?" Brooke continued.

"Yes. We were in the same class at Oxford. He was scary clever, even scared our lecturers. He and Destiny met in our second year and became engaged in our final year."

"How did you feel when she converted to Islam?"

"I thought she'd lost her mind. Not that I have a problem with Muslims of the peace-loving kind, but I just couldn't imagine the free-thinking, rebellious Destiny as a subservient Muslim wife." She smiled. "I still can't figure her in a burqa."

"Was Ushan a devout Muslim?"

"He never talked about religion in my presence. But from my observations, I'd say he was a secular Muslim."

"What were his political views?" Julian asked.

"I wouldn't know, he never participated in our discussions about national or international politics."

"When was the last time you saw him?" Brooke asked.

"A very long time ago. If my memory serves me correctly, it was a day or so before he went back home to Greece after we finished our studies. We all went partying. He had this great offer to work in Switzerland, but then he disappeared."

"Did Destiny or anyone else try to find him?"

"Destiny used all of her father's influence to get the law enforcement authorities across Europe and further afield to try and find him. She eventually gave up... After that, she left the country."

"If it's not too personal, would you mind telling us about the nature of your conversations since she left?" Brooke asked.

"It *is* personal, but if it helps to bring her killer to justice, I'll tell you."

"It could," Brooke said.

"We didn't talk politics; we had an agreement about that. I was way too conservative for her, and she too liberal for me. So, we talked about work and people—girly gossip. I got married five years after university and have three children. So, naturally, we talked about my children a lot. Destiny never married, so, we also talked about potential suitors."

Emily paused for a moment and said, "She was bisexual."

Another bit of information that seems to have escaped the Parker family, as well as Her Majesty's intelligence services. Unless you're lying, Rex noted in silence.

"My impression was she'd become quite a social butterfly among the intellectual types of Europe's universities. Over the years, there were a few of them in which she had more than just an academic interest, but none of it lasted very long. It was as if she was incapable of the commitment required for a long-term relationship. Usually, after the relationships ended, Destiny would move on to another city or country, just like she did when Ushan disappeared. Those were the kind of things we talked about."

"Did she tell you any of the names of the people she had a romantic interest in?" Brooke asked.

"No. Destiny was too discreet for that. She would mention the person's qualifications, title, and such but never a name."

"When was the last time she had a love interest that you know of?"

"Last time I spoke to her, about a month ago, she told me about an Egyptian professor she'd met in Athens."

Rex and Catia glanced at each other but remained quiet. *They* knew his name; it was Professor Nassor Almasi.

"Do you think Ushan is alive?" asked Julian.

"Your guess would be as good as mine. It's possible."

London, England

Day 5

Back at Vauxhall Cross, Brooke copied the recordings of the meetings onto a flash drive for Rex and Catia, which they immediately uploaded to the CRC servers.

A few minutes later, they were in Myles Stevens's office in conference with Richardson, Brandt, Spencer, and Thomson, providing a synopsis of the interviews.

"Ushan Ozmert played a much bigger role in the life of Destiny Parker than we ever imagined," said Stevens pensively when they finished.

"Yep," said Richardson, "and what to make of the fact that Destiny's parents and Emily Hobson didn't mention anything about Ozmert's death?"

Stevens was shaking his head. "Either they haven't heard about it, or they forgot to mention it or deliberately omitted it. Let's assume they don't know, then how did Tony Parker come to know about it?" Then he answered his own question. "Ah... I guess Destiny could've told him."

Or Tony could be making it up, Rex thought.

"After what we have learned about her the last few days, I'm wondering about Destiny's presence in The Netherlands a month ago. I'm not inclined to believe it was coincidence," said Richardson.

"Neither am I," said Stevens. "We'll look into it."

Richardson smiled. "Myles, you guys wouldn't perchance have Ushan Ozmert's fingerprints on file?"

"That would have been nice, wouldn't it?" Stevens replied. "But we'll work with MI5 to launch an investigation into Ozmert, using our combined clout with Europe's security agencies as well as Interpol and Europol."

Richardson said, "Good. In the meantime, our agents will pay the Ozmert family a visit in Greece."

Chapter Nineteen

MEETING THE OZMERTS

Alexandroupolis, Greece

Day 6

Within six hours after stepping aboard the *TOMATS* in Valletta, Josh and Marissa were back on a commercial flight, this time to Athens from where they caught a connecting flight to Alexandroupolis, where they had arrived a few hours before the Daltons. It was late afternoon when Josh and Marissa met them at the Alexandroupolis Dimokritos airport four miles east of the city.

Alexandroupolis was the capital of the Evros region in East Macedonia and Thrace. The largest city in the area, it had a little less than sixty thousand inhabitants but was an important port and commercial center of northeastern Greece.

Digger looked as if he were about to jump out of his skin when he saw Josh and Marissa. Catia was holding his leash at the time and had a hard time not being dragged across the floor in Digger's eagerness to get to them. It took a few minutes for Digger to welcome the stray members of his pack before Rex and Catia got a chance to greet their best friends.

Thanks to Joanne Sanders at the embassy in Athens, they had a rental SUV and a two-night reservation at the 4-star Grand Hotel Egnatia, all of it matching their fake passports, drivers' licenses, and credit cards.

Over dinner and late into the night, Rex and Catia brought their friends up to speed with everything that had happened since the Rhodes Island episode.

The next morning, they would travel to Feres, seventeen miles from Alexandroupolis. Josh and Marissa would wander the town's streets as tourists and talk to the locals about the town history and its people while Rex, Catia, and Digger were visiting the Ozmert family.

Feres, Greece

Day 7

Feres was a small town of about six thousand people in the area known as Western Thrace bordering Bulgaria and Turkey. Western Thrace was home to most of the Muslims who had been living in Greece since the times of the Ottoman Empire.

The town had evolved around the fortified 12th-century monastery of Panagia Kosmosotira (Virgin Mary World's Savior), which was constructed in the times when the village was still known as Vira. Located at the top of a hill in the town center, the monastery was one of the most historical sites in Greece. In 1357 the area was conquered by the Ottoman Turks who renamed Vira to Feres and turned the Panagia Kosmosotira into a mosque. Western Thrace, including Feres, became part of Greece in 1923 in terms of the Treaty of Lausanne, which ended the Ottoman Empire. The town's name was kept, but the monastery was returned to its original purpose.

It was shortly after 10:00 a.m. when the Daltons pulled up in front of a single-story, whitewashed, flat-roofed, stone house, with wood-frame windows. By Rex's estimates, the house could not have been less than a hundred and fifty years old. A few chickens moved out of the way as Rex, Catia, and Digger got out of the car and approached the thatched-roofed verandah. When they were about ten paces away, a man who Rex thought could have been born in the time when Napoleon ruled France, appeared in the front door, followed a few seconds later by a woman who looked as if she could also have been young in Napoleonic times.

"Mister and missus Ozmert, I presume?" Catia whispered to Rex.

"Uh-huh."

Catia greeted them in English but got no response. In Italian, she got the same result. She took her cellphone out, opened Google Translate's speech-to-speech app and repeated the greeting in Italian, and then held the phone out towards them to hear the Greek translation. She was rewarded with two toothless smiles from two rugged faces.

Mrs. Ozmert started talking rapidly, Catia stopped her with a gesture of her hand, pointed at the phone and with more hand gestures explained that it was necessary to get closer to each other and to speak slowly. The old couple's circumspect glances at each other and the Daltons and Digger made it clear that they were uneasy. But Catia's friendly smile and gentle tone helped the technophobes to grasp the concept, and slowly their curiosity took over as they relaxed and responded more confidently to the metallic voice speaking in their language.

After a few minutes of short-sentence exchanges, the Ozmerts invited the Daltons and Digger to join them on the verandah.

Rex and Catia had no idea how well Google's speech-to-speech translation worked in Greek. They had tested it with all the languages they could speak and were impressed with how accurate it was. Nevertheless, it didn't take long for the four of them to work out the necessary sign language to let each other know when the translation didn't make sense, and the speaker had to rephrase the sentence and try again.

It was not the quickest and easiest way to communicate, but it served the Daltons' purpose. They told the Ozmerts that they were researching the history of the area, especially the folklore. And they were given to understand that the Ozmerts were among the oldest living inhabitants.

Over a bottomless pot of near-lethal strength Greek coffee served in small ceramic cups, together with small plates of home-made baklava, the Ozmerts proudly recounted their heritage stretching back almost four hundred and fifty years. The old man's first name was Tekoz and his wife's Emel. They were Greek citizens of the Muslim faith. Tekoz was of Greek origin while his wife was Turkish. And they were proud to call themselves Ottomans.

Rex and Catia had to fight the urge to high-five when Tekoz proudly announced that he was a descendant of the revered Admiral Turgut Reis, also known as Dragut.

To prove his claim, Tekoz disappeared into the house

and returned a few minutes later with a rectangular, engraved wooden box which he opened for them to see what was inside. It was a curved-blade dagger with what looked like an ivory handle with gold inlays; the blade was about eight inches. He told them that the dagger belonged to Dragut and had been passed along the generations, a precious heirloom. He allowed Rex and Catia to take it out and have a closer look. It was impossible to tell if it once belonged to Dragut, but that it was old was beyond doubt.

The Ozmerts were crop farmers, mainly cotton, but they explained that they were too old to do the farm work anymore and have been renting their land out to a younger neighbor. When Rex asked them how old they were, Emel laughed and asked him to take a guess. He knew he was on slippery ground and went for a very diplomatic age of about sixty-five, which made both of them laugh. Tekoz was eighty and Emel seventy-six.

They had two children, twins, a son, Ushan, and a daughter, Umut. Now it was Emel's turn to disappear into the house. She returned with a framed family photo. She explained that the photo was taken on the day when the twins finished school, they were eighteen then. Rex and Catia had to take a hard look to recognize the young man staring at them from this photo as the same person who stared at them from the MI6 photos a day or two ago. On this photo, he was about two inches taller and much skinnier than his sister. Apart from the large black hornbill glasses with thick lenses, it was easy to spot that they were twins. Emel had no objections when Catia asked if she could take a picture of the photo with her cellphone.

It was apparent that Tekoz and Emel were very proud of their family history and their children. They were about to start talking about their children when a blue, two-door hatchback Toyota sedan came slowly up the gravel driveway toward the house. It was Umut. She was a senior nursing officer at the hospital in Alexandroupolis, her mother told them with proudness in her voice. She lived in Alexandroupolis and visited them on her days off. Unfortunately, she had never married and, therefore, this line of the Ozmert family would end with their deaths.

Umut had shoulder-length dark hair, which was tied in a ponytail, deep brown eyes, and olive skin. She was of medium height, and although she had obviously gained some weight since she left school, she was not overweight. She was not quite pretty, but she was not ordinary looking either. She had a friendly face, which gave the impression that she smiled often.

The Daltons and Digger were introduced, and Umut got a paw-shake from Digger. Umut was fluent in English and immediately took over the translation duties from Google. Emel fetched another coffee cup and a small plate from the kitchen and poured her some coffee and stacked the plate with baklava.

Soon after, the conversation returned to the family, and Catia asked about their son, Ushan. The long silence that followed and the sad expressions that settled on their faces almost made her regret the question.

Tekoz had tears in his eyes as he shook his head and told them that their son had died many years ago.

Umut said, "Please don't talk about him anymore. My parents have never gotten over his 'death,'" she made air quotes. "I don't mind talking about him because I don't think he's dead. But they prefer to believe it; it gave them closure and made it more bearable for them."

"Would you be willing to tell us more about yourself and your brother if we meet you somewhere in Alexandroupolis?" Catia asked. "We don't want to take up more of you and your parents' time."

"Sure. We can meet in the city later this afternoon when I'm back."

She didn't translate any of that.

Fifteen minutes later, the Daltons thanked the Ozmerts for their hospitality and all the information about their family history and made special mention of what a privilege it was to see Dragut's dagger and the family photos. They got Umut's cellphone number and agreed to meet at a coffee shop in the afternoon.

Rex was quiet as they drove back to town.

"What's going through your mind, Rex?"

"I suspect the same as yours."

"Is Dragut the Second also known as Ushan Ozmert?"

"Uh-huh."

Josh and Marissa were waiting for them at the ancient monastery. Their morning was not nearly as consequential as the Daltons. Though, both of them had learned a lot about the history of Feres and Western Thrace. The Google Translate app helped them to understand the townspeople whom they found to be very friendly and sociable.

They were, however, surprised to learn even though everyone spoke Greek and lived on Greek soil, almost all of the people they talked to told them they were Turkish. Descendants of the mighty Ottomans. And many of them expressed the hope to see the joyous day when they would be part of the great empire again.

Chapter Twenty

MY TWIN BROTHER

Alexandroupolis, Greece

Day 7

The Fleur De Lis was a charming little coffee shop in Alexandroupolis, not far from the hospital where Umut worked. It served the best coffee Rex and Catia had in days. Umut recommended the *bougatsa*, a traditional Greek pie consisting of a phyllo pastry layered with a filling of minced meat, cheese, or semolina custard. The name of the dish came from the Ottoman word *pogatsa*, a pie filled with cheese.

Rex had placed his cellphone on the table. There were no lights flickering. To Umut, it would have looked as if it were switched off, although it was busy recording their conversation.

After the server delivered their order and left, Umut told Rex and Catia about her long-lost twin brother. "As a child and throughout his school years, Ushan had been an abnormally reedy boy, as you would have seen on the family portrait my mother showed you this morning. He looked nerdy with his thick glasses, and, of course, that made him the butt of many jokes. We have always been close. I've always been very protective of him. He had few friends, but what mother nature didn't give him in physique, she more than made up for with the brains she gave him.

"He was extremely gifted. And that's not a blood-is-thicker-than-water observation; his teachers agreed. The headmaster had explained it to our parents once; only two and a half percent of the world population has an IQ of one-hundred and thirty or above. Ushan, with an IQ of one-hundred and forty-five, was part of a group of only zero-point-zero-one percent of the world population. In other words, he was more intelligent than ninety-nine-point-nine-nine percent of the world's people."

"Wow!" Catia exclaimed. "That's amazing."

"Indeed," Umut said. "The teachers at school loved him. He was a model student. They found him scholarships and financial help to get into Oxford University in England to study biochemistry. And there, as can be expected, he excelled at his studies. He quickly came to the attention of his lecturers, who saw a bright future for him as a scientist. Some of them were so bold as to predict a Nobel Laureate in his future."

Rex and Catia were impressed, though they waited for the but in the story.

"No one was surprised when a major Swiss pharmaceutical company headhunted him in his final year at Oxford. They offered him an all-expenses-paid scholarship to undertake Ph.D. studies at the University of Zurich and a posh job at their company, one of the biggest pharmaceutical companies in the world. Ushan accepted the offer."

She stopped talking, took a sip of her coffee and a bite of the savory pastry. When she didn't continue, Catia said, "And then?"

"And then he came home for a holiday after he graduated from Oxford before he had to report to his employer in Zurich. We almost didn't recognize him. He had gone through a metamorphosis since we saw him four years ago. He had gained weight. Apparently, he had taken up bodybuilding. The big glasses were gone, replaced with contact lenses. He was still lean but muscled like a gymnast. The shy, self-conscious boy that left here four years before was now a desirable, self-assured young man. He even hinted that there was a beautiful English girl who got more than just his passing attention. In short, for my brother, the world was his oyster, and the sky was the limit..."

Here comes the but, thought Rex.

"But... it was not meant to be... Everything changed within a few weeks." She paused and looked around the busy coffee shop. When she started again, her voice was soft. "It happened in a coffee house in Feres. Twenty-five years ago. I had just finished my nursing degree. We were twenty-two." She stopped again.

After a minute or so of silence, Rex asked, "What happened, Umut?"

She took a tissue out of her handbag and wiped tears from her eyes.

"Apologies, I've never told anyone about it. For twenty-five years, I *wanted* to talk about it. Please bear with me; for once, I want to tell *someone* the truth."

Catia placed her hand on Umut's and said, "We'll listen, and if there's anything we can do to help, we will."

"Thank you. Sometimes it's easier to bare your soul to strangers than friends and family." She wiped more tears away and continued.

"One afternoon during that time, Ushan and Dad went to that coffee shop to play *Okey* with some of dad's friends."

Okey was a very popular board game similar to *Rummikub*.

"In the coffee shop was this gigantic, loudmouthed man, the village bully, Dimitris Rossas, and some of his friends. When he had an audience, Rossas, who called himself a Greek Orthodox Christian, never let the opportunity pass to degrade and belittle the Muslims. Rossas went to school with us; he was a year ahead. Everyone feared him, even the teachers. He knew that we are Muslims, and he also knew that we are descendants of Dragut. One of Rossas's favorite pastimes was to degrade Dragut whenever he had the opportunity and to let everyone know that it was the Crusaders who eventually killed Dragut.

"I've never let it get to me, but for Ushan, to whom Dragut was like a deity, it was the biggest insult imaginable. When we played war games as kids, Ushan was always Dragut; it was one of the few privileges he enjoyed among his few friends. At an early age, Ushan had already devoured every bit of information about Dragut that he could lay his hands on. Some of his friends jokingly called him the Admiral; he liked it. To him, Dragut was a role model. He once told me that if Dragut were alive today, he would've restored the Ottoman empire to its former glory. I always found it strange that Ushan, who clearly was a great scientist in the making, had this almost fanatic obsession with Dragut. When I asked him about it once, he told me that everyone needs a hobby."

Rex and Catia fought the urge to look at each other. Dragut the Second was none other than Ushan Ozmert.

"Sorry, I'm digressing," Umut said. "On that afternoon, everyone in the packed coffeehouse overheard Rossas making lewd remarks about me. Everyone was staring at my father. But you saw my father today; he is a tiny man. Even twenty-five years ago, he was no match for the bully.

"I wasn't there, but a friend who was there told me what had happened. He told me Ushan got up, approached Rossas, and said, 'Excuse me, did I hear you call my sister a slut?'

"'Yes, pipsqueak, that's what I said. You got a problem with that?' Rossas had said.

"Ushan made no reply. He turned away, walked back to the table, and told Dad and his friends it was better if they all left. As they walked out the door, Rossas laughed at them and shouted, 'Not only is she a slut, Ushan, she's an ugly one too; she looks like a pack mule. Speaking of which, I think it's high time you Ottomans pack your mules and move to Turkey; you've overstayed your welcome in our country for a long time now.'"

She took a sip of coffee, took a deep breath, and continued. "No one in that coffeehouse objected. Instead, they had erupted in raucous laughter.

"The news of the incident spread quickly. By evening, my mother and I had heard about it. Later that night, I went to Ushan's room and asked him to join me for a walk around our farm. That's when I told him what Dimitris Rossas did to me..." Her voice was trembling, and she stopped talking.

Catia, sensing what she was about to tell them, tried to stop her, but Umut would have none of it.

"That bastard raped me..., two days before the incident

in the coffee shop. I would never be able to marry... have children... I didn't tell anyone except my brother that night, and now you." Her body was shaking from the sobs.

Catia moved to the chair next to Umut and placed her arm around Umut's shoulder to comfort her.

"That pig brought scandal and embarrassment over my family. I was terrified of him. He told me if I talk to anyone, he would kill me."

Rex was wondering where he would be able to get hold of this scumbag Rossas. Before he could ask, Umut continued.

"A few days later, Dimitris Rossas's family was looking for him; he had gone missing. It was a week later, in the morning, when one of the locals noted the new statue in front of the Monastery of Panagia Kosmosotira.

"On closer inspection, they found a life-size concrete statue of a man that everyone agreed bore a striking resemblance to the man who had disappeared, Dimitris Rossas. The odd feature of the figure was that the man seemed to be holding small objects in each hand and something in his mouth.

"The police removed the statue, and forensics experts discovered the body of Dimitris Rossas entombed in the concrete. The objects in his hands were his testicles, and in his mouth was his penis."

Poetic justice. Rex had to fight the smile that was threatening to take over his face.

"Needless to say, the Ozmert family was very high on the police's list of suspects. But Rossas had many enemies. Truth be told, I think the police were somewhat relieved to be rid of the eternal troublemaker. And so were many of the townspeople."

"Let me guess," Catia said, "not long after the unveiling of the statue and the police questioning, Ushan left town and never returned?"

Umut nodded. "Yes. We, my parents and I, accompanied him to the airport the day he left for Switzerland. We expected to hear from him when he arrived, but we didn't. A week after his departure, I tried to phone him but got no reply. I kept trying for a few weeks but never got a reply. I've sent emails and text messages, all without a reply. I phoned the company where he was supposed to work; they told me he never turned up.

"Naturally, we were worried, but every inquiry we made came up empty. As far as we could establish, he didn't go back to England either. For months we searched and asked, but we never heard from him again.

"And, of course, then the rumors started, many of them over the years. People claimed to have seen him. Sometimes he was in different places, thousands of kilometers apart, at the same time. Finally, a few years after his disappearance, my parents decided that Ushan had died in a foreign land. They grieved for him. They couldn't say the Ṣalāt al-Janāzah, the Islamic funeral prayer, because there was no body, but they said the Salat al-Gha'ib, the absentee funeral prayer. Since then, they've tried to accept it and live with it."

Umut looked at her watch and said, "I have to leave in ten minutes for the start of my shift. I want to thank you for listening to me. I can't tell you how much it means to me to have had the opportunity to finally unburden myself and tell someone the truth. I don't have any evidence that my brother is alive, neither that he's dead. I prefer to believe the former. But I have no idea where to begin looking for him."

Neither do we, thought Rex, *but we have to find him. Because if we don't, thousands of innocent people are going to die.*

"I'll never give up hope. One day we will find him, or he will come back on his own." With that, she took out her cellphone, opened the pictures folder, and showed them a photo of her and Ushan. "This was taken twenty-five years ago, at the airport, the day he left."

Looking at the photo, Rex and Catia agreed with Umut's earlier observation about her brother's metamorphosis; they would not have recognized the man in the photo as the same young man they saw in the family photo that morning. Without the large hornbill glasses, the likeness between them was much more apparent.

"May I email you the photo? Perhaps one day you will see him, and you can tell him that we are missing him so much." She started crying again.

Catia gave her a Gmail account, and Umut immediately forwarded the photo. Less than a minute later, Catia confirmed receipt.

"Sorry, one more question," Catia said. "Did you ever meet the English girl he told you about?"

"No. I wish I had, but he never told me her name."

"Thank you for taking the time to tell us about your brother. We promise to look for him wherever we go," Catia said without blinking an eye.

Umut thanked them again and left.

As she walked out the door, Catia looked at Rex and said, "How do we tell these kind people who are still crying for their lost son and brother that he is a monster and we're going to hunt him down?"

"We don't," Rex said softly. He was scratching Digger's ears, deep in thought. "Ushan never told his family he was engaged to the English girl. And the English girl never came to Feres to meet her future in-laws. And the Ozmert family never heard that Ushan was killed by the Camorra."

"Exactly so," said Catia.

Chapter Twenty-One

THE OTTOMANS

Alexandroupolis, Greece

Day 7

Back at the hotel, they met in the Farleys' suite and told them about the meeting with Umut. Then they uploaded the audio recordings of the conversations with the older Ozmerts and Umut to CRC's servers before phoning Brandt to give him a verbal report.

When Rex finished the report, Brandt said, "So, you reckon Dragut is Ushan Ozmert, and he's alive?"

"Yep. That's what we believe," said Rex. "We have a real name, real pictures, and real last known address, albeit it a twenty-five-year-old address."

"We'll have to see about that," said Brandt. "Get some rest."

Rex thought the Old Man sounded a bit distant, abrupt. But then, he could be like that at times. He shrugged and disconnected the call.

When the call ended, Marissa said, "Tell us everything you know about Dragut the First. I think it's good to have background information."

Catia pulled her notes up on her tablet and told them what she and Rex had gathered the past few days.

"The Great Ottoman, Turgut Reis, nicknamed Dragut, was one of the greatest Turkish leaders and commanders of all time. He operated with great success in the waters of the Mediterranean and the Black Sea, many ships and towns carried his name. He played a significant role in Turkish expansion to Northern Africa and distinguished himself in several naval battles during his lifetime. In addition to serving as a naval officer, Dragut was also the *Bey*, chieftain of Algiers, *Beylerbey*, fleet commander, of the Mediterranean, and *Pasha*, ruler of Tripoli. Under his rule, Tripoli experienced vigorous economic growth and became one of the most important cities in Northern Africa.

"He was the son of Muslim parents of Greek descent. At the age of twelve, he was captured by slavers. From that early age on, he became well versed in life at sea and learned about naval combat. The most important phase of Dragut's early career was when Turkey expanded its territory to include Egypt. During those years, he became a loyal follower of the Turkish corsair, Sinan Reis, who quickly noticed the young Dragut's prowess at sea and gave him partial command over a small warship. Not long after, Dragut got full command of his own warship, and from then on, his fame grew in leaps and bounds. His was soon the best-equipped warship in Sinan Reis's fleet. He became a close friend and confidant of the famous admiral, Hayreddin Barbarossa, who promoted Reis to the rank of chief lieutenant and gave him command over twelve galliots.

"He defeated the Venetians in the 1538 Battle of Preveza. He raided cities across Sicily, Italy, Spain, Albania, and captured the city of Castelnuovo from the Venetians. In 1540, Dragut was captured by the Genoese war fleet, and he spent the next four years as a galley slave until he was freed by his friend Barbarossa when he laid siege to Genoa with his fleet of two hundred and ten ships. In 1546, after Barbarossa's death, Dragut was promoted to the supreme commander of the Ottoman naval forces in the Mediterranean. A capacity in which he served the Ottoman Empire for twenty years until his death in the campaign for the conquest of Malta in 1565. He was buried in Tripoli."

"Now that's what most people would call an illustrious career," Marissa said when Catia ended.

"The only black mark on his résumé is his failure to conquer Malta," Josh said. "But the million-dollar question now is where is Junior, and what are his plans?"

"Rex thinks he could be on a mission to restore the Ottoman Empire," Catia said.

"If that's the case, we spoke to quite a few of his supporters this morning in Feres," Josh said.

"Okay, tell us about the Ottoman Empire," Marissa said.

Rex chuckled. "They existed for more than six hundred years; I'll have to keep to the highlights.

"Osman I, Uthman in Arabic, from which the name Ottoman derived, was the leader of the Turkish tribes in Anatolia around 1299 and was the one credited with the founding of the Ottoman Empire. At the time, the Ottoman Turks set up a formal government and started expanding their territory. They seized the ancient city of Constantinople, the Byzantine Empire's capital, and renamed it to Istanbul, ending the thousand-year reign of the Byzantine Empire.

"They were one of the largest empires in history. At the summit of their power, they ruled over what we know today as Turkey, Bulgaria, Hungary, Romania, Greece, Macedonia, Jordan, Lebanon, Israel, and the Palestinian territories, Syria, parts of Saudi Arabia, Egypt, and most of the north coast of Africa."

"Quite a spread to manage," Josh remarked dryly.

"Indeed." Rex continued. "The Ottoman Caliphate lasted for more than four hundred years from 1517 to 1922. They were the last Sunni Islamic caliphate of the late medieval and the early modern era."

Rex continued and told them many Western Europeans viewed the Ottomans as a threat, but in hindsight, historians agreed the Ottoman Empire, in fact, provided great regional stability and security. They made important contributions to science, religion, and culture. They brought some of the most popular forms of art to the world, which included calligraphy, painting, poetry, textiles and carpet weaving, ceramics, and music. They learned and practiced advanced mathematics, astronomy, philosophy, physics, geography, and chemistry.

Some of the greatest advances in medicine were attributed to the Ottomans, who invented several surgical instruments that are still used today, such as forceps, catheters, scalpels, pincers, and lancets.

They suffered their first defeat at the Battle of Vienna in 1683. Over the next century, they lost key regions, including Greece, in 1830, and in 1878 they also lost Romania, Serbia, and Bulgaria. During the Balkan Wars between

1912 and 1913, they lost nearly all their territories in Europe.

The Ottoman Empire entered World War I on the side of the Central Powers, Germany and Austria-Hungary, and were defeated in October 1918. Following the Armistice of Mudros, most of the remaining Ottoman territories were divided between Britain, France, Greece, and Russia. The empire officially ended in 1922, and the title of Sultan was abolished. Turkey was declared a republic on October 29, 1923, and reforms were implemented to secularize and westernize the country.

"Growing up around here, among people whose greatest political aspiration is to be reunited with Turkey, I'll not be surprised if the revival of the empire is exactly what Dragut Two has in mind," Marissa said.

"Yeah, history has no shortage of Walter Mitty characters who can't accept that empires and civilizations come and go like the ebb and flow of the oceans. Instead, they get starry-eyed about restoring the glory days of the past," said Rex.

Chapter Twenty-Two

CRAVINGS FOR SEAFOOD

Alexandroupolis, Greece

Day 7

Catia and Marissa had cravings for seafood, and their husbands required no convincing. Elies & Dafnes, located on the waterfront, was a new seafood restaurant in Alexandroupolis, reportedly the best in town, the concierge at the hotel told Catia and Marissa and made the booking for them. Yes, Digger would be welcome.

The weather was good. They decided to walk to the restaurant, about one and a half miles from the hotel, to give themselves and Digger a bit of exercise.

They arrived at the restaurant right on time at 8:00 p.m. Their standing rule was that they never talked about a mission until the dessert had been served. But tonight, they broke the rule and started talking about it the moment their food arrived.

"So, now we're missing only one piece of information to bring this mission to a successful end," Josh said.

"Only one?" Marissa asked.

"Yes."

"What?"

"Ushan Ozmert's new address."

"Ouch!" He shouted when her punch landed on his shoulder.

Catia laughed. "I guess that's one way of looking at it, Josh. But it's not as if we could look him up in the telephone directory."

"You don't think he would've listed himself?"

Catia was shaking with laughter. "He could've, but I am pretty sure he didn't do it under Ushan Ozmert, or Dragut, or Turgut Reis."

"What is the world coming to? You can't even find people in the telephone directory anymore. What do you reckon, Digger, you think you can sniff him out for us? It *will* save us a lot of trouble."

Digger didn't reply. He only smiled when Josh slipped him a piece of fish under the table, closed his eyes again when he realized nothing more was coming his way, and went back to sleep.

"On a serious note, if it's Dragut the Second's goal to resurrect the Ottoman Empire, what is he hoping to achieve by launching terror attacks such as the one in The Netherlands?" Josh asked.

"I think it has to do with Turkey's ambitions to become a member of the European Union," Rex said.

"You've lost me," Josh said. "Turkey wants to join the EU, and Dragut wants to bomb the place to kingdom come?"

Rex held his hand up. "Here's how I see it. Turkey is an

important gateway for the EU to the Middle East. The country also borders Bulgaria and Greece, both EU member states. Turkey's strategic location is probably one of the main reasons they're also part of NATO. The EU can benefit from having Turkey as a member.

"But for the past thirty-odd years, since their application to join the EU in 1987, they've not been successful. There were times when good progress was made, but since 2016, negotiations have stalled. The official reason given by the EU is Turkey's record of human rights violations and deficits in the rule of law. The EU's General Affairs Council issued a statement in recent years, noting that Turkey seems to be moving further away from the European Union. Of course, they'd never admit that the real problem with Turkey is that they're a Muslim country. There are no Muslim countries in the EU.

"Even so, from the little I've read, it seems as if Turkey is still bent on getting EU membership. And I think the reason for it is that once they're a member, they'd have a platform from where they can promote the idea of the new Ottoman Empire. Presenting it as a protective wall of moderate Muslims against the extremists of the Middle East. Well, that's what I think."

"So, are you saying the attacks are to drive the fear levels of the EU populace to the point where they would accept Turkey as the first Muslim country in the EU to help protect them?"

"Precisely," Rex replied. "That's what everyone has been screaming about for years, demanding that moderate Muslims stand up and stop the radical Muslims. Turkey would be the EU and the western world's knight in shining armor. At least that's how they'd present themselves."

"It sounds logical, except that it means the Turkish

government is sponsoring Dragut's terror spree. Do you think that's the case?" Josh asked.

"I'll not be surprised if it is."

"So, attacks like those in The Netherlands are to scare the people and their governments, to leave them in a state of angst, desperation, and helplessness so that Turkey can then step in and say, 'Hey, *we* can protect you from those crazy killers. Just give us our empire, and we'll make sure you're safe.'" Josh said.

"Couldn't say it better myself."

Marissa nodded slowly. "I've never been a victim of a terrorist attack, so I can't speak from experience, but I can only imagine that if I'd ever gone through something as awful as in The Netherlands, any offer to safeguard me from another event would get my immediate support."

"I think when we're back on the yacht, we should ask Martin to get one of their analysts to brief us about the current political ambitions of the Turks," Rex said. "I've seen a lot of speculation about Neo-Ottomanism, which I understand to mean a movement to promote greater political engagement of Turkey within the countries formerly comprising the Ottoman Empire."

Chapter Twenty-Three

CALL THE DOG OFF

Alexandroupolis, Greece

Day 7

It was shortly after 11:00 p.m. when they settled the bill and left the restaurant. As they went through the door, Rex noticed the couple in their mid-thirties who had been sitting across the room from them for the past hour or so also get up and make their way to the front desk. Presumably, to settle their bill as well. The woman was talking on her cell-phone in Greek while the man settled the bill.

Rex was holding Digger's leash as they walked along the deserted street.

Jack Swanson was fifty-one, too old for the kind of job he was hired to do tonight. But he had promised himself this was his last job. Over the years, he had put away enough money to fund an early retirement in warmer climes, closer to the equator. He was a former Para, as soldiers of the British Parachute Regiment were colloquially known. The First Battalion to which he belonged for almost fifteen years was part of the Special Forces Support Group under the operational command of the Director of Special Forces.

His adventure days came to an early and painful end at the age of thirty-six when he badly damaged his knee during a night jump and had to undergo knee replacement surgery. Despite the fact that he had regained almost all of his pre-accident mobility, he was relegated to a desk job. He lasted exactly three months and four days before he viciously assaulted a superior officer for which he served a year in the stockade before he was dishonorably discharged.

Although his post-accident physical condition was not what the army wanted it to be, there was a market for someone with his skills outside the military.

He liked to think of his current job as that of a problem solver. Whenever people with money had problems of the humankind and required a solution that would make the problem go away quietly and permanently, people with Jack's skills and lack of conscience were in demand. That's what his agent told him the one and only time they had met face-to-face, fifteen years ago. The agent didn't lie; there were more than enough rich people with those kinds of problems to make him rich enough to retire two years ago if he had chosen to do so. His agent also told him that most contract killers had one problem though, they didn't know when it was time to call it quits and retire. He didn't quite believe the agent then, but now he knew the man was right. Over the past two years, this had been the sixth time he had told himself, "this is the last job."

When they were about two hundred yards from the restaurant, Rex stopped to let Digger have a sniff at a lamp-post and looked back. He saw the couple about fifty yards behind them, holding hands; apparently, they were window shopping.

About ten yards further, Rex and company crossed at a pedestrian traffic light, heading into a short dark street in a semi-industrial area, which would take them through to the road leading to their hotel.

As they crossed the street, Rex looked to the right and saw the couple getting into a car with an Uber sticker in the window. The woman was on her cellphone again.

Good. I would've been unpleasantly surprised if Dragut were onto us so quickly.

The sidewalk in the short street was lined with big old trees on both sides. Behind the trees were warehouses. A few of them were dilapidated and abandoned. Only a few of the streetlights were working.

Good place for an ambush, Rex thought.

Jack had an uneasy feeling about this job. For starters, he wasn't allowed to use guns or bombs. Another concern was his crew. The five men, he was told by his agent, were the toughest and most heartless hooligans he could get in Greece on such short notice. But hooligans were not soldiers. Besides, he preferred to work alone. This was the type of job where he would have preferred to use a bomb and get it done with one big bang. But he had instructions to make it look like a mugging, not a hit job. The lack of preparation time and information about the targets also weighed on his mind.

Notwithstanding, the money was good, fantastic, actually. And half of it was already in his numbered bank account in the Seychelles. When he received the other half of the money, this job alone would have increased his total savings by fifteen percent. *That's why I took the job. Quick, easy, and lucrative.*

He raised the monocular to his eye. "Ah, finally. I've been waiting for you for more than three hours," he mumbled softly and looked at the Greek gangsters on either side of him while pointing to the end of the street. They didn't speak English, but their nods told him they'd seen the targets about a hundred yards away.

He raised the monocular again to study the four as they approached and noticed the big black dog. "Bloody hell, no one told me about a damn dog," he mumbled. But then he recognized the Service Dog sticker and smiled. *One crippled guy, one healthy guy, and two women. No challenge. This will be over in a minute, and I will have earned the easiest three hundred grand in my entire professional career. Nice way to end a career.*

———

About a third of the way into the semi-dark street Digger started growling a few seconds before four big men stepped out of the shadows from behind the trees and blocked Rex and company's way. They were about fifteen yards ahead. All of them were armed with side-handle police batons and brandishing KA-BAR combat knives with eight-inch blades.

No guns. Gangsters, Rex thought. He looked back the way they came and saw two men rounding the corner coming their way. *Boxed in.* He said to the others, "Whatever you do, don't stop walking. There are two behind us as well. They're still a hundred yards away. We have to deal with these guys in front of us first and quickly. Remember the Old Man's battle cry, speed, surprise, and violence of action."

When they were about ten yards away, the man on the left shouted in British accented English, "Stop right where you are. Put your hands on your head."

Maybe they didn't hear me. "I said, stop!" Jack shouted, but then something happened that he had never experienced in his entire life. He felt his legs taking a step back and another, but he had not told his legs to do so. Instead of stopping as he had told the targets to do, they and the dog were now rushing toward him and his men at full speed, shouting, "Geronimo!" They were less than three yards away when Jack's legs turned and steered him to the nearest tree. He didn't see his men were doing the same, and one of them tripped himself up when he turned.

Jack heard the growl behind him. He turned and kicked at the dog, but the damn dog sidestepped his kick and started closing in again.

Jack leaped up at the nearest overhanging branch, got hold of it, but immediately realized his feet were only inches from the ground. The dog would rip his legs apart; he pulled them up.

The second time the Brit shouted at them to stop was Rex's cue to deploy the surprise factor. "Now!" he shouted, and they all broke into a full sprint charging at the four men ahead of them as in a cavalry charge, shouting "Geronimo!"

As if in choreographed motion, the four thugs first took one step back then another then they gave up, turned their backs, and ran away from the crazy people with the big black dog.

In his haste to get away, one of them, a short and overweight man, had tripped himself and fallen onto his hands and knees on the tarmac. Catia and Marissa were heading for him.

Digger was like a sprinter out of the blocks after the Brit heading for a nearby tree. Digger quickly closed the gap, the man stopped, turned, and kicked at Digger but missed him by a mile as Digger deftly stepped out of the way. The Brit jumped up and grabbed the closest branch above his head. The branch held his weight, but his feet were barely off the ground. Digger rushed In. The man tried to pull himself up, but he was too slow. Digger slammed into him with full force and sunk his teeth into the Brit's crotch.

The man screamed, let go of the branch, and fell to the ground on his back with a noisy groan. He didn't move.

Josh had caught up with the second goon before he could cover ten yards. He swiped the thug's legs from under him, and he fell sideways onto the cobblestone sidewalk. Josh's kick to the head put him to sleep.

Catia and Marissa arrived just when the third ruffian got back on his feet. He took a swing at Catia with his baton, but she ducked, he missed and lost his balance. Before he could regain his balance and take another swing at Catia, Marissa pushed the probes of the stun gun into his neck. The gun was a small one, not capable of neutralizing the man like a Taser gun would have, but it was enough to send a painful jolt through his body and startle him. And that was enough distraction to allow Catia to move in and plant a roundhouse kick in his face that broke his jaw and sent him sprawling to the tarmac, unconscious.

The fourth gangster was much quicker than his compatriots. But so was Rex. He only got a few yards further than Josh's guy before Rex landed on his back and plowed him into the tarmac face first. He was going to have the mother of all headaches when he woke up, and his face was going to burn like fire where the skin got scraped away.

Twenty seconds after they had charged at the four villains, they turned around to face the two who were approaching them from behind. The street was empty. The two men had vanished like mist before the sun.

The Brit was dizzy from the fall but otherwise fully conscious yet silent and unmoving. Presumably, his immobility and silence had something to do with the fact that Digger had the guy's family jewels firmly between his teeth and was growling softly, probably as a warning that things could get a lot worse if he were to move.

Despite the seriousness of the situation, the scene with Digger and his charge was so hilarious they couldn't help but laugh.

By now, Jack Swanson had reached the conclusion that he had taken on one too many jobs. The job before this one should have been his last.

While Rex questioned the Brit, Josh and the girls quickly disarmed the three unconscious men, collected their IDs and cellphones, tied them up with their own shoelaces, and gagged them with their own socks. Then they pulled them off the street into the nearest deserted warehouse.

Rex searched and disarmed the Brit and was not surprised to find he had no wallet or ID. But finding the K iPhone was a surprise; the Brit was a professional, not the leader of a street gang. Another of Dragut's disciples?

"Who do you work for?" Rex asked.

The Brit raised his middle finger to signal to Rex to take a hike.

Rex ignored him and said to Digger, "Put a bit more pressure on, buddy, will you?"

Digger's jaws were capable of exerting pressure of more than two hundred and fifty pounds per square inch. He hadn't reached anywhere near that much when the Englishman's voice turned from baritone to soprano as he started begging Rex to call the dog off.

Rex paid no heed and said, "I need a name and address and telephone number. And photos, if you have any."

"I have none of what you want. Call the dog off. Please!"

Rex looked at Digger.

"I got instructions via Signal on my cellphone. I don't know the person."

"So, you're a hired gun?"

"Yes."

"What were your instructions."

The Brit made no reply.

By now, Josh, Marissa, and Catia had joined him.

Rex looked at Digger.

"To kill you!" The Brit shouted. "But I didn't. Please take the dog off me."

I thought you were a genius, Dragut. Sending a killer after us was your first mistake. Now I know you're alive, and I'm coming for you, asshole.

"I'd say you couldn't, but you would've if you had the

chance." Rex was tempted to kick him in the face or tell Digger to make sure the scumbag wouldn't be able to ever sire any offspring. Instead, calmly, he took the Brit's cellphone out. It was on but locked. "How do I unlock it?"

"My thumbprint. The dog, please!"

Rex grabbed the Brit's hand, twisted it violently, ignored his screams, and swiped the thumb across the screen. When the screen came alive, he gave the phone to Catia and asked her to get Greg on the line and let him explain how to change the unlock code so they could have access to it in the future.

Then Rex did what he wanted to do for the past few minutes; he kicked the Brit in the face. Then he and Josh tied and gagged the unconscious man, dragged him into the warehouse, and dumped him with the rest of his men.

Rex asked Josh and Marissa to go back to the hotel and get their stuff out of their rooms and bring the car to the warehouse. "We have to get these guys out of here and question them. I've got the bad feeling that they work for Dragut; at least the Brit does."

"Why do you think that?" Josh asked.

"He told me he's a contract killer. He doesn't know who he works for. They use Signal to communicate."

"How the hell was Dragut able to get onto us so quickly?"

"That's one of the things I'd like to ask them."

Greg had helped Catia to reset the K iPhone's login screen to a simple password. Rex thought about sending a message to the Brit's handler to tell him the job was done but then remembered the two who got away. He switched the phone off, removed the battery, and shoved it into one of the pockets in his cargo pants.

"I'll get hold of Ethan Thomson to see if he could arrange a safehouse on short notice," Rex said.

"Okay, we'll be back shortly," Josh said as he took Marissa's hand and headed for the warehouse exit.

It was 11:30 p.m., Thomson was asleep, but Rex's call assured that he wasn't going to get more of it for the rest of the night.

Chapter Twenty-Four

TO KILL YOU

Larissa, Greece

Day 8

Thomson's call to Rex to give him the address of a safehouse came through at the same time as Josh and Marissa arrived in the rental SUV. They didn't check out of the hotel; Joanne Sanders would sort that out.

They 'packed' the four captives in the back of the SUV despite their muffled protestations, which were probably about being in pain and that there wasn't enough room in the rear of the SUV for four big men.

It was 5:45 a.m. when they pulled into the double garage at the safehouse, two hundred and eighty miles from Alexandroupolis. It was an old farmhouse twelve miles outside Larissa, the fourth-most populous city in Greece, the capital of the Thessaly region, far away from the Thrace area with its abundance of Ottoman sympathizers.

At the farmhouse, everything was exactly as Thomson said it would be. There was coffee, and there was food in the refrigerator, ten rolls of duct tape on the kitchen table, as well as a plastic container with two bottles of sedatives and syringes, and the owner was absent.

They started with the Brit. Thomson was listening in from his office in Athens. Thanks to Catia and Marissa, he already had photos of all the captives. The session was recorded by Marissa on her cellphone.

The Brit was sitting on a chair. With duct tape, his arms were tied to the armrests and his legs from ankle to knee tied to the legs of the chair. Rex called Digger to come sit next to him and said to the Brit, "Do I have to explain what I will tell my dog to do if you lie to us or refuse to answer?"

The Brit shook his head.

"Speak up, we're recording."

"No. You don't have to explain."

"What's your name and address?"

By now, Jack Swanson had figured out that the four people he was sent to kill were true professionals, much better than he was—information he wished he had before taking the job. He answered truthfully.

Thomson verified it within twenty minutes.

Swanson told them that the three Greeks tied up in the basement, as well as the two who ran away and the couple in the restaurant, were ruffians hired for the night. Swanson told them he was an ex-British paratrooper who became a problem-solver-cum-assassin.

"Just for that, we should take you back to Britain and give your Para buddies a copy of this recording so they can hear from your mouth how you've dishonored their elite unit," Rex said.

Swanson didn't respond. He knew he'd lose more than

just the ability to procreate if his former Para comrades got hold of him.

He told them that he had met his agent only once, fifteen years ago. The agent didn't give a name then or ever after. He had never seen the guy again. Swanson described the agent in as much detail as he could. But it was a description that would have been applicable to at least a quarter of British males in their fifties.

Since that meeting, they had only ever communicated via online chat applications; the last year or so it was through Signal.

"How are you getting paid?"

"The last eighteen months, the payments were in Monero."

Monero was one of a number of privacy crypto coins, offering financial transactions that were anonymous and near impossible to be traced. Monero used a technique where it lined up a number of fake Monero transactions alongside the real transaction, thus obfuscating the original. Monero was very popular with organized crime syndicates and terrorists to hide their financial transactions from authorities.

"Before that?"

"Obfuscated wire transfers to my offshore accounts."

"When did you get your instructions?"

"Yesterday."

A rush job.

"How did you know where to get us?"

"My agent told me. He uploaded your photos to a temporary site on the Darknet and told me to fly to Alexandroupolis and wait for further instructions. I traveled there yesterday and waited. He contacted me after you landed yesterday afternoon and told me at which hotel you were staying. I paid the concierge at your hotel to keep me up to date with your movements. He did that and told me about your dinner plans and the restaurant you were going to."

"Hmm, maybe Joanne should also file a complaint with the hotel management about their unprincipled concierge," Josh mumbled.

"For the record. What were your orders?" Rex asked.

"To kill you and make it look like a robbery."

"How much?"

"Three hundred thousand euros."

"Preposterous!" Josh shouted in a mock British accent. "My mate over there, and he's not half as good as I am, was worth four million less than two years ago. You've been royally screwed, mate."

Rex grinned. "Yeah, I'm a bit disappointed myself. But then, I guess we're like cars; the value declines with age."

Rex and Josh sedated Swanson and dragged him down to the basement and locked him up with his Greek buddies. Marissa uploaded the recording to the CRC servers while Catia made coffee and sandwiches.

Chapter Twenty-Five

IT WAS BOUND TO HAPPEN

Video conference

Day 8

The four were seated around the kitchen table, sipping their coffee and chewing on sandwiches while in a video conference with Thomson, Brandt, Richardson, and Stevens.

"No doubt we've come to Dragut's attention," Rex said.

"It was bound to happen sooner or later," Thomson said.

"Undoubtedly, but not as soon as this. I think we might have a mole," said Richardson.

"I'm afraid that's exactly what we have, Martin," said Stevens.

"Besides everyone on this call, who knew we were coming to Greece?" asked Josh.

"My officers, Brooke and Julian," said Stevens.

"Ah... let me see... Chris McArdle, Greg what's-his-name, eh... Rehka, Spencer..." Brandt stumbled and stuttered. "Wa... way too many."

Rex was alarmed, and so was everyone else. Something was wrong with John. It was difficult to tell by looking at him on the screen, but he looked pale. "You okay, John?" Rex asked.

Brandt waved his hand dismissively. "Yeah, I'm good. Just a headache. I took some painkillers; it should be better soon."

Rex nodded slowly, hesitantly; he wasn't sure he could believe Brandt's explanation. Even so, he continued the conversation. "Add Tony Parker to that list," said Rex.

"Why? He didn't know where you were going." Stevens looked a little flustered.

"He could've guessed that we would come to Greece after all the questions we asked him about Ushan Ozmert."

"And how would he have been able to find out your travel and accommodation arrangements?"

"I don't know, but what I do know is that he's a big player in telecommunications, is he not? He would have the means to monitor electronic communications."

"Yes, he *is* big in telecommunications, but he's also an esteemed citizen of this country—a very successful businessman and philanthropist. He's from a patrician family. But obviously, you suspect him of something untoward. What and why?"

"Myles, I'm not going to apologize for my thinking. Selectivity is a luxury we can ill afford right now. It was way before my time, but need I remind you of the Cambridge Five?"

The Cambridge Five or Cambridge Spy Ring was a group of five spies recruited by the Soviet Union during World War II who were active into the 1950s. The five,

Donald Maclean (Homer), Guy Burgess (Hicks), Harold "Kim" Philby (Sonny or Stanley), Anthony Blunt (Tony or Johnson), and John Cairncross (Liszt) were known in the innermost circles of the KGB as the Magnificent Five. The name Cambridge Five derived from their recruitment during their studies at the University of Cambridge in the 1930s.

Stevens didn't look happy, probably in equal measures due to Rex's impertinent demeanor and the fact that Rex had reminded him of one of the biggest failures in British intelligence history.

Rex saw the unspoken demurral on Stevens's face and added, "Or Aldrich Ames and Robert Hanssen."

Ames was an operative who worked for the CIA for over thirty-one years while he was a KGB mole. Robert Philip Hanssen was an FBI agent who spied for the Soviet and Russian intelligence services against the United States from 1979 to 2001, described by the Department of Justice as "possibly the worst intelligence disaster in U.S. history."

Myles nodded slowly. "Painful reminders, Rex, but you're right. No one can be above suspicion. So, why do you suspect him?"

"Two reasons. I think he's lying about Ozmert's death. And Digger didn't want to greet him because he sensed Parker is a liar."

"What? You're saying a dog..." was as far as Stevens got when Richardson interrupted.

"Hold it. Trouble in Paris."

France

Like many of the former colonial powers, France had its own skeletons in the closet of history that reflected grimly on how they had treated their subjects in the colonies and those who migrated to France over the years.

The building of France's Second Colonial Empire began in earnest with the conquest of Algeria in 1830 when the French military marched into the country, toppled the local Ottoman governor, and ruthlessly suppressed the resistance movement. For more than a century, the French ruled the North African country as if it were part of France itself. During this time of empire-building, France accumulated a vast colonial empire stretching across Asia and Africa, most of it in North Africa, including Algeria, Mali, Morocco, Niger, Tunisia, and Senegal.

Following World War I, a lot of manpower was required to rebuild the French industries and to fill the labor shortage created by the large number of working-age men killed during the war. Young men from the colonies were brought to France to provide cheap labor. Thus, hundreds of thousands of North Africans, desperate to escape the poverty of their colonized homelands, jumped at the opportunity to work in France, doing the laborious jobs that most French people balked at. Far away from their families, those workers lived in overcrowded accommodations in destitution and forlornness. Even so, their meager wages were like manna from heaven for their pauperized relatives back home.

Huge numbers of colonial soldiers from across Africa fought to defend France in both world wars. In fact, Charles de Gaulle's Free French army during World War II comprised a majority of these colonial soldiers. Alas, these sacrifices received very little recognition from the French society.

Years of discrimination against the immigrants led to one of the most disgusting incidents in French history when on October 17, 1961, thousands of French Arabs gathered in Paris to protest in support of the Algerian independence movement. French police fired live ammunition into terrified crowds of unarmed protesters. Many were captured and then drowned in the Seine. Historians estimate that as many as two hundred people were killed that day.

In the years that followed, a new generation, descendants of black and Arab colonial soldiers and laborers, was born in France. They had no ties to their parents' homelands, yet they found that they were not accepted in France either, where they were stereotyped as socially delinquent, indigent, and extremist. By 2017 it was estimated that ten percent of the French population were of Muslim background, mostly descendants of the country's erstwhile colonial territories.

The millions of Muslims who were marginalized, disenfranchised, and without community institutions to guide and support them, became easy targets for extremists. For many of the second and third-generation Muslims of France, things were unbearable in the suburbs. They had lived their whole lives without equal rights, dignity, access to jobs, or proper housing, and there were no signs that their lot would improve in their lifetimes. A 2010 Stanford University study showed that a French Christian citizen had a two hundred and fifty percent better chance of getting a job interview than an equally qualified French Muslim candidate. And the discrimination had worsened since the Charlie Hebdo attack in January 2015. The French had been living under a state of emergency since 2015 and had suffered a series of Islamist militant attacks that killed more than two hundred and thirty people in two years.

There were six million Muslims in France, fifteen thousand of them were on the watch lists of various security agencies. Too many to watch properly. The Direction générale de la sécurité intérieure, (General Directorate for Internal Security), DGSI, tasked with counterespionage, counterterrorism, and the surveillance of potential threats on French soil had an estimated three thousand three hundred employees. By comparison, the Australian Security Intelligence Organization, ASIO, had one thousand eight hundred employees for a population of twenty-four million, and a Muslim population of about half a million. In other words, France allocated less than ten percent of the resources Australia allocated to security intelligence relative to the potential threat.

The poverty-stricken Muslim suburbs of France's cities were fertile recruiting grounds; jihadi candidates were plentiful. The message of the recruiters was simple; France exploited and humiliated your parents, they destroyed the countries of your ancestry, and now they hate you too. Do you want to keep trying to be like them, or do you want to take revenge? It was, therefore, no surprise that more than a thousand French citizens joined the terrorist group, Islamic State (ISIS).

Providing them with weapons and explosives was easy. In terms of the 1985 Schengen Agreement, national border controls were removed and replaced by controls only at the European Union's external borders. That left Western Europe with little to no control of population movement, which created a situation where extremists and weapons were able to move freely between the Schengen area countries. Military-grade assault weapons and explosives were streaming across the EU borders from the Balkans and former Soviet-bloc states. It was estimated that there were between ten and twenty million illegal weapons in France.

Paris, France

Day 8

It was bound to happen. The city, the target, and the method. The target was the Paris Metro, the underground railway system. The method was a rail passenger's darkest nightmare, a bomb on a jammed subway car at the peak of rush hour.

For decades, security experts had been warning about the vulnerabilities of metropolitan train systems to terrorist attacks. Their analysis showed that existing security systems would not prevent terrorists from bringing explosive devices into the metro.

And the terrorists knew all about it, which was why they liked to launch attacks on public transport. Since 1970 there were at least three hundred and eighty-seven attacks on trains, buses, and passenger ferries in North America and Europe. Attacks in enclosed environments like subway stations were the deadliest. In Europe, close to seventy-five percent of casualties from terrorist attacks occurred in underground train stations, even though those attacks accounted for only thirteen percent of all attacks.

Unlike airports that had massive checkpoints and bag scans, public transport was hard to secure and easy to access, and at rush hour, they were packed with unsuspecting targets. Not only that, the rail systems were essential to the economic well-being of the community. Thus, the terrorists got a double whammy by killing infidels and disrupting their economy in one fell swoop.

The Paris Metro with fourteen lines, one hundred and thirty-two miles of track, and three hundred and three stations had a ridership of seven million people a day. It was described as the second busiest metro system in Europe and one of the best transport systems in terms of service density, frequency, and safety. As for safety, those who made that claim were proved wrong on this day.

A regular user of the metro said on her blog, "*On busy Paris subway lines such as 'la ligne treize,' it's important that during rush hour (Monday through Friday, roughly between 7:30 and 9:00 AM and 5:00 and 6:00 PM), you follow the métro untold politeness code… Or common sense.*"

On this Friday, at precisely 7:45 a.m., the terrorists, who might have read that request but ignored it, or never read it, or had an entirely different view of what politeness and common sense meant, set off their bombs. Fourteen of them. One per train on each of the fourteen lines of the Paris metro.

No one of the survivors was able to tell the investigators if the suicide bombers had screamed the traditional 'Allahu Akbar' before the bombs were detonated because they were not close enough, those who were within earshot were dead. Survivors in the carriages furthest from the bombs heard the explosions, those who were closer lost their hearing when their eardrums burst before the sound could reach their ears.

Of the bomb carriers, only tiny pieces remained. Eight hundred commuters, most of whom would never have heard the sound of the explosion, only felt the searing ball of fire and the blast wave that swept them off their seats and feet, like sheets of paper in a tornado, smashing their bodies against the walls of the car before darkness descended upon them, forever.

More than two thousand five hundred were injured, many were critical, many more would be added to the death toll in the hours and days to come.

It was the worst terror attack ever in Europe. Globally, it was the third-worst in modern history, outdone only by al-Qaeda with 2,996 deaths in the Nine Eleven attacks in America and Boko Haram's January 2015 killing of more than 2,000 villagers in Baga, Nigeria.

The bombs were simple in construction. Each of the fourteen bombs consisted of two kilograms of Semtex, a general-purpose plastic explosive manufactured in Czecho-slovakia, popular with terrorists because it was near impossible to detect, packed inside laptop computers stripped of all internal parts. The modified laptops were carried in backpacks, and all fourteen were detonated in synch. It was unclear if the bombs were set off remotely or by the martyrs or by a preset timing mechanism.

The entire Paris Metro system was paralyzed in an instant, shut down, and wouldn't run for days. French police and security services and ambulances started arriving on the fourteen sites within minutes. Stations were evacuated and locked down, and streets were sealed off. The gruesome task of collecting and matching body parts had commenced. What was left of some of the bodies would fit into a container no bigger than a shoebox. Other bodies were torn in half; some bodies were missing limbs or heads; some limbs and heads were missing bodies.

Within two hours, the French President and Prime Minister had visited each of the fourteen scenes of carnage.

At the press conference afterward, the mournful President declared it to be the saddest day in French history since August 22, 1914, when, during the Battle of the Frontiers, on that single day, 27,000 French soldiers lost their lives. His statement included the usual vow to hunt down the perpetrators to the ends of the earth and bring them to justice.

The reality, however, was the perpetrators hadn't claimed responsibility; therefore, just like the Dutch, the French security agencies could only speculate. Notwithstanding the lack of identity of the terror group, for law enforcement and security agencies across Europe, it was the worst nightmare scenario imaginable; the existence of a highly sophisticated, well-organized, unidentified terror organization able to orchestrate two of the most devastating attacks in European history seven days apart without any forewarning whatsoever.

They knew more attacks were on the way. What they didn't know was who, where and when.

Chapter Twenty-Six

SOMETHING'S WRONG WITH THE OLD MAN

Video conference

Day 8

The French who had more than their fair share of terrorist attacks over the years were much more adept at responding to them than the Dutch. Still, apart from the difference in the number of victims, the bottom line was the same as in The Netherlands a week before. Even though they were on high alert since The Netherlands attacks, the French security services had no prior intelligence. Not even a hint. Like the Dutch and the rest of the world, they had no idea who was responsible. Of course, the suicide bombers were radicalized Muslim youths, but who recruited them, trained them, armed them, planned, and coordinated the attacks? Who funded the operation? How long have they been planning this? And what was next?

The fact was, Dragut had just upped the ante. The citizens of Europe were in a panic. And if The Netherlands and Paris were indicative of things to come, the next attack was going to be worse. That realization was likely the reason for Stevens friendlier demeanor when they finally returned to the topic of Tony Parker.

"Myles, I assume you don't have personal experience with military dogs?" Brandt said.

It didn't escape Rex that Brandt's speech was slightly, almost indiscernibly, slurred. *Maybe it's the painkillers.*

"Correct, I don't," said Stevens.

"Keep it short," Brandt mumbled.

Everyone frowned.

Rex pointed at himself and raised his eyebrows.

"Yes, you," growled Brandt.

Rex nodded. *Something's wrong with the Old Man.* "Well, I can keep you busy for a while with what I've experienced with Digger over the years. But the quickest way to explain it is to say Digger is a team member. Just like every human team member has a unique skillset, so does Digger. Among many others, he has sensory capabilities we can't fathom. Most relevant to the current discussion is his capability to smell and sense human emotions and conditions. He can detect fear, sadness, pain, anger, deceit, illness, I can go on.

"Over the years, I've learned to pay close attention to Digger's behavior around humans. Especially when he meets someone for the first time. He has never failed to alert me about someone he didn't like. Of the new people he met the past few days, he didn't like Tony Parker and Emily Hobson, although I got the impression she's afraid of dogs. I suggest we put surveillance on both."

Stevens was quiet for a beat before he spoke. "I accept that it's possible. However, as you know, surveillance of UK citizens inside the country is MI5's jurisdiction. I'll talk to them, but I'm afraid, with the lack of evidence, human evidence that is, it's not going to be easy for them to get authorization."

"Hopefully, with the Paris attacks, they'll understand how important it is to immediately follow every possible lead no matter how underwhelming the evidence," Richardson said.

"I think we need to also keep an eye on the Ozmerts," Rex said. "Digger likes all of them, and so do Catia and I. But Dragut could be watching them."

Stevens smiled. "*That*, MI6 can take care of without asking anyone's permission."

"Excellent," said Richardson.

"Unless you have something else for me, I'd like to get over to MI5 immediately," Stevens said.

Video conference

Day 8

After Stevens left, Brandt took a sip of water and said, "So, Martin, I suppose the first thing is to get those fancy face-detection computers of yours to search your databases for Ozmert?"

Brandt acted and sounded normal again.

"Yep and the databases of Five Eyes and the Mossad and other allies."

"I suggest you don't include Turkey in that list of allies," Rex interjected.

"Why not?"

"I've got this theory about them," Rex said and told them why he thought there could be a link between Dragut and the Turkish government. "I think it might be worthwhile hearing one of your specialists about the ideology and goals of the current Turkish government. I know the current President of Turkey has been making overtures about Neo-Ottomanism and the protection of people of Ottoman descent in neighboring countries. To me, it sounds as if the Turkish President took a leaf out of Hitler's book. He used the same excuse to invade and annex Czechoslovakia's Sudetenland."

"Okay, I'll get an expert on Turkey to enlighten us. As for finding a photo match for Ozmert, if the facial recognition system doesn't find it on the first run-through, we'll get artists to modify the photos to reflect aging, disguises, cosmetic surgery, and such before we run them through the databases again."

"I've been thinking about this Ozmert guy since hearing his story," said Josh. "His sister got raped and insulted. It's horrible. But he got his revenge when he killed the scumbag who did it. Then, instead of carrying on with his life and earning himself a Nobel Laureate, he vanished, never contacted his loved ones, and became a terrorist rivaling the likes of Osama bin Laden. Right?"

"Get to the point, Farley," snapped Brandt.

"We're missing something, and I think it's what happened during those four years in England. I think that's where he had a change of heart and decided on a different career path, not because his sister was raped. We have to look into that."

"Yeah, well, twenty-five years later, no one remembers anything," retorted Brandt.

"Hang on, John, Josh is onto something there," said

Rex. "What about Destiny's other friends? Admittedly, Emily told us she wasn't aware of anyone as close as the two of them were, but she also told us what a private person Destiny was. We've only talked to four people who knew her, three of them family. There must've been more. Privacy or not, it's not as if she were living under a rock in the desert. What about those friends or associates who brought her to the attention of MI5 in the first place?"

Brandt made no reply; he just glowered at Rex.

"I'm now wondering if Almasi and Destiny knew each other during their student years," Richardson added. "They were about the same age and went to the same university. If that proves to be correct, what should we make of Almasi's so-called defection?"

"Martin, though Almasi knew much more than he told us, I'm also sure if he were a plant, he would still be alive," Rex responded.

"But which parts of Almasi's report should we believe and which not?"

"The man is dead! How the hell will we know?" growled Brandt.

An uneasy silence descended as everyone stared at Brandt, shocked, and surprised at his sudden outburst. All but Thomson and Stevens knew John Brandt. They knew he had a short temper; diplomacy was not exactly one of his stronger traits. Even so, there was no cause for his belligerent tone.

Even Rex, also not known for his tactful mannerisms, was taken aback by Brandt's atypical behavior. *We need to get this call over and find out what's wrong with the Old Man. Problems with Christelle Proll? Maybe.*

Despite his concerns about Brandt, Rex said, "Well, unless I'm missing something, Almasi's twenty-page report contained only two pieces of actionable information. One, there exists a group of experts and academics helping an unidentified person to plan acts of terror against big cities within the borders of the European Union and Jerusalem. Two, said unidentified person, the mastermind behind the cabal, might be using the pseudonym Dragut.

"Vague information to be sure, but our investigations proved it to be accurate and critically important."

"He didn't tell us anything about Destiny Parker," said Richardson.

"Not only her, Martin, he didn't tell us *anything* about his personal life at all."

"Hmm, good point."

"So, I'm of the opinion there is nothing to be gained from trying to analyze Almasi's motives. What we got from him is what we'll have to work with. He might have known Destiny when they were students or not. How will knowing that help us find Dragut?"

"You're right, it doesn't," agreed Richardson.

Rex noticed the almost imperceptible grin on Brandt's face and wondered about it. *From growling to smiling in minutes.*

"Notwithstanding, we'll have to investigate Miss Parker's penchant for affairs with intellectual types," said Catia. "We have to find out which universities she frequented over the years and whom she recruited."

"Recruited?" Thomson frowned.

"For Dragut's brains trust."

"Ah, of course."

"Words such as seduction and blackmail are coming to mind," added Rex.

"Okay, we've got our work cut out for us," said Brandt. "We need a team to find Almasi's colleagues in the Delphi Group. Another team has to investigate Ozmert's life while at university. Ozmert's photos have to be fed to the facial recognition databases. Tony Parker and Emily Hobson have to be put under surveillance." Brandt was back to his usual self, the efficient and meticulous CEO and mission control specialist.

"Martin and Ethan, for the sake of plausible deniability, I want you to mute your speakers for a few minutes."

They grinned and did as requested.

Chapter Twenty-Seven

MAKE A COLD TRAIL HOT

Video conference

Day 8

When Brandt was satisfied that Richardson and Thomson couldn't hear, he said, "Greg, the IT team needs to get into some serious hacking and cracking.

"I want you and your IT team to start up those computers and break into the airlines' databases. I am not holding my breath that they will still have data about passengers of twenty-five years ago, but you need to find out if they do.

"Break into the Turkish and Swiss border control databases. I am a bit more optimistic that they might have data going back that far. Ushan Ozmert, I'm sure, left Feres under his real name, with his real passport. Did he indeed travel to Geneva? If so, where did he go after that?

"That's to say, I want you to make a cold trail hot."

"On it, boss," said Greg with a big smile.

"Furthermore, just in case MI5 experiences a bout of morality about civil rights and privacy, I want you to put electronic tabs on Tony Parker. Dig into his finances as well as his social and private life. The same goes for Emily Hobson and Umut Ozmert. Nothing is sacred. We want everything you can get."

"And Joanna Sanders," said Rex.

All eyes darted to Rex.

Brandt spoke first. "The woman in the embassy in Athens. She knew..."

"All about our travel and accommodation arrangements," Rex completed Brandt's sentence for him.

Brandt took a deep breath and let it out slowly before he signaled to Martin and Ethan to rejoin the conference.

"Rex identified your fuckin' mole," Brandt growled without preamble.

"Who?" Richardson and Thomson asked in unison, ignoring Brandt's uncharacteristic use of profanity.

"Joanna Sanders," said Rex.

Thomson's face had gone pallid. He whispered, "Of course, she made all travel arrangements for Rex and the team to Alexandroupolis."

Rex nodded slowly. "And for Reece Cole when he went to Rhodes Island to meet with Almasi. Right?"

"Yep. She did. She's in charge of all travel and accommodation arrangements and the associated expenses, including the per diems."

"Dammit. As if we don't have enough trouble as it is. Ethan, get counter-espionage onto it immediately," said Richardson. "Arrest her on suspicion of espionage, keep her in solitary, no computer or phone access. We need to know who she's been sending the information to. If she's not the mole, then who else has access to that information?"

"On my way," Thomson said.

"Ethan, before you go. Would she know where we are right now?" asked Rex.

"Let me think." Thomson closed his eyes as he ran through the events of the past twelve hours. A few seconds later, he said, "No, I am sure she doesn't. I personally made all arrangements for the safe house, and I didn't tell anyone else. She doesn't have access to that information. So, unless my telephone and office had been bugged since security swept it yesterday afternoon, you're safe there for now."

"Good."

"If there's nothing else, please excuse me, I've got a mole to catch."

When Thomson left the conference, Rex said, "We'll have to decide what we're going to do with our prisoners. We don't think the Greeks are anything but mobsters for hire. Even so, it's important to find out who they work for and the connection to Swanson's agent. Maybe we'll be able to track him down.

"Swanson should be taken to the UK for further interrogation. This guy has been killing people for a living for the past fifteen years. I'm sure there's still much he can talk about."

"Yeah, well, good luck to the Brits with getting any information out of him if Digger isn't there to put the squeeze on him, so to speak," said Josh.

When Rex, Catia, and Marissa finally stopped laughing, Brandt snarled, "The hell's so damn funny?"

Josh told them.

When the hilarity ended, Richardson said. "Okay, I'll talk to Myles, I'm sure he would be very much interested in having a chat with Swanson. With or without Digger's help. I'm just wondering how we're going to get him out of Greece."

"We'll think of a way." Brandt grinned and looked at Rex. No doubt thinking of the masterful stunt which Rex and his team pulled off six months ago in Shanghai when they smuggled a very senior Chinese general out of China to the United States. For weeks after, the Chinese security police were consuming inordinate quantities of indigestion tablets and pulling their hair out as they tried to figure out how it happened.

"I don't think it's a big deal, Martin," said Josh. "Unless we lay a complaint with the police, which we won't because we have none to complain about, Swanson is only a British tourist who lost his passport when he was mugged in the streets of Alexandroupolis. After that dreadful experience, he wants to go home, desperately. Get the British embassy to issue emergency travel documents for him. We'll take care of the rest. We've got a plan that will assure he'll be eating bangers and mash in a British prison in no time."

Richardson laughed. "Okay, I'll see if I can organize it through Myles. Let's take a break. I'll let you know as soon as Ethan has news about the mole."

"Good idea," said Brandt sounding tired.

When the screen went blank, Marissa said, "Josh, I hope you'll share *our* plan with us at some stage so that we also know what *our* plan is."

"In due time, my dear. I'm still working on it."

Chapter Twenty-Eight

WHAT NOW

Larissa, Greece

Day 8

After checking on the prisoners, the four were in the comfortable chairs of the family room, each with a mug of coffee in hand, when Marissa asked, "What's wrong with the Old Man? He's like a bear with a sore tooth."

"We all know John, he won't be nominated for a mister congeniality contest, but I've never seen our Old Man behaving like that, not unprovoked," added Josh.

"Agreed," said Catia. "I haven't known him as long as any of you, but I am also worried. Could it be that he and Christelle had a fallout?"

"The thought crossed my mind," said Rex. "Even so, the Old Man would never allow his personal life to interfere with an operation. I'm going to call Chris."

"Yes, please do that," said Marissa. The concern notice-able on her face.

Chris McArdle answered the phone almost immediately. "Hey Rex, you must've read my mind. I was about to call you to set up a meeting. The Old Man wants to talk to all of us in an hour."

"Okay, we're not going anywhere. Call us when you're ready. Now, the reason I called *you* is to find out what's the matter with him. Is he okay? His behavior in the meeting was, to say the least, erratic."

"I know, it's been going on for a while now. He's forget-ful, and the last day or so, he's been having these mood swings, almost by the minute. We're worried about him."

"What does Rick say?"

Rick Longland was CRC'S resident psychologist.

"He had a long chat with John about two weeks ago. After that, John went away for a few days. Christelle has been in touch with Rick, and she arrived here yesterday."

"Christelle is there on the ranch?"

"Yes."

"We were thinking there could be trouble in paradise; he and Christelle breaking up or something?"

"No, it's not that."

"So, you know, but you're not going to tell me."

"Yes, it's better that he tells you."

"Tell me what?"

"Wait for the call, Rex."

"See you soon," said Rex in frustration and ended the call.

"I've got a nasty feeling he's got a health problem," whispered Catia when the call ended.

They went quiet for a long while, everyone consumed by

their own thoughts about the man they all loved and respected. All hoping Catia was wrong, including herself.

"Josh, Digger, let's go and check on our prisoners," said Rex, breaking the silence.

Josh and Digger got up and followed Rex. None of them mentioned they had checked the prisoners less than twenty minutes ago. Neither did they mention they could have looked at the video feed from each of the rooms where the prisoners were kept on Marissa's computer.

Video Conference

Day 8

Four pairs of eyes belonging to worried faces immediately settled on John Brandt when the video call went live. Christelle was sitting next to him. She looked beautiful and elegant as always, but she couldn't hide the disquiet on her face. No introductions were necessary, she already knew everyone on the call.

It was a surprise to see Rick Longland there. He was not just a shrink with no idea of what the men were doing out in the field. He himself was a trained Delta Force operator and had passed through the grueling CRC training and taken part in more than a few missions before he was appointed to his current role. He knew what made a good agent and what they were up against when on missions. And he knew what was required of a good CEO to lead those agents. Over the years, he'd become the Old Man's confidant and soundboard.

Everyone noticed the slight shaking of his hand as Brandt brought the glass of water to his lips. "Okay, now don't interrupt me," he started after putting the glass down. "We need to make a change to CRC's command structure for this operation. I've been diagnosed with an aggressive but, thank God, benign brain tumor. The damn thing is playing havoc on me. I forget things, I'm irritable, etcetera. I won't bore you with the details. In this condition, I'm a danger to my agents.

"I spoke to Chris and Rick; we're in agreement, Rex has to take over as CEO right now. The doctors wanted to operate immediately. I told them I can't fit them into my schedule right now and to pound sand until I can, which will be when this mission is over."

Slowly all eyes moved from Brandt to Rex.

Inwardly, Rex's mind was in turmoil, outwardly, he seemed impassive.

"Dalton, don't stuff it up. I'll be right next to you all the way, and I *will* kick your ass if you make a mess of things." His speech started slurring ever so slightly toward the end. In a whispered voice, an almost pleading tone, he said, "Get it done before I lose my mind, Rex."

In Greece, Josh's face was white as paper, Marissa and Catia were wiping tears from their eyes, and Digger whined softly as he made the rounds to each of his pack to console them.

Rex put on a fake smile and said, "Don't worry, John, you can't lose your mind because you don't *have* one to lose."

Catia punched him in the shoulder.

Brandt smiled wryly.

McArdle took over. "John and I already spoke to Richardson and Stevens. There were no hums and haws, they're happy to continue with you in place of John. And just to let you know, Rex, you have Rick's and my unreserved loyalty and support."

"And mine," Christelle said.

"Thanks. That's good to know," said Rex quietly.

Josh cleared his throat. "There are two people and a dog that I want on my team when I'm going on a mission, John Brandt and Rex Dalton. I don't care who drives and who's in the passenger seat. Just as long as the dog and both of you are there. So, John, quit talking about that losing your mind BS."

"Hear! Hear!" said Marissa as she wiped the tears from her eyes.

Catia said nothing; she was also fighting the tears. She and Rex often spoke about John's offer to Rex about eighteen months ago to take over the helm at CRC. Rex was on the fence, she was not. She wanted him to take the job. They had considered every possible angle but always ended at the same place. And then they left it hanging for the next time it came up.

But this was not how it was supposed to happen. Not that Rex wasn't capable of taking on the role, but up 'til now, John was still more than capable of doing his job as efficiently as always. And that was probably the main reason Rex kept postponing his decision. "Don't fix what's not broken," he kept telling Catia. But now it *was* broken... or maybe it was only cracked and could be repaired.

"If I'm to run this operation, let's get on with it," said Rex in a solemn voice.

Brandt chuckled. "Spoken like a true leader. Chris, give him the briefing."

McArdle said, "Here's the situation in terms of the high-level support we have for the mission. The CIA will supply and back us up as on previous missions. POTUS has been briefed. He wants results. The British Prime Minister has been briefed, MI6 and MI5 have been ordered to cooperate fully. He wants results, that's to say, stop them before they reach Britain's shores. On British soil, MI5 takes the lead, elsewhere we're in charge unless circumstances dictate differently.

"The French President has been briefed, and the Director of the DGSE has ordered Christelle's replacement, Francois Renou, to work with us. The French President wants results. The people responsible for the Paris Metro bombing he wants to be brought back to France, dead or alive. The three leaders, POTUS, the UK PM, and the President of France, are talking to the Dutch to get their cooperation and support."

"Thanks, Chris. Let's hope we'll get the same support from other countries as and when we need them," said Rex and woke his laptop from sleep mode, brought a blank Word document up on the screen, and named it Operation Dragut. He inserted three columns on the page. The left column he titled Facts the middle Assumptions and the right, Actions.

"Good. Let's fill it in."

Catia took Rex's laptop and put it in front of her on the table; she could type sixty words a minute using all fingers. Rex only used two and struggled to reach thirty and made double the number of typos.

A big smile had settled on Brandt's face. "Please excuse me. I've got to take my meds and get a nap. Doctor's orders."

Rex paused and looked at Brandt. "Did I hear you correctly, you're doing what a doctor told you?"

"Yeah, well, shit happens when your fiancée, your

shrink, and doctor conspire against you," said Brandt as he and Christelle got up to leave.

Josh's quote of Bob Dylan's 1964 song, "Times they certainly are a-changin," brought a smile to everyone's face.

"Christelle, one of your most important functions is to supply John with his medications and make sure he takes them. Force-feed him if necessary. If he gives you any trouble whatsoever, call me," said Rex.

Christelle laughed. "You heard that, John? Any trouble whatsoever."

"Dalton, you're skating on thin ice," said Brandt.

When he and Christelle were outside the CRC operations room, Brandt whispered to her, "Now I can relax. The mission couldn't be in better hands."

"I don't have a single moment's doubt about that, John. Rex is more than capable of handling it."

Christelle called Rex an hour later when Brandt was asleep and thanked him for taking over from John without protest. "He is a lot calmer now that he knows you're there. It's the first time in two days he's gotten sleep, I'm told."

"It's a lot of pressure on him and me, Christelle. There's nobody that can do it better than John; he knows that. I'm nervous."

"Don't be. He says you're much better than him. I'm not lying, that's what he said. And don't forget, I've seen you in action; I agree with John. He was very worried you wouldn't want to do it."

"What's the prognosis, Christelle?"

"The doctor says he has to have that operation very soon, within the next few weeks, no more than three. The operation itself carries low risk, according to the specialist. He reckons John has a ninety-plus percent chance to make a full recovery but only if the operation is not delayed for too long. Otherwise, there's a risk of permanent brain damage."

"What should we expect over the next few weeks as the tumor grows?"

"Lethargy, forgetfulness, moodiness, blurred vision, maybe loss of hand-eye coordination. The red light would be a seizure. If that happens, he has to get the surgery immediately."

"Thank you again for being with him during this time, Christelle. We'll do our bit. You keep an eye on our Old Man and let us know when you think it's time for him to go to the hospital rather than be with us."

"I will Rex, I will... I love him. He's going to be okay."

"Tell him, we, the five of us including Digger, say he doesn't have our permission to fall off his twig. We expect him to keep on chirping until *we* tell him it's time to stop."

It took Christelle a few seconds to figure out what Rex meant. She laughed. "I'll tell him."

Chapter Twenty-Nine

THE MOLE

Athens, Greece

Day 8

Thomson and the FBI agent in charge of counterespionage, Louise Bell, confronted Joanne Sanders behind closed doors in her office. She denied any wrong-doing for about ten minutes until Bell pointed to her handbag and said, "I say in that bag is a private cellphone. And on it, I'm going to find evidence that you told someone about the team that was sent to Alexandroupolis. And if I look further back, I'll find a message telling someone about Reece Cole's trip to Rhodes Island eight days ago. Right?"

Sanders denied it.

Bell said, "Well, in that case, prove me wrong. Give me the phone. Or should I take it out myself?"

Very reluctantly, Sanders handed the phone over and

started crying. She told them she was forced to do it. She didn't want to but had no choice. "She blackmailed me."

"Who?"

"Claire."

"Who's Claire?"

"I believed she loved me. She lied, she used me."

It took another twenty minutes to get it out of her that she was a lesbian, but she'd kept it secret all her life, even got married and had two children to hide it. She met Claire at a function at the Dutch embassy six months ago. They fell in love, or at least Sanders thought they were in love. But it was a disaster. Claire didn't care about her; she used the information about Sanders's sexual orientation against her and threatened to tell her husband and children. She had photos and videos of their trysts. Her husband was an analyst for the CIA, also stationed at the embassy in Athens. Their children were attending university back in America.

Thomson shook his head. "We don't live in the middle ages anymore, Joanne. Homosexuality is not a social disgrace. You know that as well as I do, yet you've betrayed your country to keep it a secret. How selfish are you?"

She made no reply.

"Do you have a photo of Claire?" Bell asked.

"No, she never wanted me to take a photo of her."

"And that never struck you as odd?"

There was no reply.

"What did she look like?"

Sanders gave a description of a tall, skinny, blonde woman who spoke English with a British accent. It was useless.

Thomson took his cellphone out and showed her a few photos. "That's the woman you're talking about. Right?"

"Yes. But how... Where did you...?"

"Her real name is Destiny Parker, a professional assassin. She's the one who killed Reece Cole. The information you gave this woman enabled her to kill him. That's not all, she killed another man, Professor Almasi, that same day, in the same place, only seconds later. Two murders Ms. Sanders. You're an accomplice in both."

Sanders was sobbing uncontrollably. But Thomson and Bell had little to no sympathy; two people were dead because of her, and four more were almost killed the night before. And many more were about to die if Dragut wasn't stopped.

"But she blackmailed me. I would never have done it if..."

"You'll get an opportunity to plead your case before a court," said Bell. "You've only told us about one incident. I'm sure there are many more. You'll get time to come clean on those as well. Right now, we want to know who you told about the team going to Alexandroupolis."

"I told Claire, ah... whatever her name is."

"No. You didn't," said Thomson.

"How would you know what..."

"She's dead, Ms. Sanders, has been since about two minutes after she killed Professor Almasi eight days ago," said Thomson. "And you know that. Stop lying. How many more have to be killed before you come to your senses?"

Sanders let out a long and weary sigh, admitting defeat.

It took another hour to find out that two days after Destiny's death, Sanders was approached by another woman, speaking fluent English but with a German accent, of whom she also had no photos, only another vague description. The woman apparently had copies of the compromising material Claire had made and explained the deal was still the same; as long as Sanders supplied the information about all travel and accommodation arrangements made by her, the secret would be safe.

"How much did they pay you?" asked Bell.

"Nothing! I didn't do it for money. I..."

"So, when we check your bank accounts, which we will, we'll find no evidence of payments?"

Sanders made no reply.

"I thought so."

The information was on Sanders's phone. All of it. Even the information about the private charter she booked for Rex, Catia, and Digger the day they had to leave Rhodes Island in a hurry as well as the travel and accommodation arrangements she made for the Daltons and Farleys for their trip to Alexandroupolis.

The last entry had been made an hour before Thomson and Bell stepped into her office. It was the travel information for one of the senior staff at the embassy going to Paris. The information on the phone was dooming. The frustration was the information had been transferred via the Signal app on her phone to another Signal user whose handle was Bumblebee, and because it was Signal, there was no number or IP address to trace.

Chapter Thirty

THE SNIFF OF A CUCUMBER SANDWICH

Video Conference

Day 8

Brandt got two and a half hours of sleep after taking his medication before Richardson's video call came through. On the call were Rex and his team at the safehouse in Greece, Thomson in Athens, Richardson in Langley, Stevens in London, Spencer onboard the *TOMATS* in Valletta, and from CRC HQ in Arizona, Brandt, McArdle, Christelle, and Greg.

Brandt looked much better, the color had returned to his face, and he was smiling. Christelle was next to him. When Brandt looked away from the screen at McArdle, she quickly showed Rex a thumbs up.

Nothing had to be explained about Rex's role as mission leader; everyone had been informed prior.

Thomson started by giving them an update about the

mole hunt and told them Joanne Sanders would be on her way to America soon. Her husband would be informed and evacuated with her. In due time she would be brought before a court and charged. Probably with treason, which carried the death penalty. She would not get bail. To be sure, the Sanders family was facing tough times, three of them totally innocent, and that because of the peccadillos of one member of the family.

"Let's hope we've seen the end of moles in our midst," sighed Thomson. "But that's probably wishful thinking."

"Probably," said Richardson.

In Greece, it was late afternoon; the sun was about to set. Rex and his team hadn't slept in more than thirty-six hours. The news of the Paris attack, the shock of Brandt's health setback, the mole who almost got them killed, and the clock ticking relentlessly toward the next terror attack, which only they could stop, were all weighing heavily on them. Yet, there was no end in sight.

"We have to decide what to do with your prisoners," said Stevens. "I don't care what you do with the Greeks, but I've got a keen interest in Swanson."

"I want to question the Greeks to find out who they work for and then let the Hellenic Police know where to find them," said Rex. "Ethan, you'll have to make arrangements with the police to pick them up when we're done with them."

The Hellenic Police was the national police service, one of the three security forces of Greece. They were responsible for anything from road traffic control to counterterrorism.

"I will see how far I can get with them and keep you posted. They've been surprisingly cooperative so far," Thomson replied. "But we'll have to coordinate it. You finish the questioning and let me know when I should contact the police."

"Will do," said Rex. "Now, Swanson. What's the status with his emergency travel documents, Myles?"

"Done," said Stevens. "Just let me know where you want them dropped off."

"We've got a CIA jet on standby to fly you to London," said Richardson. "Ethan has been smoothing things over with the EYP to ensure that you won't have issues when you have to clear customs."

The CIA had a fleet of 'private' jets stationed all over the world, registered in dummy corporations of which the ownership was so obfuscated it would take a lifetime to unravel.

"Excellent. Okay, give us an hour or so to wrap things up here," said Rex. "We'll let you know when we're ready to leave."

It took a little over an hour to get the information Rex and the team wanted from their Greek prisoners. It would have been much quicker if any one of them could speak Greek, but as it were, they had to rely on Google Translate. Fortunately, they didn't need much information, only the name and address of their employer.

The three of them were in a bad way. One had a broken jaw, thanks to Catia, and was in a world of pain. The second one had very little healthy skin left on his face, and the third one's face looked like he had gone head to head with a twenty-ton truck. They were hungry and thirsty. None of them felt much loyalty toward their boss anymore. It was only the fear of what would happen to them if they betrayed their boss that kept them from spitting it out immediately.

However, with a bit of help from Digger, Rex and Josh

convinced them that what their boss would do to them would pale in comparison to what would happen to them if they kept refusing to give up the information.

The three men, in separate sessions, gave up the same name, address, and telephone number—Savvas Rallotis, the main crime boss in Alexandroupolis.

The team had a brief discussion about what to do about Mr. Rallotis and decided that he would have been told by the two who escaped what had happened the night before and would have gone into hiding. Although Rallotis could potentially lead them to someone higher up in Dragut's food chain, it was not a certainty. They agreed it was better to get Swanson back to London, get their ducks in a row, and then send a team after Rallotis.

Rex phoned Thomson and told him they were done. Half an hour later, after receiving confirmation from Thomson that the police were on their way, Rex and company were on the road to Athens. In the back of the SUV, Swanson was in a diazepam-induced deep sleep, totally unaware of his surroundings.

Athens was two hundred and ninety miles away. About four hour's drive, including a stop to refuel and get some supplies from a pharmacy. They would take turns to drive and sleep.

Athens, Greece

Day 8

At 11:30 p.m. Rex and company pulled into the darkest corner of the public parking at Athens International Airport, also known as Venizelos Airport. An ambulance staffed with two men and a woman dressed in the uniforms of paramedics were waiting for them. They had a gurney with them. The woman handed Rex a sealed envelope in which were Swanson's emergency travel papers.

It took only a minute to transfer the unconscious Swanson whose face was completely covered with bandages, from the back of the SUV to the gurney, secure him with straps, put a 'drip' in his arm, and roll him into the back of the waiting ambulance.

Rex and the team bundled into the back and were transported to the waiting Gulfstream jet.

On the tarmac, before they could enter the plane, they were stopped by a customs officer. He spoke broken but passable English.

"Passports."

Despite the fact that the officer would have received instructions to ask no questions, stamp their passports, and get out of their way, he made a bit of a show of authority, possibly to emphasize his importance in the matter, although he had no idea what was happening.

He slowly opened each passport, looked at the photo, and then at the faces in front of him. Apparently satisfied that he had matched all photos and faces, he took his time to retrieve a small stamp and pad out of his pocket, stamped the passports, and handed them back.

He paid no attention to Digger. Rex, however, did and was relieved to see Digger was relaxed. The officer was just a bit arrogant, not truculent.

But then the officer pointed at the gurney and said, "Who that? My boss, she says only four people and dog. Not five."

Damn, Ethan, did you forget to tell them about our patient? Rex was ready to reply when Josh spoke.

"He's our friend. He got mugged and was injured very badly. We're taking him home."

"What wrong?"

"He got kicked in the head by some muggers. We took him to the hospital. He's got some brain damage; he needs brain surgery urgently. Other body parts also got crushed... a little more than would've been comfortable. It's bad, we need to get him to London very quickly."

"Papers."

Rex handed him the papers, an official temporary emergency passport for Jack Swanson, and a letter from a 'doctor.' There was a photo in the passport, but the officer had no face to compare it with. He looked at the 'doctor's letter' and frowned. Probably because it consisted mostly of medical terms in Latin and very few English words. All of it in nearly indecipherable handwriting, a physician's trademark, but actually Josh's handy work. The officer shook his head in defeat and tried another angle.

"You American, he English?"

"No shit, Sherlock," Josh mumbled. "Yes," he replied, more audibly.

"Why you friends?" The officer sounded incredulous.

Josh looked stumped, but only for a second or two; Josh Farley was seldom at a loss for words when in a tight situation. "I know, buddy, it's sometimes hard for me to believe, too. But you can take my word for it, over the past two hundred and thirty-odd years, since the end of the War of Independence, during which, by the way, we kicked their asses, we've buried the hatchets and learned to like each other. Just like the Bible says we should. You know, love thy neighbor, do unto others, and all that.

"The only gripe they have with us these days is that we've apparently ruined their language. That despite the fact that we understand each other perfectly maybe with the exception of their insistence to call the john a loo. But then, they've got a bit of a reputation for being whiners."

Rex and the girls were struggling very hard not to explode in laughter at Josh's eloquent antics and his hitherto hidden biblical and history knowledge.

The officer's slack jaw betrayed the fact that he, ten to one, understood nothing of what Josh had just said. He cleared his throat, officiously, nodded slightly, and said, "Have good travel. Hope friend is better."

"Thanks, buddy. We appreciate your concern about our dear friend. We've got high hopes that he'll be on the road to better health the moment he gets the first sniff of a cucumber sandwich."

Rex and the girls were still laughing when the plane took off.

And Josh knew he hadn't heard the last of it.

When the plane reached cruising altitude, they high-fived and plunged back into their seats, reclined them, and closed their eyes.

Chapter Thirty-One

TALKING TURKEY

En route to London, England

Day 9

It was a four-hour flight to London. On the trip from Larissa to Athens, each of them got about two hours of sleep. They were in need of much more. The space and luxury of the jet were exactly what they needed. But soon after closing their eyes, Richardson came through on the video screen. The expert on Turkey was ready to brief them.

"I know you're tired and dying for sleep, but this will take no more than half an hour. I suspect when you get to London, there's not going to be time for this." Richardson didn't wait for responses; he went straight ahead and introduced the expert.

Blake Hudson was a middle-aged man with the air of a university professor with his longish and disheveled hair and tortoiseshell glasses. He was seated in Richardson's office in Langley, facing the big video screen.

Hudson started the PowerPoint application on his laptop. "I understood from Deputy Director Richardson that you want an overview of current policies and political thinking in the Turkish government. I will get to that soon, but please allow me to give you a brief historical introduction to explain what is driving their current thinking."

He paused, and when everyone had nodded, he continued, "At the end of World War One, the Ottoman Empire signed an armistice with the allied powers. However, when the Allies signaled that they were planning to take away almost all of the empire's holdings and leave only Turkey, renewed fighting broke out. It was only in July 1924 when the Treaty of Lausanne was signed, which ended the conflict and defined the borders of the modern Turkish Republic. In the treaty, Turkey gave up all claims to the remainder of the Ottoman Empire, and in return, the Allies recognized Turkish sovereignty within its new borders. The treaty was set to be reviewed a hundred years later in 2023.

"The first president of the Republic of Turkey was Mustafa Kemal Atatürk, a former field marshal. He was a revolutionary statesman and author, and undertook extensive social reforms, modernizing Turkey into a secular, industrial nation.

"All was going well between Turkey and its neighbors and the former Allied countries for more than eight decades until the current president started making noises about revising the Treaty of Lausanne. He is quite vocal about his displeasure that Turkey had been forced to cede the Aegean islands to Greece. He regularly laments that the treaty has left Turkey too small."

"Sounds a bit like Hitler's cry for *lebensraum*," Brandt noted, sounding like his usual self.

Hudson nodded but didn't reply.

"The President often talks about Ottoman descendants, minorities living beyond the current Turkish borders that need protection from Turkey. And Turkey's pro-government media have shown a newfound interest in a series of imprecise, even crudely drawn, maps of Turkey with new and 'improved' borders. It is not as if Turkey is posing an imminent threat to former Ottoman regions, but the rhetoric cannot be ignored."

"Let me guess," said Rex, "The Western Thrace region in Greece is one of those regions included on those maps?"

"Yes, it is."

Dragut and the Turkish president... birds of a feather... Rex thought.

"The President upset Greece and a few others when he recently said, 'Turkey cannot disregard its kinsmen in Western Thrace, Cyprus, Crimea, and anywhere else.'"

"And he's getting support for his ideas beyond Turkey's borders. Bosnia regards Turkey as their best ally, and the Turkish media promotes the idea that Turkey is the natural protector of Bosnia's Muslims."

"Our quick, and admittedly unscientific poll in Feres, in said Western Thrace region, showed most of the people there consider themselves Turks, not Greeks," Josh said.

"Yes, that's how many people in former Ottoman regions feel, and it's being exploited by the Turkish President in his rhetoric," Hudson said. "Turkey, as you know, is already a member of NATO and has been striving to become a member of the European Union. However, due to human rights issues, they are not currently in the good books of the EU. Not only that, Turkey's irredentism, that's their policy of advocating the restoration of the Ottoman Empire, is raising eyebrows. If they were to become an EU member, they'd be the first Muslim country to attain membership.

"About the accusations of human rights abuses, they were quick to point out the EU's hypocrisy and failure to meet its own standards when one of their ministers worded it thus: 'Today there are around two million siblings within our borders who fled from Syria and Iraq. Two million here, hundred and thirty thousand in the whole of Europe. Where is your commitment to human rights, the Universal Declaration of Human Rights? Wasn't it you who were protecting the oppressed? What happened to the European Union acquis? Where are you?'"

"Ouch!" Said Richardson.

Hudson smiled and continued. "The major aspirations of the Turkish president are for his country to become the leader of the world's Sunni Muslims and the restoration of the Ottoman Empire.

"But his fall from grace with the European Union is impacting on the fulfillment of his aspirations in a negative way. Therefore, he has been deploying extortion tactics to get the EU to open the door for them by weaponizing the refugee crisis from Syria. A 'Weapon of Mass Migration' as some call it.

"Here are the President's exact words about it recently: 'Hey EU, wake up! I say it again; if you try to frame our operation there as an invasion, [referring to the conflict in Syria] our task is simple: we will open the doors and send three-point-six-million migrants to you.'"

"That would be catastrophic for the EU," said Rex.

"It will be," replied Hudson. "Despite declarations that the term Neo-Ottomanism does not signify an ideal to resurrect the dead empire but rather the ascendance of Turkey to a position of a dominant and influential political entity among the former Ottoman dominions, observers are alarmed by the President's statements such as:

"What we call Syria and Iraq today is not different from what Mardin, Diyarbakır, Gaziantep, or Hatay was for us in the last century. To see those who live in Syria and Iraq as different from our citizens would shame us in the eyes of our fathers and martyrs."

"Turkey is larger than Turkey. We cannot be imprisoned in seven hundred and eighty thousand square kilometers. The borders of our hearts are elsewhere. Our brothers in Mosul, Kirkuk, Skopje, may be outside our natural boundaries, but they are within the borders of our hearts, at the epicenter of our hearts."

"And now the EU finds itself between a rock and a hard place," said Brandt.

"Indeed. If they allow Turkey as a member, on the one hand, they would tacitly be agreeing to their expansionist policies. On the other hand, they are fully aware that Turkey might have a moderating influence on the Sunni Muslims, the cradle of Islamic extremism.

"One final comment. Don't forget, Turkey has one of the most powerful armed forces in Europe and Asia. They have the second largest standing military force in NATO after the United States."

After Hudson had left the room, Rex said, "One more thing to investigate."

"What?" asked Richardson.

"The link between the President of Turkey and Dragut Junior. Dollars to donuts, they're well acquainted."

Chapter Thirty-Two

AN AFFAIR TO HIDE

London, England

Day 9

On arrival in London, MI5 officers met Rex and the team and took Swanson into their custody. An MI6 driver in a TX$ model black cab delivered them to their hotel a few minutes past 5:00 a.m.

They had about five hours before they had to go back in conclave at MI6 headquarters to plan their next steps— enough time to take a shower and get more sleep.

Half an hour before they were to be picked up by the MI6 cab, Rex got a call from Greg and Rehka. They wanted to update Rex with the first results of the CRC IT team's efforts.

Rex put his phone on speaker for Catia to participate.

Greg reported that they couldn't find information about Ushan Ozmert in the airlines' databases because they didn't keep accessible records that far back. They might have them, but they were probably on some offline storage devices in archives.

However, the border control agencies stored information for thirty years before moving it to offline archival systems. The Swiss and Greek databases showed Ushan Ozmert leaving Greece and arriving in Switzerland on the same date twenty-five years ago. But those were the last entries in both countries' border control records. Taking that information on face value, Ushan Ozmert should still be in Switzerland.

"At least we know his sister didn't lie to us about that part," said Rex.

Greg also told Rex they'd easily gained access to Umut Ozmert's phone and downloaded all information which they were in the process of preparing for analysis. It was all in Greek. Nevertheless, using Google Translate, a quick peek at the incoming and outgoing calls for the past six months showed no international calls in or out.

Rehka told Rex, thus far, all efforts to get into Tony Parker's and Emily Hobson's phones had failed. But the records of Tony's and Emily's mobile phone service providers were easier to access. From those records, they were able to collect information about who they communicated with.

"Found anything interesting, like the Queen's cellphone number?" Rex quipped.

Rehka laughed. "No. But I *can* tell you Tony Parker and Emily Hobson lied to you; they phone or text each other at least twice a day. I don't know the contents of their communications yet, but they don't always have short conversations."

Rex's mind was processing at warp speed. "Do you have the data in front of you?"

"Yes."

"Check if they called each other on the day when we interviewed them."

A minute or so of silence followed before Rehka said, "Yes, there are three calls on that day. She called him in the morning, and he called her in the afternoon, and later she called him again."

"Time?"

"11:00 a.m. she called him. Call duration, ten minutes fifteen seconds."

"Probably talking about the meetings with us later in the day."

"2:35 p.m., he called her. Duration fifteen minutes eleven seconds."

"Shortly after we left his office, giving her a detailed account of our meeting."

"4:56 p.m. she called him again, and they talked for seven minutes twenty seconds."

"Her report to him about her meeting with us."

"You want me to send you the data?"

"No, not yet. But what you can do for me is make a report of all of their cellphone activities covering the last six months—date of the call, time of the call, duration, and who initiated the call. And their GPS locations when the calls were made and received. My meeting starts soon, please email it through as soon as it's ready and send me a text. Oh, and could you please also make a separate list for all incoming and outgoing international calls on both their phones?"

"Sure. It should be ready within the hour."

"Thanks, Greg, Rehka, excellent work. Keep at it. I've

got the feeling you guys are going to get us the break-through on this operation."

When the call ended, Rex said to Catia, "I'm surprised, I thought Tony was the only one lying to us. What are they hiding?"

"An affair would be my guess."

Rex stared at her for a while. "Possibly... but then why pretend that they've had no contact, haven't seen each other in donkey's years?"

Catia smiled. She'd never heard that expression but immediately knew what it meant. "Do you think that's why Digger didn't like him and Emily?"

"I'm not sure. I got the distinct impression Emily is terri-fied of dogs. I understand that. I've been scared of dogs since early childhood until Digger and I became friends. And to be honest, I am still scared of dogs, just not of Digger.

"Tony wasn't scared of Digger. Besides, Digger couldn't know that they were going to lie to us about their relation-ship when we walked into their respective offices. The ques-tions that triggered their lies came much later. He never ceases to surprise me with his skills, but I'd be hard-pressed to believe Digger would have known that in advance."

She looked at Digger where he lay on the couch. "You're the Einstein of dogs, Digger. What would it take for you to learn a human language?"

Digger woofed once, jumped off the couch, and did the down-dog stretch while letting out a long noisy yawn.

"And what exactly does that mean?"

Digger didn't answer.

Rex laughed. "I think he said, 'The same effort as for you to learn K-nine.'"

Catia laughed. "Of course. So, if Digger is to be

believed, Tony Parker could be hiding more than just an extramarital affair?"

"Yep. And maybe Emily as well."

"We know much more than we did nine days ago, yet, I feel we still know almost nothing," said Catia.

"That's true. Dragut is still a few steps ahead of us. What we have are mostly assumptions and theories. But it's a good start. I firmly believe if we just work our way through all the theories we have, something will come out of the woodwork. If we just had more time, but I suspect we don't. The first two attacks were seven days apart. Going by that, we've got five days before the next attack."

Chapter Thirty-Three

DRAGUT HUNTING

Video conference

Day 9

The virtual meeting initiated from a secured meeting room at MI6 headquarters in Vauxhall Cross was attended from CRC headquarters by Brandt, Christelle, McArdle, and Greg, from the *TOMATS* it was Spencer, and from Athens, Thomson. Stevens brought with him Julian and Brooke, whom he had assigned fulltime to the mission.

To everyone's relief, Brandt looked rested and back to normal.

Richardson started the meeting. "Rex, you're in the driver's seat."

Rex nodded. "We've got a serious lack of information and many theories. Even so, I think we have enough to formulate the big picture, which is Turkey's, or at least their current president's and his loyalists', desire to revive the Ottoman Empire or parts thereof."

"Agreed," said Christelle. "It's the *raison d'etre* for the Delphi Group."

"Good, let's keep going."

"Add to that Ushan Ozmert is alive, he's Dragut, and he's acting in collaboration with the Turkish government or factions within," said Catia.

Everyone agreed.

Marissa said, "And Turkey is trying to get EU membership to use it as a platform to launch their bid for the restoration of the Ottoman Empire in exchange for protecting the EU countries from Islamic extremists."

"Agreed," said Josh. "And because the EU is dragging their feet, Dragut Junior and cronies decided to shoot and bomb their way through the front door."

"Agreed," said Richardson. "Turkey was among the first to condemn the attacks. The Turkish President suggested in a speech on the day of the attacks in The Netherlands, it was time for the EU to resume talks about Turkey's membership. The day after the Paris train bombings, he repeated that and added that Turkey has a lot to offer to the EU on the security front and urged them to take up his offer."

"Okay. Anything else to add?"

There were none.

"That's the big picture then. Let's analyze the information we have. I'd say our inquiries about Destiny Parker and Ushan Ozmert have come to the latter's attention, and he's getting nervous. Hence he sent a paid assassin after us."

"That, as far as I'm concerned, was proof of life," said Brandt.

"Which means we are digging in the right spot and got too close for comfort," said Josh.

"Yes, we did," said Rex. "And it's clear, Dragut has eyes on us. Even though we've neutralized one of his informants, Ms. Sanders, for an operation of the size he's got going here, we can be assured he'd have an expansive intelligence network."

Everyone agreed.

"So, we're going to do more of the same; put more pressure on him. We're going to increase it relentlessly on all fronts forcing him to make mistakes."

"It sounds like you have a plan, Rex," said Stevens.

"I do. Dragut is hiding in a forest. We're going to shake the trees of his forest, cut them down, uproot them, set them on fire if necessary, every one of them, and keep at it until we find him. Not one tree at a time; all of them at the same time. We have the resources to do it.

"We already know five trees in desperate need of attention: Destiny Parker, Jack Swanson's agent, the President of Turkey, Tony Parker, and Emily Hobson."

"Good. Let's talk about Tony Parker and Emily Hobson. I am afraid the news is not good," said Stevens. "MI5 is not willing to put tabs on them unless we can provide more tangible information. I told them Tony Parker misinformed us when he told us his sister visited the Ozmert family in Greece and about his death. But MI5 was quick to point out it was more than likely that Parker was only repeating what his sister told him. It is something, they said, we could resolve by having another meeting with Parker and asking him where he got that information.

"I told them he could be lying about other things. Such as no contact with his sister. But they quickly pointed out it was baseless speculation. Given their objections, I thought it wasn't a good idea to tell them about your dog's warning. Nonetheless, I'm not giving up on my brethren at MI5, but it's going to take a bit longer than I hoped it would."

"We don't have time for that. How about he and Emily lied to us about knowing each other much better than they tried to make us believe?"

"What do you mean?"

"They're in regular contact, like twice a day or more," said Rex.

"How would you know?"

"There's no question like that," said Rex with a straight face.

Stevens stared at Rex from across the table for a long moment, processing what he heard, and then started laughing. "Ah, I see, don't ask, don't tell?"

"Uh-huh. But ask MI5 to do you one favor; let them ask GCHQ to check Tony's and Emily's phone records for, say, the past two to three weeks."

GCHQ, Government Communications Headquarters, was the British intelligence and security organization responsible for providing signals intelligence (SIGINT) to the government and armed forces of the United Kingdom. They were based in 'The Doughnut' in the suburbs of Cheltenham, about eighty-eight miles out of London. The doughnut-shaped building was the largest secret intelligence operations building outside the United States. The GCHQ was the British equivalent of America's NSA.

"What will they find?"

"Exactly what I told you. They call each other twice a day on average. But both of them told us they haven't had contact for a quarter of a century. Right, Brooke, Julian?"

"Exactly," said Brooke. "In fact, both of them made a bit of a scene trying to remember the other's name."

Julian confirmed Brooke's statement with a nod.

"Interesting. Why would they...?" Stevens murmured.

"Catia thinks, and I concur, it could be to cover up an extramarital affair," said Rex. "But it could just as well be for another reason, which is why we need to find out what it is. We can either confront them with what we have now, or we can get more information and confront them then."

"I'm for the latter," said Stevens without hesitation, and everyone else agreed. "I'll have another chat with our MI5 friends."

"Good. Let's move on to Destiny Parker," Rex continued. "She and Ozmert, in all likelihood, maintained contact for the past twenty-five years. We know she liked to hang out with academics, according to her self-proclaimed best friend. We assume some of her academic friends might be associates of Dragut, constituting the Delphi thinktank. And, after learning how Ms. Parker had recruited Joanne Sanders in Athens, it's probably safe to assume not all of the associates are volunteers. We need to find as many of them as possible."

"Agreed," said Richardson. "Maybe we should start with Muslim academics in Western Europe. Hopefully, we don't have to get them all, just one with the right information might be enough."

"Ozmert had been recruited by someone during his university years, or he came up with the idea of the new Ottoman Empire on his own," said Josh. "I think a deep dive into Ozmert's university days might produce more leads."

Rex nodded. "Myles, it's in your domain, how'd you like to proceed?"

"I'll talk to my counterpart at MI5 to provide agents to work with Julian and Brooke."

"I'd like Josh and Marissa to be part of that team," Rex said.

"No problem."

"You don't expect pushback from MI5?" Richardson asked.

"Maybe, but that will only be until the Prime Minister gives them a direct order. Don't worry, they'll come to the party."

"Excellent," said Rex. "Christelle, I'd like you to work with Catia, Digger, and I on the academics at the universities of Europe."

Christelle nodded. "I'll talk to Francois Renou to open the doors for you and assign some agents to help us."

"Martin, Myles, I'd like to have your permission to contact Yaron Aderet to see if I can enlist the help of the Mossad. As you know, they have an extensive intelligence network across Europe with their *sayanim* system. I'm sure they'll have useful information about the intellectuals we're seeking."

"You have it," said Richardson.

"Same here," said Stevens.

The Mossad, a small intelligence agency compared to those of the USA, the UK, and other western European countries, had devised a brilliant plan to overcome their limitations by recruiting helpers, *sayanim*, Jewish volunteers across the world.

The *sayanim* were bankers, restauranteurs, homeowners, hoteliers, owners and managers of guest houses, rental car companies, travel agents, lawyers, doctors, nurses, journalists, large corporates, and many others. It was estimated that across the globe, they numbered more than ten thousand, and whenever needed, provided mission support to Mossad's covert operations—free of charge. One of the benefits of the Jewish diaspora was what the chief of the Mossad called it.

"Now, Ethan, I've been wondering about the Hellenic police's investigation into the killing of Cole and Almasi, as well as the attack on us at our hotel. We haven't heard much from them, have we?"

"No, we haven't, but that's my fault. With all that's been going on, I haven't been bugging them enough. I'll make work of that immediately after this meeting."

"Good. Maybe they have information about where Destiny lived. Have they searched her residence? Who were her friends and associates? If they've done a proper job, there must be something useful for us. Also, those thugs who attacked us at our hotel, who sent them?"

"On it," said Thomson.

Richardson said, "Ethan, if you get any resistance from the police, let me know. I'm sure a call from POTUS to the Greek Prime Minister will open the doors."

"Will do," said Thomson. "So far, they've been cooperative."

Rex smiled. "Not done with you, Ethan. We still have Savvas Rallotis, the crime boss in Alexandroupolis. He seems to be the only one who could possibly know who the agent is. Greg's team will put electronic tabs on him. Will you be able to put a physical surveillance team on?"

"No problem. I'll brief a team as soon as we're done here."

"Martin, this is for you *and* Ethan. The police took names, addresses, and statements of everyone who was at the Castle of the Grand Master at the time of the killings. Catia and I think Destiny Parker had backup there. We took videos and photos, trying to capture as many faces as possible. I think we should put a team of analysts to task to check out everyone that was there, try to match faces with statements, and check them against the facial recognition databases of security agencies across Europe."

"I'll assign a team from here to assist you with that," said Richardson. "Ethan, you'll have to get us that list of witnesses and let me know."

"Will do," said Thomson.

Rex continued. "Ozmert and the President of Turkey might have a connection. Martin, it would be good if you could put a team on to conduct in-depth research into the backgrounds of current Turkish politicians and officials. See if one or more of them perchance wandered the streets of Feres during the time Ushan Ozmert lived there."

"On it," said Martin.

"Do you want the *TOMATS* to stay here in Valletta?" Spencer asked.

Rex thought about it for a moment. "I can't think of a reason to move you anywhere for now. It's close enough to reach Greece, Turkey, and Italy within a day or two if required. I'd suggest you brief the crew to be vigilant just in case Dragut discovers the yacht and gets it in his head to send more knuckle-draggers our way."

"Okay, we'll sail around the islands for the next few days," Spencer said.

"Good. Anything else we need to discuss?"

"One more thing, Rex," said Stevens. "I can make one of the meeting rooms available here at HQ to serve as mission control center if you want."

"That would be perfect. Thanks, Myles."

"Ahem. Myles, only one request, would you mind if I put an espresso machine in the room? Not that we don't like English tea, but we're addicted to Italian espresso. I'll pay for the machine and the coffee beans," said Catia.

Josh and Marissa immediately chimed in and said they would contribute to the cost.

Myles chuckled. "No problem, Catia, we're used to people with weird tastes visiting us from time to time. I'll ask them to set up a coffee machine for you. The cost will be on British taxpayers."

"Thanks, Myles. Now that we've defeated the coffee crisis, is there anything else?" Rex asked.

There wasn't.

"Dragut hunting season is now officially open. In the words of the notorious John Brandt, 'Let's do it to them before they do it to us.'"

Everyone smiled, and Brandt's smile reminded Christelle of a proud father wanting to tell the world, "Now that's my boy I've been telling you about."

Chapter Thirty-Four

AN OLD MAN IN A WHEELCHAIR

London, England

Day 9

The Great Bell, better known as Big Ben, London's relentless reminder of humanity's race against time located at the north end of the Palace of Westminster, was playing the 20-note sequence of the Westminster Quarters melody, signifying the lapse of another fifteen minutes since the clock struck 7:00 p.m. as the Daltons and Farleys stepped out of the SIS Headquarters building. It was a stark reminder of what the Romans called *tempus fugit* literally translated as 'time flees' or 'time escapes' or more colloquially, 'time flies.'

They decided to walk to their hotel, the Park Plaza Riverbank, which was less than a mile away, to give everyone a chance to stretch their legs after a day of meetings. They walked through the Vauxhall Pleasure Gardens, also known as the Spring Gardens, and entered The Black Dog pub. The venue was Catia's choice because she thought Digger might like it. And by all accounts, he did. The place was noisy, the people were jovial, the beer was excellent, so were the beef and ale pies.

Big Ben told them it was 8:30 p.m. when they left The Black Dog and made their way to the hotel. There were still more than two hours of sunlight left. The sidewalks, which the English called pavements, were busy but not crowded. They were about two hundred yards from the hotel when Rex felt Digger pulling on his leash and looked down at him. Digger had stopped to look back at something behind them. Rex looked back, it was an old man with a long silver-gray beard, hornbill glasses with thick lenses, in a wheelchair pushed by a young woman with dark hair.

Something stirred in Rex's mind. *I've seen this before... Rhodes Island, the Palace of the Grand Master. The old man in a wheelchair...* He looked closely at them and realized it was not the same people. But then what was it that got Digger's attention? Is it possible that his curiosity was stirred because the couple looked remarkably similar to the old man and his helper he saw nine days ago on Rhodes Island? Maybe.

By now, Josh, Catia, and Marissa had also stopped, turned around, and were staring askance at Rex and Digger.

"What's up?" Josh asked.

"Give us a minute," Rex said. He waited for the couple to pass them, nodded a greeting, which they returned with friendly smiles. *Hmm, definitely not the same people.* Rex kept his eyes on Digger, but he was happy, no warning signals. Digger stared at the passing couple and then turned his gaze to Rex, waiting for him to start walking again.

Rex started walking, and then it struck him, and he stopped again.

The watchers!

Rex looked up and saw the questioning gazes of his companions. He looked around, there was no one else nearby, he took a step closer to them and said in an urgent whisper, "I think I know who the watchers were at the Palace of the Grand Master."

Catia turned and looked at the disappearing old man in the wheelchair and remembered. "Rex! What made you..."

"Our resident four-legged genius." Rex pointed at Digger. "Let's get to the hotel."

They went straight to the Daltons' suite, scanned it for bugs, found none, and sat down on the couch and chairs in the lounge area.

Rex and Catia told them about the old man and his minder they saw that day at the Palace of the Grand Master.

Catia had her laptop out and was calling up the photos and video footage from their visit to the palace. Within minutes she had two photos and a video in which the old man and his caretaker were clearly visible. She and Marissa quickly cut the images of the couple out and saved them as new images then they started to zoom in on each of them.

"It's not the same people," Rex said, "but I think they bear a striking resemblance to the couple we just saw on the street."

"Okay, I agree, they do, but what makes you think they were the watchers?" Josh asked.

"Digger," Rex said.

All eyes turned to Digger, where he was lying on the carpet busy with serious matters, attacking the kong filled with jerky.

"C'mon Rex. You already said the couple we saw on the street was not the same people you saw on the Island that day. Digger won't make that kind of mistake," said Marissa.

"I don't think that's what he was trying to tell me. I think he was just saying, 'hey, look there is an old man in a wheelchair being pushed by a woman just like we saw the other day', or..."

"Or... is it possible that he smelled trouble with that couple on the Island and now he's telling you? Nah, I can't even begin to fathom how that's possible," Josh murmured.

"Wait, I think I might know how to solve the puzzle. A long shot, but worth trying." He picked his satphone up, dialed Ethan Thomson's number, and put the phone on speaker.

"What's up, Rex?"

"I need an urgent favor from you."

"Say the word."

"Is Joanne Sanders still there at the embassy?"

"Yep, still in custody. She'll be here for a few more days."

"Is she still in a cooperative mood?"

"Yes, very much so."

"Excellent. In your inbox are a few pictures of a woman and an old man in a wheelchair. We took them that day at the Palace of the Grand Master on Rhodes Island. I want you to show them to Sanders and ask her if that is the woman who contacted her after Destiny Parker was killed."

"Shit! That would be a major breakthrough. Got the pictures. What about the guy in the wheelchair?"

"I doubt that Sanders would know who that is."

"It sounds as if *you* know."

Rex chuckled but made no reply.

"I'll get on it immediately."

When the call ended, Rex turned his attention back to the others in the room, staring at him with wrinkled eyebrows. He smiled and said, "Coffee, anyone? I'm making."

He got three orders for coffee and a barrage of questions, which he more or less ignored with his comments. "To be revealed shortly. Mug or cup? Be patient. Milk and sugar?"

Rex was spared a severe beating by his wife and friends when Thomson's call came through ten minutes after he had served everyone their coffee.

"The answer is yes; Sanders knows that woman. She's the one who replaced Destiny Parker. Rex, one day you'll have to tell me how you figured this out."

"That was easy, Digger gave me the idea."

"Digger... Riiiiiight... of course... how stupid of me. You'll still have to explain it to me."

"It will cost you four bottles of seven-star Metaxa brandy, a bottle for everyone here in the room with me, and a big bag of real American jerky for Digger."

"Deal. Now, who's that old man in the wheelchair?"

"That, ladies and gentlemen, I believe, is Ushan Ozmert, aka Dragut."

A long contemplative silence followed before Catia said, "I guess the facial recognition team has an urgent job coming their way?"

"Right. Let's get back to Vauxhall Cross, we're not going to get much sleep tonight," said Rex. "In the meantime, Ethan, it would be extremely helpful if you could get us the witness statements from the Hellenic police. Among them should be the statements of those two."

Half an hour later, they were in the mission control room that Stevens had set up for them. Stevens and his agents, Brooke and Julian already had Richardson, Brandt, Christelle, McArdle, Greg, and Spencer dialed in on the secured video conference. Thomson would join them as soon as he had wangled the witness statements out of the Hellenic Police.

Rex told them what they discovered and his idea that the old man could be Ushan Ozmert in disguise.

There was an almost tangible excitement and anticipation among the group.

Richardson picked up his desk phone and summoned the head of the facial recognition team to his office.

Scott Armstrong entered Richardson's office a few minutes later.

"Over to you, Rex," said Richardson after the introductions.

"Two things. We want you to take the images of that woman in the pictures on the screen and run them through your databases to find a match. The second request is to go to work on the image of the old man in the wheelchair; we suspect he's in disguise and might, in fact, be the person in these images." Rex brought the pictures of Ushan Ozmert that they got from MI6 and the Ozmert family up on the screen. "The images are twenty-five years or older. We hope you'll be able to match them if it is the same person. Or would that be a problem?"

"It won't be. Our identification algorithms have an error rate approaching point zero eight percent these days. There are eighty nodal points on a human face. Those are endpoints used to measure variables of a person's face, such as the length or width of the nose, the depth of the eye sockets, the shape of the cheekbones, distances between facial features, and such. In other words, if that old man is the same person you have on-screen now, our computers will tell us. A disguise won't fool them."

"Okay, Scott, show us what you can do," said Richardson.

"Can I use your phone?" Armstrong asked.

"Go for it."

A few minutes later, Olivia Simpson, Armstrong's best facial recognition expert, took a seat at the table, opened her laptop, and downloaded the images. She took the images of the dark-haired woman and fed them into the system and said, "Okay, that one is in the system, it could take up to two hours or longer before we get an answer. Let's now look at the old man."

Her fingers were flying over the keyboard as she called up all the old photos as well as the new ones and the video and fed them to a program that would help her make the comparisons.

As Olivia hammered away at the keyboard, Armstrong explained, "When it comes to disguises, there are ways to deceive our algorithms, face masks and suchlike, but in this case, it's obvious the old man didn't go to that extreme. Not many people realize that disguises have limitations; you can make someone look older, but it's near impossible to make them look younger. The same goes for weight, you can make lean people look fatter but not the other way round."

Marissa feigned a deep sigh. "Yeah, don't I know all about that."

Josh placed his hand on her arm and said, "Don't worry, you're still the most beautiful girl who ever fell in love with me."

It earned him a kiss on the cheek to the delight of everyone else in the meeting.

A few minutes later, Olivia looked up from her screen and said, "We've got a fifty percent match on the first run. Let me take that beard and glasses away and age the face of the young guy a bit."

Three minutes later, she said, "Bingo! Ninety-five percent. The old man in the wheelchair is the same person as the young man in your photos. Here's what he looks like without disguise." She brought the new image up on the screen next to the twenty-five-year-old images.

There was no doubt, it was the face of Ushan Ozmert.

Everyone started clapping their hands.

Richardson thanked the two analysts and excused them.

Rex was quiet, thinking. *Ushan Ozmert, if only I knew then what I know now, your parents would indeed have only one living child. The people killed and maimed by your guns and bombs would all be alive and unharmed. And the Ottoman Empire would have remained in the recesses of history.*

———————

"What was Dragut doing there?" Richardson spoke the question on everyone's mind.

"Overseeing the operation to stop Almasi from passing on the information about the Delphi Group," said Myles.

Richardson nodded. "Yes, but he's a man who's been hiding in the shadows for more than twenty-five years. Why would he risk exposure? Why not send someone else?"

"Keep in mind," Rex said, "Ozmert is also a sentimental kind of person. At least about Ottoman history, he is. He worships Turgut Reis, even adopted his nickname. Since his childhood, he'd been playing Admiral Turgut Reis and dreaming about restoring the Ottoman Empire. Rhodes Island became part of the Ottoman Empire in 1522, and the Palace of the Grandmaster was their command center on the island. So, it's possible that he was there also for sentimental reasons. However, we could speculate in perpetuity. The fact is, he was there, and he got a good look at Catia, me, and Digger. Probably took photos of us as well. I suggest we move on."

"Agreed," said Richardson.

Stevens was shaking his head. "You know, Rex, I took your tales about Digger's abilities with a pinch of salt, but please accept my sincerest and deepest apologies, and please convey same to Digger. I'll never doubt the two of you again."

Richardson echoed that.

"Okay, I'll let Digger know," said Rex with a big grin on his face.

"It will teach you all to never doubt any of my agents," Brandt smirked. "Especially not Agent Digger."

"Well, I have to confess," said Josh, "I actually bribed him with half of my fish a few days ago when we were in the seafood restaurant in Alexandroupolis to find Dragut for us. And he came through like a real trooper. I'm going to give him a whole fish to find the address for us."

Digger, apparently, had no interest in the praises showered upon him. Maybe it was because he was fast asleep on the floor between Rex and Catia.

"And that brings us to the crux of the matter," said Rex. "The addresses for Dragut and his wheelchair operator."

Just then, Thomson joined the conference.

"What happened?"

"Not much," Josh deadpanned. "The old guy in the

wheelchair was Dragut. Digger knew it all along but waited until now to tell us."

Thomson blinked a few times before joining the mirth. "He doesn't perchance have their address as well?"

"He might very well," said Josh. "But there's a process to follow to get him talking. We'll kick it off as soon as he wakes up."

Thomson laughed and shook his head. "Okay, on a serious note. It took a little arm-twisting and name-dropping to get copies of all the witness statements, but I got them in the end. The police did a great job and took photos of all witnesses, which they attached to their statements, including yours. The two we're interested in for now are Georgios and Fillia Pipatros, father and daughter, both from Athens."

"Which, of course, is all bullshit," growled Brandt.

Christelle placed her hand on Brandt's arm and smiled at him. He relaxed.

"Exactly," said Thomson. "The lead investigator told me the address exists, but no one there has ever seen or heard of the Pipatroses, and it goes without saying the phone numbers don't exist. According to him, the Pipatroses were the only witnesses who gave false addresses and telephone numbers."

Rex nodded slowly. "No surprises there. Nonetheless, I think we've made progress. Let's see what the database search for Ms. Pipatros produces."

Half an hour later, Richardson's phone rang. It was Armstrong. Richardson put it on speaker.

"Sir, we have a match for the woman. Sarah Sulzer, according to her Facebook page. Originally from Berlin, Germany."

"Your algorithms check Facebook images as well?"

"Yes, sir. We pretty much capture every photo that goes on the internet, including anything that is uploaded to any website or accompanies an email. The problem is she is 'dead'; her Facebook page has been dormant for more than three years. The last post on the page is a eulogy. Apparently, she was killed in a car accident outside Paris."

"In other words, another dead end, so to speak," said Richardson.

"I wouldn't know about that, sir. I'm sending you the link to the Facebook page for the social media analysts to study."

Richardson thanked Armstrong and ended the call.

Brandt was shaking his head. "Another living dead to chase. That bastard is not going to make it easy for us."

"That's for sure," Rex said. "Greg, can you get Rehka to look at that Facebook page to see who Sarah Sulzer's friends and family were and delve into her life? Get every scrap of information about her from the day she was born."

"Will do."

Rex had gone quiet as he stared at the images on the screen. Everyone was staring at him, but he didn't realize it until Catia touched his arm and said, "Rex?"

"Huh... Sorry. I was just wondering about Ozmert and Sulzer. I'm sure they don't live on Rhodes Island, which means they must have traveled there and back from wherever they live. And that means somewhere there could be official records, CCTV footage and such, about their coming and going. It could be at the airport or any of the six harbors of Rhodes Island."

"I'll see if I can get that information," said Thomson. "But keep in mind they could just as easily have bypassed all those entry points if they arrived on a yacht, anchored offshore, and took a small boat to land."

"Yep, that's a possibility, but we won't know until we've studied the official records."

"Agreed."

"Are we in agreement, our discoveries of the past few hours don't change our plans of earlier today?"

Everyone agreed.

"Okay, let's get on with it. Shake the trees."

Chapter Thirty-Five

HEY JACK

London, England

Day 10

By dawn the next morning, with Big Ben relentlessly announcing the lapse of every quarter of an hour toward the next attack or the capture of Ushan Ozmert, Operation Dragut was rapidly gaining momentum.

Myles kept some of his friends over at MI5 busy throughout the night and got their cooperation to put tabs on Tony Parker and Emily Hobson. Physical surveillance would follow if electronic surveillance produced anything of value. Rex didn't tell Myles that Greg and Rehka were, in the meantime, still hammering away at hacking into their computers and phones.

Rex and Catia had a long video call with Yaron Aderet in Jerusalem to brief him fully on Operation Dragut and how the Mossad could help. Aderet was, as always, more than willing to assist in any manner he could.

"For now," Rex said, "it would be most helpful if you could assist us in finding one or more of the Delphi Group's thinktank members."

Aderet promised to assign two of his staff to it immediately.

By mid-day, Myles stopped by the mission control room and told Rex et al. that Jack Swanson was the epitome of uncooperativeness. He had been telling his interrogators that he was illegally captured while on holiday in Greece and transported to the UK and that he'd done nothing wrong. And he was threatening them with lawsuits that would bankrupt the country.

"Would you mind if Digger and I pay Swanson a visit?" Rex asked. Seeing the frown on Myles's forehead, he quickly added, "I promise I won't lay a hand on him, and I'll keep Digger away from him."

"O-k-a-y, I'll take you there but..."

"Don't worry Myles, you have my word, I'm not going to make any trouble for you, neither will Digger."

Five minutes later, Myles, Rex, and Digger entered the interrogation room after briefing the investigating officer about the scheme.

"Hey, Jack, good to see you again. How..." was as far as Rex got before Swanson threw himself off his chair onto the floor and curled into a ball protecting his crotch with his cuffed hands and legs.

He whimpered, "Get the damn dog out of here! Now! Get him out!"

Rex and Digger ignored him and took a few steps closer. He kneeled down and said to Digger, "Hey buddy, now look at that, Jack is not happy to see us. Do you think you could do something to let him know we came in peace?"

Digger growled.

Swanson screamed, "Nooooo!" And lost control of his bladder.

Rex and Digger took a few steps back. Rex said, "Ah, well, I guess that's the end of the friendship then. Digger..."

"Stop it! Please. I'll talk to you. I'll tell you everything you want to know. Just take the dog away."

Rex grinned as he and Digger headed for the door. Mission accomplished.

Myles was shaking his head when they were outside the room. "If only all interviews could be as easy as that. Maybe I should recommend to the director to get a dog or two to help us."

Rex laughed. "Not a bad idea. But you could let the officer know there is one thing Swanson fears as much or more than Digger, and that's his former Para buddies."

"I'll let him know."

Within the next few hours, Swanson's interrogator learned that he knew nothing more about his agent than he had already told Rex. His phone didn't produce much either because it didn't store the metadata about his calls and text messages.

The interesting bit they got when they started looking into his finances was that all his Monero payments came from an IP address in Malta. It was not entirely surprising that the cryptocurrency transactions were executed from Malta; the majority of the world's crypto trading volume moved through companies based there. It was another lead to follow up.

After divulging that information, Swanson started telling

them about his hit jobs over the years. In the process, quite a few unsolved cases under investigation by MI5 got solved.

Josh's brainchild: tracking down Ushan Ozmert's university friends and associates, was a bit more of a challenge than getting Swanson to talk. Josh, Marissa, Brooke, and Julian soon realized they would need access to student records at Oxford University. And, dealing with university officials was every bit as painful and frustrating as dealing with government bureaucrats.

It required a personal phone call from the director of MI6 to his old friend, the rector of the university, to get their cooperation. Only then was Josh's team able to start making a list of Ozmert's erstwhile classmates and friends. And then the real work would start as they had to track them down and interview them. It was going to be a long and arduous process.

Thomson reported that he had dispatched two agents to Alexandroupolis to put surveillance on Savvas Rallotis, the crime boss. It would soon become apparent that Rallotis's word was law in Alexandroupolis; even the police feared him. He thought he was untouchable and invincible. As is often the case with people with a misplaced self-aggrandizing streak, Savvas also had a few vices; good food in abundance, lots of wine, and women, willing or unwilling, he didn't care, nobody refused him.

He sounded a lot like Dimitris Rossas, the guy who raped Ushan Ozmert's sister and ended up in a concrete casing with some of his body parts in odd places.

Rumor had it that Savvas was looking high and low for his three missing men and the people who abducted them. He had placed a fifty-thousand euro reward on the heads of the abductors.

"Bloody hell. What an insult," Josh said when he heard about the reward. "Only three days ago, we were worth three hundred thousand. Rex, we better get this mission over before we're worthless."

Chapter Thirty-Six

TWO CANDIDATES

London, England

Day 10

Back in the mission control room, Rex and Catia returned to the quest to find the members of Dragut's advisory team. Their mission was going to be a lot more challenging than Josh's.

Christelle had provided a list of Muslim academics, clerics, and influencers of interest on the French security agencies' watch lists. In the spy business, political correctness was not part of the lexicon. They worked with the facts. Facts untainted by political correctness. Those facts were undeniable; Muslim radicals were responsible for the vast majority of terror attacks in Europe since 2001. Racial and religious profiling was a necessity; therefore, among others, Muslim clerics and academics and influencers were watched by default. Not all of them all the time and not to the same level for all; some were just checked randomly, others constantly.

She also asked her successor at DGSE, Francois Renou, to get the cooperation of the EU Intelligence and Situation Centre (EU INTCEN) and Club de Berne. Due to the growing rift between Britain and the EU caused by Britain's decision to leave the EU, known as Brexit, it was thought it would be better for Myles not to be involved in the requests for information.

EU INTCEN was the European Union's intelligence body under the authority of the EU's High Representative. Their mission: to provide intelligence analysis, early warning, and situational awareness to the EU Member States.

Club de Berne, as the name suggested, was a less formal organization. Constituted in 1971 in Bern, Switzerland. They were an intelligence-sharing forum between the intelligence services of the twenty-seven states of the European Union (EU) plus Norway and Switzerland. They operated on the basis of voluntary exchange of information, had no secretariat, and took no-decisions. The Counter Terrorism Group (CTG), created after 9/11, was an offshoot of the Club and shared terrorism intelligence among members.

When Big Ben chimed at 5:00 p.m., Rex had the list of targets provided by Aderet's analysts.

Greg's team was already hard at work on Christelle's list, hacking into their computers and phones, analyzing their internet activities and financial transactions. It was a shotgun approach, to be sure, but there was no other way. They had to study each and every one of them.

Aderet's list was added to Greg's queue, which by 7:00 p.m. had grown to forty-six when Christelle dropped the list of names from EU INTCEN and Club de Berne.

It was a few minutes past 8:00 p.m. when Greg and

Rehka appeared on the big screen in the mission control room.

"I finally managed to get into Tony Parker's computers. I'm still working on Emily Hobson's," said Rehka.

"We're all ears," said Catia.

"So far, there's nothing exciting about Parker's personal or his company social media activities; it's all about marketing and branding. As expected, his financial activities show a vast and complex conglomerate of trusts and companies, some of which his main UK-based company owns the controlling shares in and some in which he has made substantial investments but doesn't control.

"He has fixed assets such as houses and offices in Paris, Rome, Madrid, and Lisbon. Holiday homes on the Algarve in Portugal and on the French Riviera, Côte d'Azur, as the French call it. It will take a while to unearth and untangle all of it.

"However, what I thought might be of interest to you is his regular trips, as in once a quarter, to Malta where he has two companies registered. Thus far, I've not been able to get into his bank accounts there."

Rex nodded. "Malta again," he said softly. "Hmm, but maybe his interests in Malta are for tax purposes. They have very attractive tax schemes with effective rates as low as five percent for foreign-owned companies versus an average of twenty-two percent offered by other European countries. It's a mecca for investment funds, banks, and financial-services firms from all over the world."

"That's what I have at the moment," said Rehka. "Oh, he and Emily are still keeping up their daily communications, and although I can't yet tell you what they're talking about, I can tell you that the record of the GPS coordinates of their phones over the last six months, which is as far back as I looked, show they were in each other's physical company at least once a week."

"Great work, Rehka. Keep on digging," said Rex.

They were about to end the call when Greg said, "Hang on, I just got a message from the team. They have two potential candidates for closer scrutiny. Give me a sec."

A minute later, Greg looked up from the screen of his laptop and said, "Two of them. Yunus Albayrak, Turkish by birth, a professor in international security studies at the University of Lyon. Our algorithms flagged his name because he has been dabbling in cryptocurrencies. The team hacked into his computer and found his cryptocurrency wallet addresses and login credentials, enabling them to look at all his transactions. He has a substantial portfolio of Bitcoin and other cryptos, and guess what?"

"He received Monero payments from Malta?" Rex whispered.

"Precisely. To the tune of a hundred and fifty thousand US dollars, the last nine months. He converted all of it to Bitcoin."

"Okay. Who's the second one?"

"Özdemir Tozlu, Greek by birth, operating an import-export business out of the Kreuzberg neighborhood in central Berlin, known as Little Istanbul or the Turkish Quarters. Our algorithms also flagged his name because of his cryptocurrency activities. Substantial amounts of Bitcoin, Monero, and other cryptocurrencies have been going through his accounts. Looking at his transactions, my first impression is that he's their financial officer. Almost all of his dealings in cryptos are going through Binance, the world's biggest cryptocurrency exchange, based in Malta."

"Malta seems to be a common denominator," Rex

murmured. "I want you to delve into those crypto transactions."

"Will do."

Catia ran a quick Google search on her laptop and said,
"That name, Özdemir, seems to be an Ottoman name. The
surname, Tozlu, is Turkish. Do you have a place and date of
birth or any other details?"

"Not yet. We'll get it," Greg replied.

Rex pulled the list of names up on his computer,
searched for Tozlu, and saw the name had been supplied by
the BND. They were Germany's foreign intelligence agency,
Federal Intelligence Service, or *Bundesnachrichtendienst* in
German, acting as an early warning system to alert the
German government about threats to German interests.
They depended heavily on wiretapping and electronic
surveillance.

Rex's phone started ringing. It was Christelle.

Chapter Thirty-Seven

BAD NEWS

Video Conference

Day 10

Christelle started without preamble. "Rex, I'm sorry to be the bearer of bad news. John took a turn for the worst. He collapsed when he got up from his chair. We're in the CRC plane on the way to Phoenix. A team of specialists is preparing to operate as soon as we arrive."

The blood drained from Rex's face. It was as if a bucket of ice water had been dumped over him. He swallowed hard and said, "Is he still unconscious?"

"Thank God, no. He regained consciousness fairly quickly. He wants to talk to you. Hang on, I'll give him the phone."

"How are you, son?" Brandt said in a weak voice.

"I'm good, John. But I'm told you're not."

"Don't worry about me, I have no intentions to check

out yet. I'll get through it. I have to; Christelle is waiting on me to marry her, and I'm not going to disappoint her."

"That's a *very* good reason to hang in there. Another is that you don't have my permission to check out. I'm the CEO now, and don't you forget that. I'm ordering you to stay alive." Rex's voice broke off as he struggled to get control of his emotions.

"Listen to me, Rex. I don't want you to miss a beat because of me. Get hold of that son of a bitch. When I open my eyes after the surgery, I want it to be to the news that Dragut is dead or in custody."

Rex took a deep breath. "John, I can't promise you that the sun will rise tomorrow morning, but I can promise you I'm just as sure we're going to get him. Maybe not by the time you wake up after your surgery, but it won't be long after. I think we're just days away from nailing the bastard."

"Tha... goo... enough... me," John mumbled.

"He's tired, Rex," said Christelle, "but he's got a smile on his face now that he has spoken to you."

"Thanks, Christelle. I'll let the others know. Keep me posted, twenty-four-seven, please," whispered Rex.

"I will. He's going to be all right, Rex. He's strong and healthy, he'll get through it, and I'll be right next to him every step of the way."

Rex nodded slowly and whispered, "Thanks Christelle."

One would have been able to hear a pin drop in the mission control room when Christelle ended the call. Everyone was staring at Rex.

Rex's voice was soft and filled with restrained emotion. "John has taken a turn for the worst. He and Christelle are in the CRC plane on the way to Phoenix. The doctors are on standby to operate on him."

Catia and Marissa were wiping tears from their faces.

Josh said nothing. He got up slowly and made his way to the espresso machine. Brooke and Julian stared at their computer screens. Digger was on his feet standing between Catia and Marissa, making soft, comforting noises.

It was a shock; they didn't have to say it to each other. Neither did they have to tell each other it was a situation they had no control over other than to pray and hope. In the meantime, Dragut was still out there, planning his next massacre.

"Four coffees and two teas?" Josh asked.

Everyone nodded.

"Jerky or peanut butter in your kong, Digger?"

Digger looked at Josh when he heard his name but didn't move. He shifted his gaze between Rex, Catia, Marissa, and Josh in turn as if he wanted to know if they're okay.

Catia scratched his ears and said, "Thanks, Digger, you're a great comfort. You can go and get your kong, we're okay."

Josh forced a few pieces of jerky into the kong and gave it to Digger.

By the time everyone had their drinks in front of them, Myles had joined them. Rex had Richardson, Spencer, and Thomson on video conference.

They all listened in shocked silence as Rex told them about Brandt.

The reaction was the same as before. It was sad, it was emotional, and it was not in their hands. They soon concluded the best they could do for their friend, and the world was to redouble their efforts to get hold of Dragut.

They were still talking when Rex got a message from Greg. They had three more candidates. One in Paris, Riyad Messaoudi, from Algerian descent, a dealer in Middle East ancient artifacts. It was no secret, illicit dealing in ancient artifacts was one of the ways terror organizations funded their operations.

The second candidate was Fareed al-Moradi from Germany, a senior lecturer in International War Studies at the University of Potsdam, bordering Berlin. He had no dealings in cryptocurrencies, but his field of study made him an ideal candidate for Dragut's brain trust.

The third was Waleed Hajjar, Egyptian, a professor in Islamic studies at the Humboldt University of Berlin, one of the world's foremost scholars about the Ottoman Empire. Again, no crypto dealings, but his expertise in the Ottoman Empire is what flagged him.

"Three from Germany so far and all of them in Berlin or surrounding areas," said Rex. "I think we need to have a chat with the BND."

"Martin and I can help you with that," said Stevens. "We're old acquaintances of Tilmann Wieser, one of the three vice presidents of the BND. Wieser is in charge of *Internationaler Terrorismus und Internationale Organisierte Kriminal-ität*, Terrorism and International Organized Crime."

"Excellent. See if you can get a video meeting with him for starters, but I think it might be worth going over to Berlin to have a face-to-face with him.

"In the absence of Christelle, I'll take it on myself to talk to Francois Renou to put surveillance teams on Yunus Albayrak, the professor in international security studies at the University of Lyon. And the guy in Paris, Riyad Messaoudi."

Big Ben said it was 9:30 p.m. when the call ended.

Video Conference

Day 10

AN HOUR LATER, STEVENS and Richardson introduced Rex to Tilmann Wieser of the BND. The three older
men knew each other from the Cold War days and still had
regular contact with each other as new threats emerged in
the form of Islamic terrorism as well as Russian and
Chinese expansionism.

When Rex was introduced, Richardson mentioned the
relationship with CRC and John Brandt.

"Hmm, one of John Brandt's boys," said Wieser. "How
is the old fox?"

Rex shook his head slightly. "Not good, I'm afraid." He
told Wieser about Brandt's health issues.

"I'm so sorry to hear that. Please let him know if you
can, I send my regards and best wishes, hoping he'll get
better very soon. I don't know if you know, but John saved
my life once during a mission in East Germany. Were it not
for him, you would be talking to someone else now."

"I'll ask him to tell me about it," Rex said.

"But that's not why you called me. Let's get on with it."

Richardson and Stevens filled Wieser in about the operation to track down Dragut and then handed it over to Rex.

"Thanks for your cooperation so far, Herr Wieser," Rex
started.

Wieser smiled. "You speak German?"

"Yes. My mother was German."

"Good. But please call me Tilmann. I don't like formali-
ties when dealing with friends." Wieser smiled. "Yeah,
believe it or not, Martin, I've decided to forget about the

NSA spying on our Chancellor." He was referring to the scandal that erupted over President Obama's head when Wikileaks revealed that the NSA had been spying on the German Chancellor. At the time of the discovery, there was a big commotion, but it got buried later when it became evident that Germany was also spying on allies.

Rex grinned and continued. "Thanks for the list of names you've provided. We're studying them now and already have three names we would like to have a closer look at. Of most interest is a man by the name of Özdemir Tozlu."

Wieser held his hand up. "I know about the list and approved that it be provided to you. But I'm afraid that's as far as my knowledge goes. It would be best if I set up a time for you to meet with the senior agent in charge of the watch lists, Andrea Degen. Wieser had a quick look at her electronic calendar and said, "She's got an hour free tomorrow morning at 10:00 a.m. You want me to book that timeslot?"

"Thanks, Tilmann, but I was wondering if it would be okay if we fly over and meet with her in person?"

"No problem. In that case, I'll ask her to clear her schedule so that she's available for the day."

They spent a few more minutes talking about the mission before ending the call.

Chapter Thirty-Eight

SINGING THE STAR-SPANGLED BANNER

En route to Berlin, Germany

Day 11

Since the Joanne Sanders debacle, it was decided that they would not use commercial airlines. The CIA jets would transport them wherever they wanted to be, and they would make all their own travel and accommodation arrangements.

On the two-hour flight over to Berlin, which started at 6:00 a.m. in London, Rex and Catia took stock of the situation.

The attacks in The Netherlands and France were still big news. Although the media was still rife with speculations about the identity of the anonymous culprits, most of their time was spent on debating possible solutions. And, probably because of the prominence given to the Turkish President's statements, there was a rapidly growing number of politicians and intellectuals expressing the opinion that maybe it was time for the EU to open the doors for Turkey to become a member. The benefits of doing so were very obvious, they contended. And more than just a few news outlets started supporting the idea.

As the media kept the debate alive, they inadvertently stoked the fires of fear raging in the hearts and minds of the people of Europe who realized that they hadn't seen the last of these kinds of attacks and that their country's security agencies were unable to protect them.

Why not Turkish EU membership? Or is it Islamophobia? The Turks are secular moderates. They've got the second-biggest military in NATO. Speaking of which, why can they be members of NATO but not the EU? What can we lose? As it is, we're being slaughtered, and they seem to be the only ones who can protect us.

No doubt, Dragut would've been smiling from ear to ear when he listened to the debate. He was getting exactly what he wanted. A few more attacks, a little more media support, and the EU would start begging Turkey to join them.

"On another topic," Rex said to Catia, "I've been thinking a lot about Ozmert's disappearance. I disappeared for two years after that ambush in Afghanistan, but that was different. I tried to start a new life, even considered cosmetic surgery at some stage. My intentions were to reenter society and try to live a normal life."

Catia smiled. "I'm very glad you didn't get that surgery and just as glad that Josh and Marissa hauled you out of obscurity."

"So am I." Rex smiled. "The hardest part of my self-imposed exile was to be in love with someone who didn't even know I loved her."

Catia laughed and kissed him on the cheek. "It worked

out in the end. And I thank God for that every day. As for Dragut, I agree with you, his motivation to disappear would have been different than yours."

"Yep, he would have been using different methods. Other than his appearance at the Palace of the Grand Master, for whatever reason, I'll not be surprised to learn that he secluded himself for the past twenty-five years."

"Agreed. The question is, where? I don't think he'll be living in some city in plain sight."

"You're right. Perhaps he's in a rural area, away from people, surrounded only by a select few he can trust. And never shows himself to anyone but the few he trusts. And even then, maybe *they* don't even know who he really is."

"It's difficult to imagine that in this day and age where every human is on a computer system somewhere, it's even possible to live such a secret life that he would never show up on any system anywhere. Never give fingerprints. Never have a bank account. Never go to the doctor or hospital. Never get a driver's license."

"But, as the mastermind, he must have ways and means to communicate with his underlings. And I'm sure he must, at least occasionally, communicate with the President of Turkey or his delegates. I just wish I could think of a quicker way to drive him out into the open."

"Well, until we can think of a better way, your plan to shake as many trees as hard and often as possible, is still the best."

Rex smiled and nodded. "Did I ever tell you that I love you?"

"Never," said Catia and started laughing before throwing her arms around his neck and laying a passionate kiss on him.

About fifteen minutes before the plane landed in Berlin, Christelle's call came through. The surgery took almost six hours.

"*Six hours?* That's a very long time. Were there problems?"

"No problems, Rex. The duration is not an indication of success or not, it was just a long, very delicate and complex procedure. The lead surgeon is happy that the tumor has been removed completely and there were no complications."

"Thank God," Rex whispered.

"The doctor said if John had waited another week it could have been too late. He's now in the recovery room, and as soon as he has stabilized, they'll move him to the ICU. He will be kept under sedation for a few days. The healing of the wound will take ten to fourteen days, and it will take four to eight weeks to recover. The doctor said John will feel very tired for a few weeks, but that will gradually disappear. He also said John's good physical condition will help a lot to speed up his recovery. I can't tell you how relieved I am, Rex."

"I can imagine. Thanks for the good news, Christelle. With you there, we all know John is in the best possible care he could ever be. We appreciate it very much."

"I love him, Rex."

"And that's what's going to have him back in the saddle, singing the Star-Spangled Banner in no time."

Christelle laughed.

"We're about to land in Berlin, we've got an appointment with one of Tilmann Wieser's senior staff to talk about the people on their watch lists."

"Tell Tilmann I say hi. He's a good guy. You can expect

full cooperation from him and his staff. But if you don't, just let me know. I'll get into his ear; he owes me a few favors."

"Okay, thanks for that. Tell John he's in our thoughts and prayers, and we're making good progress."

"Will do."

Chapter Thirty-Nine

GERMAN COOPERATION

Berlin, Germany

Day 11

At the airport in Berlin, Rex and Catia were met by a driver from the US Embassy who took them to the newly constructed BND Headquarters in Chausseestrasse in the Mitte district in the center of Berlin. It was the workplace of some four thousand people. The complex was located close to the former Berlin Wall, about three hundred and eighty yards from the canal which, during the Cold War, marked the border to West Berlin known as the Chausseestrasse Crossing Point. The BND was the first intelligence organization in the world to have a visitor center that was open to the public.

Andrea Degen was a shapely woman in her late forties to early fifties. Graying blonde hair coiffed in a short volumized bob, above average height, strong facial features, and striking light-blue eyes, dressed in a dark gray formal pants suit, all lending her an air of authority.

She was fluent in English and friendly in a professional manner. The embodiment of German precision and efficiency. She loved Digger at first sight. She told them that she grew up in a small town, and they always had German Shepherds as pets.

She had all the files ready on her computer and showed them to Rex and Catia on a wall-mounted big-screen TV. As they worked through the information, she copied what they wanted onto a flash drive.

Rex and Catia had been given the assurances by Wieser that Andrea had the highest possible security clearances and he had informed her about the operation.

They started with Fareed al-Moradi and Waleed Hajjar. It soon became apparent that the two academics were, more likely than not, just that, academics with no ulterior motives and no history of radicalism.

Andrea agreed to request increased surveillance on them, and then they moved on to Özdemir Tozlu. His was a different story altogether. He received a degree in commerce from Heidelberg University and was fluent in Greek, Turkish, German, and English. The first piece of electrifying information was Tozlu's place of birth and his age; Feres, Greece, and he was forty-eight. Rex estimated him to be little over five foot ten and about a hundred pounds overweight. He was slightly olive-skinned, had a balding head, salt and pepper beard, and was wearing golden wireframed glasses.

"In other words, a contemporary of Ushan Ozmert," said Catia.

"Indeed. And there is more as you'll see soon. But

please allow me to digress just a little to tell you about the Turkish community in Germany."

Rex and Catia nodded.

"Turkish immigrants are the second biggest immigrant group in Germany. The largest Turkish community outside of Turkey. Almost three million of them of which more than two-hundred thousand call Berlin home, making them the city's largest ethnic minority. But, according to the Berlin Institute, they integrated very poorly into German society. In fact, they ranked last on the institute's integration ranking scale.

"Of course, there are a variety of factors contributing to their reluctance or inability to integrate. One of them, the guidance by the Turkish President in a speech during a visit to our country when he urged Turks in Germany to integrate, but not assimilate."

"And let me guess, he didn't explain how to integrate but not assimilate?" asked Catia.

"Exactly. His statement was met with a lot of criticism, but as it is in politics, that's where it ended. No retractions or explanations; the president's statement still stands."

"No surprises there," said Rex.

Andrea scrolled to the next page and said, "As you can see there, Özdemir Tozlu is a cousin of the Turkish President."

Rex and Catia stared at the screen then at each other and then at Andrea. Rex said, "Frau Degen, in the past five minutes, you've given us some of the most valuable information we could've hoped for."

She smiled and continued. "I'm a little surprised that you didn't know about it already. Tozlu's relationship to the President of Turkey is common knowledge around here. And the

Turkish community, at least in Berlin, holds him in high regard for that. He's a fiery supporter of the Turkish President and his ideals of Neo Ottomanism. Despite being born in Greece, Tozlu insists that he's an Ottoman, not a Greek. He's an influencer in the Turkish community and quite outspoken about the ideal to revive the Ottoman Empire. As far as we know, he doesn't preach violence to achieve the goal, but he certainly has a lot of support for the idea."

Andrea's phone started ringing. She looked at the screen and said, "My apologies. I *have* to take this. It won't be long." She got up and stepped out of the room.

"Now we're cooking," said Rex to Catia when the door closed behind Andrea. The excitement was unmistakable in his voice. "Tozlu is the connection between Dragut and the Turkish government."

"And I'm willing to bet he helped Dragut build the concrete statue of the man who raped his sister," said Catia.

Andrea returned, apologized for the interruption, and continued.

Within the next ten minutes, they learned that Tozlu often visited Malta. A fact that had Rex wondering if Dragut could be on Malta. After all, it's the only failure on Dragut Senior's résumé; he had been unable to conquer the island and died trying.

Tozlu also traveled to Austria regularly, at least once a month for two to three days at a time; he had offices and warehouses there.

"Do you have a list of friends, family, and associates for Tozlu?" Rex asked when they got to the end of the file.

Andrea opened another document and pulled up a list of names with addresses and thumbnail photos.

Catia took her cellphone out and opened the images of

Ushan Ozmert, Nassor Almasi, Destiny Parker, and Sarah Sulzer. "We're looking for matches to any of these."

"Let's have a look," said Andrea and clicked on the first thumbnail photo which brought up a large image.

Within minutes they had gone through all the images and found one match: Sarah Sulzer.

"Not entirely surprising, she is from Berlin," said Catia. "But it confirms our theory that Tozlu and Ozmert are in contact with each other."

What are the chances that Sarah Sulzer can be found at that address? Rex wondered in silence.

It was almost mid-day when Rex said, "I'm starving. Frau Degen, it would be an honor if you'd join us for lunch. You can pick the place."

Rex always wondered how large Digger's English vocabulary was. He knew it was much bigger than he could imagine; but he had no doubt all words associated with food existed in Digger's dictionary. He opened his eyes when he heard the word lunch, got to his feet, and started wagging his tail in anticipation.

Andrea said, "My pleasure. While we're on the topic of Turkish immigrants, I suggest we go to the Turkish Quarters in Kreuzberg, known as Little Istanbul. They have some nice little restaurants with excellent food there. It's only three and a half kilometers from here. Just a few minutes by train."

Chapter Forty

LUNCH IN LITTLE ISTANBUL

Berlin, Germany

Day 11

Shortly after 12:15 p.m., they got off the train in the heart of Kreuzberg's Turkish neighborhood in Adalbertstrasse and walked to a restaurant. The casual restaurant served traditional Turkish food with lamb dishes and kabobs. The service was efficient and friendly, and the food was excellent. Digger especially liked the lamb fed to him under the table by Rex and Catia.

Rex noticed a man in his late seventies, maybe older, of Middle Eastern descent sitting at a table on his own, sipping Turkish coffee. He had a laptop open in front of him, Bluetooth earpieces in his ears, and he was talking softly to someone. He paid Rex et al. no attention. Rex couldn't help but find it strange to see someone of that age so *au fait* with modern technology.

After lunch, they took a stroll through the popular Turkish market on Maybachuferstrasse, home of Berlin's largest outdoor Turkish market. Merchants were hawking fresh produce, baked goods, fresh fish, cheese, spices, flowers, clothing, toys, electronics, leather goods, table linens, and a surprising amount of fabric and sewing designs lined the almost kilometer-long market on Maybachuferstrasse.

The Turkish Market drew a diverse crowd. Some were dressed in formal office attire, probably office workers on lunch breaks, holidaymakers in casual wear, and locals dressed in Muslim garb. Many different languages from all over Europe and Turkey could be heard.

When they exited the market at the far end, Rex's attention was drawn to a young man approaching them on the same side of the road as they were, because Digger was staring at him. The young man was staring in front of him as if not aware of his surroundings. He had a backpack on his back, and he was bent slightly forward like someone carrying a heavy load on his back.

Then Rex noticed Digger looking across the street and saw another person of interest, a young woman, pregnant by the looks of it. She was covered in a full-body niqab. But her gait was awkward, not like a heavily pregnant woman, rather like one carrying a heavy load around her abdomen.

Rex stopped and studied them more carefully. Digger's hair on the back of his neck stood on end, and his tail was ramrod straight as he growled softly.

Lee Child, the world-renowned author of the Jack Reacher series, said in his book, Gone Tomorrow, "Suicide bombers are easy to spot. They give out all kinds of tell-tale signs. Mostly because they're nervous. By definition they're all first-timers." And although it's a fiction book, Child had it right.

All over the world, there are posters in public places and on public transport alerting people to keep a watchful eye out for people acting suspiciously. The problem was the posters did not begin to describe the characteristics of a 'suspicious person.'

It was a combination of many signs, body language, behavior, clothing, and more that had to be assessed. Perhaps it was the country's lack of experience with suicide bombings that made the U.S. Department of Homeland Security state that there was 'no specific profile' for those who engage in suicide bombings.

The Israelis, however, disagreed. They based their opinions on their experience of more than three hundred such bombings since 1993, two hundred and forty-two of them since 2000. Their statistics showed, among others: thirty-two percent of suicide bombers had a high school education, a quarter of them had a college education. The majority were single and were males between the ages of seventeen and twenty-three. The rest were older men and women, and children. The Chechen rebels bucked the trend, their suicide bombings had mostly been carried out by women but not for fanatical religious reasons. They did it to revenge the killing of loved ones by Russian security forces.

Before their 'big' day, suicide bombers would have gone through prolonged indoctrination and would be in a hypnotic state when the time came for heaven's gates to be opened for them.

As for general demeanor, the Israelis advised to be on the lookout for people displaying nervousness, a blank stare, preoccupation, and many others. Look for people seeming to be praying fervently as if talking or whispering to someone. Profuse sweating that is out of sync with weather conditions could be another sign. So were signs of a beard that had been recently shaved or the hair cut short. And weird as it may sound, some suicide bombers want to smell nice when they arrive in paradise, therefore, will sprinkle themselves lavishly with herbal- or floral-scented water.

On this day in Maybachuferstrasse, Berlin, it was a combination of Digger's inexplicable but astounding ability to sense danger, Rex's training, experience, and constant awareness of Digger's behavior that set off the alarm bells in Rex's head.

The young man was about twelve paces away from them moving very slowly, almost hesitantly, when Rex noticed the sweat glistening on his face and his lips moving in silence. His hands were empty—*no switch*.

Catia and Andrea were standing next to him on either side, Digger was two yards in front of them, protecting his pack. Rex pulled the quick release on Digger's leash to free him.

"We've got a problem. Two suicide bombers. The young guy with the backpack approaching us, and the young pregnant woman in the niqab across the street. We don't have much time. They're heading into the market."

Andrea's first reaction was to get her phone out to call the police.

It was not going to work. The bombers were going to enter the market in the next thirty yards. There could be more of them. There was but one course of action—stop them right now.

Rex said to Catia, "Take Digger and go for the woman, I'll go for this guy in front of us. They don't have triggers in their hands, not yet anyway." There was a lot more he could say to Catia, but it was not necessary, she was trained to handle a situation like this. But Andrea was not.

When Rex and Catia started moving, Andrea saw a police officer at the entrance to the market and ran to him.

Seconds later, the policeman with Andrea short on his heels ran into the market, started blowing on a whistle, and screamed at the people, "*Bomben! Terroristen! Lauf! Raus jetzt! Machen sie schnell!*"

The people listened and fled away from him to the opposite side of the market, screaming and shouting to the others.

The young man with the backpack was now about five paces away from Rex. He had broken into a full sprint. He was two paces away when the young man's eyes shot wide as he realized Rex was coming for him. He only had time to stop walking before Rex punched him in the throat. His hands flew to his throat. Rex moved in behind him, got hold of both arms, pulled them back behind him, and ripped the backpack off. He looked around, saw a drain opening below the edge of the sidewalk, and threw the bag into it. There was no explosion. The young man was on the ground, loudly gasping for air.

Catia and Digger ran toward the young woman. She noticed them only when they were a few yards away. She stopped, turned, and tried to run away, but Digger got to her in two strides. Her hands were empty, no trigger. The woman went still as Digger snarled in her face. Catia ripped the niqab away and saw the bomb. She saw the cellphone connected to it. She tried to unstrap the bomb, but quickly realized it was going to take too long. She grabbed the cellphone and ripped the battery out. There was no explosion. She removed the straps holding the bomb to the woman's body and removed the bomb.

From across the street, Rex shouted, "Throw it in the drain!"

Catia turned, saw the drain opening Rex was pointing to, and dumped the bomb in it.

She and Rex pulled their quarries to their feet and frog-marched them to the market.

In the meantime, pandemonium had erupted inside the market as people were falling over each other to get away. And then three earsplitting explosions, sounding almost like one, decimated everything within the blast ranges of the bombs.

Rex and his prisoner were thrown to the ground by the blast wave that came from the front. The bomb that he had thrown into the drain had exploded, but all of the effects stayed below ground level. He looked to Catia and saw she was still on her feet. Her bomb had not exploded. It was obvious, the bombs had been exploded remotely. And Rex couldn't help but think of the old man with the laptop in the restaurant.

Then he realized that the other explosions happened somewhere inside the market. And that meant Andrea, the police officer, and everyone inside must have run right into the path of the other bombers.

"Shit!"

Rex jumped to his feet, pulled his captive up, and pushed him toward the market. He and Catia arrived with their captives at the entrance at the same time. All they could see down the passageway was smoke and debris. She grabbed some silk scarves from the racks of one of the clothing shops and tied their prisoners up.

Rex asked Catia and Digger to keep a watch over the prisoners while he went find Andrea.

He found them about halfway down the street in a horrific scene of blood, body parts, wounded, and burned victims screaming in pain. Of the police officer, little other than parts of his uniform containing some of his limbs remained, he was about fifteen yards ahead of Andrea when the bombs went off.

She was not moving. However, Rex quickly established that she was alive but unconscious. Her left arm got blown off at the elbow. Rex looked around and found some cloth among the remains of a material shop and used some of it to make a tourniquet which he placed around the bleeding stump to stem the blood flow.

Within minutes the sirens of the police vehicles and ambulances could be heard.

Chapter Forty-One

WE HAVE TO GET AHEAD

Berlin, Germany

Day 11

Within hours, the death toll stood at forty-five with a hundred and fifty wounded. A lot less than the attacks in The Netherlands and France. Even so, it was a devastating and gruesome tragedy that could've been much, much worse, was it not for Digger's keen senses and the Daltons' death-defying actions.

Rex's and Catia's biggest problem in the immediate aftermath, while helping the wounded, was to keep out of sight of the media who had descended upon the scene like vultures.

They were relieved when Tilmann Wieser and some of his senior staff turned up within an hour. Rex and Catia told him what happened and asked him to help keep their involvement, identities, and pictures out of the media. He understood and used his influence to do so.

The two would-be bombers were taken into custody by the first police officers arriving on the scene. But it became evident within minutes that the police would not get much information from them now or in the future. They were just the bombers; they didn't know anything or anyone for that matter. And they were both mentally disabled. It was a well-established, tried, and tested method of ISIS and al Qaeda to use mentally disabled people for these kinds of jobs.

As the rescue teams and paramedics pulled people and bodies and pieces out of the rubble, it became clear that many of the dead and injured were Turkish. The final score was that twenty of the dead were Turks, and so were seventy-nine of the wounded.

The immediate question on the lips of the security and law enforcement agencies and politicians was, why the Turkish Quarters? The Turks were Muslims. The bombers, dead and alive, it was quickly established, were all Muslims, two of Turkish origin, one Algerian, and one Syrian. Two men and two women, youngsters.

The German Chancellor visited the scene and made the usual statement: "We will find you and bring you to justice." But who they were going to find and bring to justice neither she nor her security agencies knew.

No one claimed responsibility; although the media was rife with speculation that it was some crazy right-wing Neo-Nazi group. But they didn't offer any explanation as to how it came about that a Neo-Nazi group was able to recruit Muslims to bomb fellow Muslims.

Within hours someone discovered the website. It was a group who called themselves GfG, Germany for Germans. No one had ever heard of them. Nonetheless, GfG claimed responsibility, saying the Turks were parasites sucking Germany dry and had it coming for years. Many believed it without giving any consideration to the anomaly that the website had only been launched an hour after the attack and consisted of only one page.

Late that night, Rex and Catia were with Tilmann Wieser in his office. He told them that Andrea was doing well. He told them that he was inclined to believe it was the Neo-Nazi group who did it. It took some effort from Rex and Catia to change Wieser's mind, which they achieved only by enlisting the help of Stevens and Richardson on a video conference and have them explain to Wieser what was really going on.

"This was Dragut's work. A false flag operation aimed at getting the German Turks to ask Turkey to protect them," explained Richardson.

"And if you don't believe us, watch the news," said Stevens. "Within the next twenty-four hours, the President of Turkey is going to say something along the lines of, 'If Germany can't protect their Turkish citizens then Turkey might have to do it for you and, by the way, it's time for Europe to stop beating around the bush and let Turkey into the EU.'"

They didn't have to wait twenty-four hours; the statement came within the next hour.

Before sunrise, the owner of the website, Klaus Schrötter, was in custody and soon admitted there was no GfG. He had been paid a substantial amount of money to set up the whole ruse, the name, and website, and post the messages that were supplied to him. It was a job he got on the Darknet, where he advertised his services as a hacker. His anonymous client paid him in Monero.

The accounts of Tozlu, to which Greg and his team by

now had unfettered access, showed he was the one who made the payments to Klaus Schrötter, in Monero, transferred from Malta.

Wieser required no more convincing; the attack was the work of Dragut. He informed the President of the BND who, in turn, briefed the Chancellor.

Berlin, Germany

Day 12

Rex, Catia, and Digger had breakfast early. After breakfast, Catia bought a big bunch of flowers before they went to the hospital to visit Andrea. Under the circumstances, given her injuries and the effects of concussion, she was doing remarkably well. Understandably, she was not in high spirits, but she had a positive attitude and was very grateful for the Daltons' actions saving not only her life but the lives of countless others.

After the hospital visit, they went back to the BND headquarters for more meetings with Wieser and the investigators.

Christelle called and reported that Brandt was still in the ICU under sedation, but his condition, according to the doctor, was stable and satisfactory.

By late afternoon Rex had enough. He was struggling to hide his irritation with the lack of action.

When they were alone for a few minutes, he told Catia that they were wasting time. He was fed-up with being one step behind Dragut.

"We have to get ahead. Get our hands on Tozlu. The scumbag should've been in custody by now with his feet held to the fire. But no, the BND wants to analyze and strategize and not offend anyone. I am going to get us out of this politically correct quagmire and find Tozlu, and then I'm going to offend him big time by beating the shit out of him."

Catia placed her hand on his arm and said, "I agree, Rex. That's exactly what has to be done, but first, take a few deep breaths."

He smiled, took two deep breaths, got his phone out, and called Greg.

"Greg, I have a bottle of your favorite whiskey that says you can track Özdemir Tozlu down for me within the hour."

Greg laughed. "Make that two bottles, and I'll tell you right now."

"Deal."

"He's in Austria. In Vienna to be more precise. He traveled there early yesterday morning. He's due back in Berlin in two days. Give me ten minutes, and I'll tell you where he's staying. But that will be two bottles of strawberry daiquiri, Rehka's favorite."

"Deal."

Half an hour later, Rex thanked Wieser for BND's help. Wieser, in turn, thanked them profusely for preventing a bigger carnage and saving Andrea's life. They shook hands, and the Daltons left for the airport.

From Berlin to Vienna was a little over three hundred and seventy-two miles, about an hour with the CIA jet.

By the time the Daltons boarded their plane, Josh and Marissa were already almost halfway to Vienna in another

CIA jet from London. The two planes would land within half an hour of each other in Vienna.

The CIA chief of station in Vienna had been fully briefed by Richardson and was expecting them.

Chapter Forty-Two

THIS IS A JOB FOR ME

Vienna, Austria

Day 12

They arrived in Vienna shortly after 6:30 p.m. Josh and Marissa were already there, waiting for them.

Thanks to the CIA COS in Vienna, who had assigned two surveillance teams to Tozlu the moment he got off the phone with Richardson, they already had eyes on Tozlu when the Daltons and Farleys arrived. The case officer in charge was Charles (Chuck) Evans, a tall, dark-haired, forty-something, jovial guy from Texas.

Tozlu had no way of knowing that the concierge at the Hotel Kurt von Francois in Philharmoniker-Strasse in the Vienna city center where he stayed was on the CIA's payroll. He was one of many concierges throughout the city working with the CIA when required. A short conversation between Evans and the concierge earlier told him everything they needed to know. An envelope stuffed with five-hundred euros in cash, slipped unobtrusively into the concierge's hand, also gave Evans and one of his agents access to Tozlu's room. When they left the room fifteen minutes later, it was bugged wall to wall with minuscule but powerful video and audio recording devices, even in the bathroom.

The five-hundred euros also got them some personal information about Tozlu. He was a regular at the hotel and must have been a happily married man because, with each visit, the concierge had to arrange company for him. It was one of the unadvertised and very discreet services offered by the hotel to their top clientele, managed by the concierge exclusively.

Chuck Evans shared all of this with Rex and company during the drive from the airport to their hotel.

The answer to their question of how to get their hands on Tozlu was obvious; they had to set up a honey trap for him.

Marissa said, "This is a job for me. I've been trained for it. I don't want any arguments."

"Had enough of me?" Josh asked, clearly not thrilled with the idea.

Marissa gave him a withering look. "I'm not answering that."

Josh recognized the look on his wife's face and knew it was best to remain silent. It did nothing to improve his mood, though.

"You have a problem," said Rex. "You don't speak Turkish or German."

"Of course I don't, I'm from France, arrived only last week. France is going down the drain. That's why I am here looking for a better life. Besides, the file about him provided by the Germans says he's fluent in English."

"You don't have to do it, Marissa, we can work something out," Catia said.

"Would you rather trust *me* to do the job or someone you don't know?"

"No contest, Marissa, but I'd never ask you to walk into such a dangerous situation," said Rex.

"Look, I appreciate the concern, but let's sit down and plan it out in detail. if I feel uncomfortable about my safety, I'll let you know."

"On that proviso, I agree," said Rex.

With that, the matter was settled, and Josh steamed in silence.

No one saw the little smile playing on Rex's face. He had a plan to make sure this incident wouldn't cause any strain in the Farleys marriage in the future but was not ready to reveal it yet.

The next morning, they would have the recordings of Tozlu's escapades of that night. One more night, and they would have enough evidence to give them the upper hand in their upcoming negotiations with Tozlu.

Marissa phoned Rehka and asked her to get every bit of information she could find about Tozlu so that she could prepare to impress him the next evening.

It was Evans's job to make arrangements with the concierge for Tozlu's companion for the next evening.

Vienna, Austria

Day 13

Marissa was the only one having croissants at breakfast.

"Taking this French thing seriously, I see," said Josh, pointing to the croissants on her plate, clearly still sulking about Marissa's decision to be the honey trap.

"You don't know?"

"What?"

"Croissants are not French, they're Austrian."

Now everyone, including Digger, was looking at her as if she was from Mars.

Marissa smiled. "Okay, children, pay attention. Mommy is going to tell you about the history of croissants."

They stopped eating and listened.

"Many people, like yourselves, believe the croissant is a quintessentially French pastry. It's not. The *kipferl*, as it was called back in the thirteenth century when it was first baked, is the ancestor of the croissant. The modern croissant's story dates back to 1683 when the Ottomans tried to tunnel underneath the walls of Vienna during the siege of the city. The bakers, working through the night, heard the noise and raised the alarm. King John III of Poland arrived in time to defeat the invaders. Afterward, the bakers, wanting to celebrate the victory, created a pastry that would symbolize the crescent moon that appears on the Turkish flag. The *kipferl* —the German word for crescent.

"It was only in 1770 that the *kipferl* made its way to France when the Austrian-born Marie-Antoinette married the future king of France, Louis XVI, that the royal bakers baked a *kipferl* in her honor, which they subsequently named, 'croissant.'

"Questions?"

There were none, but she got thunderous applause from her audience and, what she thought to be, a congratulatory woof from Digger, but it could also have been that he got excited when his pack was so happy.

Shortly after, Christelle called to let them know that Brandt was making good and steady progress and that the doctor thought he could be moved out of the ICU within the next twenty-four to thirty-six hours.

Chapter Forty-Three

TOZLU'S COMPANIONS

Vienna, Austria

Day 13

By 9:00 p.m. Rex, Catia, Digger, and Josh were in the room next to Tozlu's. Chuck Evans was in the restaurant keeping an eye on Marissa from a few tables away. Three of his agents were in cars in strategic positions around the hotel. All of them were in contact with each other. Rex et al. had eyes on every part of Tozlu's suite. Marissa had microphones on her handbag, her little stun gun inside, and the two-way radio app on her cellphone was on. In short, Marissa was protected nearly as well as the President of the United States.

For the next hour and a quarter, they listened to Tozlu's and Marissa's dinner talk. Over a bottle of wine and excellent food, they talked about themselves first, all of it fake stuff; well, at least large parts of Marissa's tale about growing up in France with her French father and American mother, from whom she had picked up the American accented English. Soon they moved on to world politics. That part didn't last long as they more or less agreed that international politics were such a mess anyone who claimed to understand what was going on was either lying or crazy. About halfway through dinner, the conversation moved to art and music, the things that made Vienna a great and famous city.

To the eavesdroppers, it was quite clear; Tozlu was a well-read and intelligent man. But Marissa was orders of magnitude better, and also well-prepared for the occasion. She had him all but eating out of her hand by the time they finished dinner.

By 10:20 p.m. they entered Tozlu's suite.

Marissa went straight to the liquor cabinet and poured cognac for both of them from the crystal decanter. She handed him one of the crystal glasses, feigned taking a sip from hers, and said, "Enjoy your drink while I get into something more comfortable."

"Excellent idea," said Tozlu as he downed his drink in one big gulp and reached for the decanter.

She went to the bedroom, closed and locked the door, and sat down in the recliner. Evans had shown her photos of the inside of the suite. She knew exactly where each bug in the room was. She looked at the one closest to her, put on a dazzling smile, and mouthed the words, *I love you, Josh.*

She waited ten minutes, went into the bathroom, flushed the toilet, washed and dried her hands, and headed for the lounge.

When she stepped into the lounge, in no state of undress, Tozlu was in dreamland on the couch. The rapid action sedative, midazolam, mixed into the cognac by Evans earlier, worked as advertised. Tozlu would regain consciousness in a few hours.

She opened his eyelids, checked his pupils, felt his pulse, and showed a thumbs up to the video camera above the TV on her way to unlock the door.

Josh was the first one through the door and pulled his wife into a bear hug. "You were brilliant. Sorry I've been such an ass about it."

Marissa just laughed and kissed him.

"Showtime," said Rex.

They carried Tozlu to the bedroom, undressed him up to his boxer shorts, and laid him out on the silk sheets on the bed. Catia was the photographer. She ordered Rex and Josh out of the room.

They followed her orders.

Within ten minutes, Catia and Marissa had more than twenty good quality photos of Tozlu and Marissa in various compromising poses. When Marissa's photoshoot was over, and she was again dressed respectably, Catia gave their spouses permission to reenter the bedroom.

Rex turned to Josh and said, "Your turn, buddy."

"My turn for what?"

"To get into bed with the stud."

Josh was speechless; his mouth was opening and closing like a fish out of water, but no sound came out. It was the first time in his life that Rex saw his friend so bewildered. Rex was struggling not to laugh. Fortunately, he had forewarned Catia and Marissa; they kept straight faces.

"You can't be serious."

Marissa said, "C'mon Josh, what's sauce for the goose is sauce for the gander. Take it off, but *please* keep your underwear on, and get in that bed. Hurry up, we've got to get him out of here ASAP."

Josh studied each of their faces, looking for signs of hoodwinking. Finally, he turned to Rex and said, "Why not you?"

Rex was still able to keep his poker face, but only just. "A number of reasons." He held up one finger. "You're much better-looking than me."

"Yeah, right."

Rex raised the second finger. "You look the part much more than I could ever—"

"Are you saying I look—"

Rex held his hands up in defense. "No! Not at all. But how can I put it... You've got pizazz, I don't."

"What the hell does that mean?"

"Hmm, tell you what, let's skip that one. The main reason is, I'm the CEO now. It will be very bad for CRC's image if it comes to light that the CEO is a man who engages in extramarital affairs."

"Bullshit!"

That was as much self-control as the three could muster before they exploded in laughter.

Josh was shaking his fist at Rex. "Dalton, the last thing I want to do is kill you... but take note, it's still on my list."

They enjoyed the humor for a short while and became serious again. Marissa told Josh that many a truth is spoken in jest and that it could be very helpful if they indeed had a few photos of Tozlu in bed with a man.

Josh knew it was true, and relented, but only after he extracted an agreement that Marissa would take the photos on her phone and that the Daltons, including Digger, were outside the room for the duration of the photoshoot. And that no copies would ever be made of what was going to be on Marissa's phone. "Oh, and you keep it very short."

Seven minutes later, Josh's modeling career was over. He

was still grumbling when he and Rex tied Tozlu up, gagged him, and shoved him unceremoniously into a wheelchair. They switched Tozlu's laptop off. They swiped the screen of Tozlu's K iPhone with his thumb to unlock it, and before switching it off and disassembling it, Catia disabled the GPS location-tracking feature.

Greg was waiting for Rex to tell him when to switch off the security cameras and lights in the hallway. Rex gave him the signal. Within seconds Greg confirmed it was done.

Josh opened the door, and in the lights of their cellphones, they wheeled Tozlu out of the room, ten yards down the hallway, and into the service elevator, which Greg also had control of. They all went down to the basement.

In the basement, they made their way to the parking area where they loaded Tozlu into the back of the black Mercedes SUV with tinted windows, provided by Evans. Within minutes they were on the way to a safe house on the outskirts of the city. Actually, it was more like a small castle than a house, on a small farm. The safehouse came compliments of one of Yaron Aderet's *sayanim*.

As soon as Evans got confirmation from Rex that they were out of Tozlu's room, he and his agents moved in. They packed all Tozlu's stuff and cleaned his room, even replaced the linen, towels, etcetera. They wiped the place down to remove fingerprints and DNA.

Greg and his team would see to it that the hotel's electronic records reflect that Tozlu had checked out that morning, and that day's CCTV footage would confirm it.

Özdemir Tozlu had disappeared.

Chapter Forty-Four

A CHAT WITH TOZLU

Vienna, Austria

Day 14

At quarter past midnight, after arriving at the safehouse, Tozlu was carried to the family room and dumped on one of the couches; he was still unconscious. The two Mossad agents onsite, a man and woman, showed them around the place, helped them set up their equipment, and then withdrew to the guesthouse a hundred yards away from the house.

The four of them quickly set up the family room with hidden video cameras and microphones and connected them all to the secured video conference with MI6 in London, CIA in Langley, CRC HQ in Arizona, Thomson in Athens, and Spencer on the *TOMATS* in Malta. Catia and Marissa would watch the interrogation on their laptops from the kitchen.

Shortly after 12:30 a.m., Tozlu groaned softly a few times before opening his eyes. Immediately an expression of shock and fear took over his face. Opening one's eyes to find two men with ski masks and a mean-looking big black dog staring at you would have that effect on anyone.

He was sitting in a comfortable chair in the family room. Rex and Josh had removed all his restraints. They believed Tozlu wouldn't require much of the rough stuff to get him talking. Of course, the option to use enhanced techniques was always available if Tozlu proved them wrong.

Digger also seemed to be content to not scare the living daylights out of the prisoner, although his presence must have been intimidating.

Rex and Josh made as if they didn't know Tozlu was awake. "One of my favorite methods to get a guy talking is to use an electric drill to bore a hole into his kneecap. I've never had anyone who required a second hole before they started talking," said Josh.

"I like that. We'll try it if he's not talking when I'm finished pulling his finger- and toenails out," said Rex.

"Maybe we should let the dog have a little fun with him as well," said Josh.

Rex said, "Yeah, I haven't fed him today, he must be really hungry, he'll probably devour this guy."

"But, to be honest, I'd rather shoot the son of a bitch in the head and be done with it," said Josh.

Tozlu groaned loudly this time to get their attention.

Rex and Josh turned and looked at him, feigning surprise.

Rex said, "Hey, Tozlu, you're awake. We were just talking about you."

"Who are you, and where am I?" Tozlu demanded feebly.

"It's not important who we are or where you are, except to say you're in serious trouble." Rex continued and explained to Tozlu that they had irrefutable proof of his trysts of the past two days on video.

Tozlu denied it vehemently until Rex played a short clip of the romp with the Austrian hooker the night before and said, "How will your wife and children feel when they see that?"

Tozlu didn't reply.

"I thought so. And that was the mild one of the three recordings we have. I almost feel sorry for you when we show your wife tonight's clips. A woman *and* a man in one night."

"That's a lie! I've never been with a man. I'm not homosexual."

"Let me show you the video. Tonight, you definitely were."

Tozlu dropped his head in defeat and whispered, "You set me up. You drugged me..."

Rex ignored him and said, "Tozlu, as a Muslim yourself, you probably know better than I do that Muslims don't take kindly to homosexuality. I've heard they throw gay men off the top of buildings or inject glue into the anuses of 'un-manly' men—killing them slowly. I am not sure if that's what the Muslims of Berlin would do to you. Do you want to find out?"

Tozlu only shook his head and made no reply.

Rex continued. "Now, if your debauchery is not enough to get you skinned alive by your wife and fellow believers, let me tell you about the really serious stuff.

"You claim to be a Turk, an Ottoman no less. Yet, you were involved in the killing and maiming of your kinsmen two days ago at the Turkish market on Maybachuferstrasse in Berlin."

"I had nothing to do with that!"

"No, that's not true. You paid the families of the bombers, and you paid an incompetent idiot to set up a fake website claiming to be a Neo-Nazi group taking responsibility for the bombings. You were involved, Tozlu.

"You funded the operation that killed forty-five people, twenty-five of them Turks, including five children below age ten and two infants. Your bombs also injured and maimed a hundred and fifty, including more than seventy Turks. I can't even begin to imagine what the Turks of Berlin will do to you when we release this information.

"Oh, by the way, your bombs also killed a police officer and one of the injured is a woman who lost an arm, she works for the BND. I spoke to her boss earlier; let me tell you, they're pissed, they can't wait for you to return to Berlin. Apparently, they've got something very special in mind for you; some nasty trick they learned from the East German Stasi during the Cold War. I don't know what it is, but it apparently involves battery acid and a slow, agonizing death."

"I have no idea what you're talking about," Tozlu said.

Josh, very much relieved that the footage of him and Marissa would not be shown, pulled Tozlu's laptop closer, turned it so Tozlu could see the screen, and showed him the crypto transactions on the laptop.

That was the final straw.

"What do you want?"

"Your cooperation to find your old school friend, Ushan Ozmert," said Rex.

The look of surprise on Tozlu's face gave it away. He dropped his head into his hands and went quiet for almost a minute. Finally, he looked up and said, "I want to make a deal. My freedom in exchange for the information."

"We're not negotiators, we're the executioners. All we can do for you is to choose the method of your execution. Our choice will depend on your cooperation and the value of the information you give us," said Josh.

"But Tozlu, make no mistake, we are *very* keen to put you through a world of pain before we kill you," added Rex.

To add weight to their threats, Rex and Josh removed their ski masks.

Tozlu was intelligent enough to understand the significance of that. Allowing him to see their faces meant they were definitely going to kill him. He was sweating profusely. "I'm not afraid to die. I will go straight to Jannah."

Rex shook his head. "Wishful thinking. Jannah is for people who lived an exemplary life. You drink alcohol, you're an unrepentant adulterer, homosexual and murderer, to name only a few. Besides, even if Allah would overlook your atrocious sins, I doubt you would be welcome in paradise if you arrived there wrapped in a pigskin, which is what we're going to do before killing you."

Tozlu shuddered visibly, let out a long sigh in defeat, and started talking. He started with his childhood in Feres. How he and Ushan were buddies, Ushan helped him with his schoolwork, and he protected Ushan from the bullies. He told them how he and Ushan had drugged and killed Dimitris Rossas, who had raped Ushan's sister, and put him in a cement cast.

He and Ozmert had lost contact after that for more than twenty years.

Yes, he was a cousin of the President of Turkey, the president's father and his mother were siblings.

He had very little contact with the President, maybe

once or twice a year when visiting his family who were all now living in Istanbul, Turkey.

Then out of the blue, about four years ago, Ozmert turned up in Berlin and invited him to spend a weekend with him on a farm about sixty miles out of the city. That's where Ozmert and two representatives of the Turkish President recruited and initiated him into Operation Delphi— the scheme to restore the Ottoman Empire. Tozlu thought the name had something to do with the Oracle of Delphi.

Yes, the President knew all about Delphi, but Tozlu had no idea how it came about that the President and Ozmert knew each other. Nonetheless, during that weekend, it became clear that Ozmert and his uncle had known each other for quite a few years already.

Tozlu was the financial manager. He was well-versed in financial matters and understood all about cryptocurrencies and how they offered a level of security, which made it almost impossible to trace transactions back to their origin. His import-export business with the warehouses and distribution network was ideally suited for Operation Delphi activities. Tozlu's job was to administer all the payments to the contractors. But other than long strings of numbers and letters making up electronic wallet addresses to which he had to transfer crypto money when told to do so, he had no personal information about the recipients. He wasn't sure where the money came from except, of course, that it was transferred into the Operation Delphi's cryptocurrency account held at an exchange in Malta.

Rex showed him a collage of photos which Catia and Marissa created and included pictures of Destiny Parker, Nassor Almasi, Ushan Ozmert, Tony Parker, Emily Hobson and a few unknown people they got from Google Images, as well as Tozlu's wife and two sons, copied from Facebook.

The latter, of course, to scare Tozlu into believing his family was in danger. But, other than his family and Ozmert, Tozlu didn't know anyone else.

They talked about Swanson's agent, but he didn't know him either. However, his cryptocurrency wallet address was on the laptop, and with that came the IP addresses.

That was all Greg needed. Knowing the IP addresses of the parties to the transaction, the payer and payee, it was possible to trace the entire money flow and through the IP addresses track down the physical addresses. It took Greg less than half an hour to locate the physical address upon which Stevens arranged with MI5 to dispatch a SWAT team to arrest the man.

In the meantime, Rex and Josh continued the questioning.

Chapter Forty-Five

Vienna, Austria

Day 14

Two hours later, Rex and Josh gave Tozlu what they told him was his last meal, tea and biscuits, before he was tied up and gagged with duct tape. They went into the kitchen to talk to the others.

Rex and Josh, and for that matter everyone that was dialed into the conference, were getting despondent about the lack of real earthshattering information coming from Tozlu. Thus far, except for the details of the crypto transactions, he hadn't told them much that they didn't already know or suspect.

And Stevens had more disappointing news to add. The SWAT team went to the address provided by Greg and found a woman in her mid-fifties there who was in mourning. Her husband, Damian Henderson, had been killed in a motorcycle accident two days before. Apparently, he was a big motorcycle enthusiast and a speed devil to boot. According to her, the police thought that he was traveling at a very high speed when he lost control of his bike and slammed into the railing of a bridge, killing him instantly. No foul play was suspected. They had been married for less than a year. She claimed to know very little about her late husband's work other than he traded the stock and commodity markets.

The SWAT team had taken her into custody for further questioning, searched the house, and confiscated several computers and a stack of documents. Analysts were working through the information.

Richardson sighed deeply. "One dead end after another. My guess is we're not going to get much joy out of Henderson's widow, computers, and documents, either."

"Maybe we'll find out who contacted him to arrange all the hit jobs," said Stevens.

Richardson shook his head. "I'll be surprised."

"I agree, it's frustrating," said Rex, "but we're shaking the trees and things are falling out of them. Not as much as we hoped, but so far, every tree has delivered something. We've got confirmation about the Turkish president's involvement. We've gained access to some of their financial information, and I'm sure Greg and his team still have a lot of information on Tozlu's laptop to uncover. You know the adage, 'follow the money.' And I've got a gut feeling that Henderson's accident was not what it seems. Myles, my suggestion is that you ask MI5 to confiscate the wreckage of the motorcycle and let a team of experts have a good look at it. If I'm right, it means Dragut is getting nervous, he knows we're closing in on him, and he's tying up loose ends."

"I'll let MI5 know," said Stevens.

"Okay, we'll go back to Tozlu now. We've only skimmed the surface so far. We haven't talked about Dragut yet, and I still have to show him the photos of Sarah Sulzer."

Five minutes later, Tozlu had been untied and ungagged, given two headache tablets and a glass of water.

"Who's this woman?" Rex showed Tozlu Sarah Sulzer's photos.

He started shaking his head, but his wide-shot eyes and body language gave it away. "I don't know her."

Digger started growling and took a step toward him.

Rex said, "Tozlu, you're making a grave mistake by confusing our kindness with weakness." He looked at Josh, who retrieved a pair of pliers from his backpack and handed them to Rex.

Rex walked over to Tozlu and grabbed his left hand.

Tozlu screamed. "Stop! Don't do it. I'm sorry I lied. I won't do it again. I promise I won't. I know the woman; her name is Martina Streicher, she works for me."

Rex stood back. "One more lie and your fingernails are coming off. Five for each lie, and then I move on to your toenails."

"I won't lie again."

"You can try, but the dog will tell me. If you don't believe me and you don't care much about your finger- and toenails, try it. What kind of work does she do?"

"She sources products for my import-export businesses across Europe and the world."

"And shares her bed with you. Right?"

"Yes."

"What's her address?"

"Apartment 102, at number 6 Wetsarpstrasse, Bavarian

Quarter, Berlin. But she's not there much; she travels around most of the time."

"Where is she right now?"

"Istanbul, due back in Berlin today, we have a meeting scheduled for 11:00 a.m. today."

"Which you will not be attending. What do you import and export?"

"Food, clothing, materials, electronic goods."

"Weapons and explosives?"

Tozlu hesitated. Rex picked up the pliers and Digger snarled.

"Yes!"

"What kind of weapons?"

"Assault rifles, handguns, hand grenades, explosives..."

"Where to?"

"It only started about six months ago. So far, I've moved stuff to The Netherlands, Paris, Berlin..."

"More innocent people you helped to kill and mutilate. There'll be no Jannah for you, Tozlu. Where else?"

"The latest shipment is destined for Brussels."

"Where is the stuff now?"

"In one of my warehouses in Berlin." He gave them the address.

"When will it be transported to Brussels?"

Tozlu hesitated.

Rex picked the pliers up from the table and Digger growled.

"It will leave my warehouse in two days at around five o'clock in the morning. It'll be hidden among a shipment of Turkish coffee, tobacco, and leather clothing items."

By now, Richardson was already on the phone to the CIA COS in Berlin to assign surveillance teams to Martina Streicher and the warehouse.

"Now back to the woman, Martina Streicher. She knows all about Delphi, doesn't she?"

Tozlu nodded.

"Speak up."

"Yes, she does. Ushan asked me to employ her. She's our go-between."

"And she's the one telling you where to ship the weapons and explosives, and how much to pay to whom and when?"

"Yes."

"What's her cellphone number?"

"It's on my phone under her name."

"Martina Streicher has one of these phones as well. Right?"

"Yes."

Josh had an idea. He called Rex out of the room and told him.

Rex agreed.

Josh took the phone, put the battery back in, and switched it on.

Josh said to Tozlu, "Do you communicate with her via text or voice?"

"Both, but mostly text messages."

Rex was paying close attention to Digger and was satisfied that Tozlu was honest.

Josh said, "You're going to type a message to Martina on your phone. You're going to tell her you're postponing today's meeting to the same time tomorrow. You've come across a very good business opportunity in Vienna, and your phone has been playing up the last day or so, she might not be able to reach you."

Tozlu nodded.

Josh handed him the phone and said, "Type the

message, but don't send it. Any monkey tricks, and you'll be the sorriest Ottoman on the planet."

Tozlu took a few minutes to type the message and handed the phone back to Josh. He had one look at it, saw it was in German, and gave it to Rex.

Rex studied it carefully and sent it.

"Tozlu, for your part, I sincerely hope she replies very soon," Josh said.

It was 8:12 a.m.

The reply came less than a minute later. Rex translated it. "No problem. I've got lots of admin work to do. See you tomorrow. Miss you very much. M."

"One more message," said Rex. "This one to your wife. Tell her the same story, and she can expect you home by tomorrow night."

Tozlu typed the message as ordered. Rex checked it, Tozlu's wife was a third-generation German-Turk who spoke very little Turkish.

A few minutes later, Tozlu's wife's confirmation message came through, and a note that she and the children were missing him.

Rex went to the kitchen and spoke to Richardson. "Martin, you need to tell the surveillance teams to keep out of sight. We've got one chance with this woman to lead us to Dragut. I have an idea about the weapons in the warehouse as well. If we mess it up, we're back to square one. The teams should be aware that the woman might have a protection detail, and so would that warehouse."

"I'll let them know to take great care."

Chapter Forty-Six

WHERE'S DRAGUT?

Vienna, Austria

Day 14

"Your friend, Ushan Ozmer, where is he?"

Tozlu held his hands up in defense. "I honestly don't know. I'm not lying. From the very beginning, it was made clear to me that I would never be allowed to know where he is and never to ask or try to find out. Over the past twenty-five years, I've seen him only once, which was, as I've told you before, about four years ago on the farm for the weekend. Over the course of that weekend, the organization's standard operating procedures were drilled into me. Compartmentalization was the keyword, everyone operated in isolation from the others and only knew what needed to be known to fulfill their duties.

"Part of the rules were that Ushan and I would never communicate in person again. All our communications were put on a password-protected thumb drive and carried between us by Martina. Nothing ever went on email or any internet application, including chat programs and such. And, of course, we never used a phone, not even the K iPhones."

"Okay, you've made your point," said Rex. "And I'm getting irritated with your attempts to evade my question. One more time, think carefully, your life depends on this one. It could be the difference between a bullet through the head, or a long and painful death over many days. Where is Dragut?"

Tozlu said, "I want to make a deal first. What's going to happen to me? I can't go back to Germany. He will find me and have me killed."

"Don't worry about going back to Germany or Dragut killing you," said Josh. "You can only die once, and we're first in the queue. The biggest problem you have right now is that we don't make deals with terrorists. You have no principles; you betrayed your friends and family and the Ottomans. You're responsible for the death and injuries of thousands, and that's just over the last two weeks. We haven't even talked about all the other atrocities you've been involved in since teaming up with Ozmert. Why would we want to make a deal with a lowlife like you?"

"Only because I might be able to help you find Ushan. I've got nothing else to offer."

"Where's Dragut?"

Tears had started to well up in Tozlu's eyes. He whispered, "I think he's somewhere in Greece. Maybe on one of the small islands or somewhere near Athens."

"What makes you think he's there?"

"According to the transactions on Martina's corporate

credit card, that's where she travels most often and spends a lot of her time."

Got a bit sloppy with security measures, Dragut, Rex thought.

The next moment a message popped up on Rex's laptop screen. It was Greg. "On it, boss. We're pulling up the credit card details right now."

"Great," Rex typed and turned to Tozlu. "How is Operation Delphi funded?"

"I don't have any insight into the organization's funding sources, but Ushan told me that weekend he had made in the order of a hundred and fifty million when he cashed in eight thousand Bitcoins."

"Enough to start a damn world war," Josh mumbled.

This was the moment Rex knew they were finally closing in on Dragut.

"What had Ozmert been doing in the twenty-odd years until you saw him again?"

Tozlu shrugged. "He was vague about it. He hinted that he'd been making an intense study of the Ottoman Empire, Islam, and Middle Eastern politics. Working on a master plan to restore the Ottoman Empire to its former glory and recruiting people to help him do it."

"How did he fund his lifestyle in the time before he sold his Bitcoins?"

"He didn't tell me, and I didn't ask."

Chapter Forty-Seven

THAT'S THE PLAN

Video conference

Day 14

Tozlu was tied up and gagged and locked up in a room without windows or furniture in the basement.

When Rex and Josh arrived in the kitchen to start the planning session, Christelle dialed in to give them an update about Brandt's progress. He was no longer under sedation, "and the first thing he wanted to know was if Dragut had been captured. I told him you're getting close. He seemed very pleased to hear that. He's still weak and, at times, a little incoherent, but the doctor said that's normal. He's making good progress."

"Thanks for the update, Christelle," said Rex. "The good news is a big relief for all of us. Please give him our best wishes. You can tell him we got Dragut's scent, and if everything works in our favor, it won't be long now."

"Will do. Thanks for your thoughts and prayers."

When Christelle was gone, they turned their attention back to Dragut.

Stevens reported that GCHQ's electronic surveillance of Tony Parker and Emily Hobson, thus far, confirmed Catia's notion that they were having an affair, but nothing more nefarious than that had been uncovered.

Thomson reported that his agents had been watching Savvas Rallotis, the Alexandroupolis crime boss, for the past few days and were able to get a good idea of his daily rituals and routines.

Rex said, "I think we can leave him out of our plans for now. We know it was Henderson who contracted him to send his goons to kill us."

Everyone agreed.

"Martina Streicher or Sarah Sulzer or whatever her name is," Rex said. "I believe she's going to lead us to Dragut. Or am I the only one thinking that?"

Thomson said, "No, you're not. We have to get into her apartment while she is out to meet with Tozlu, bug the place, put GPS trackers on her travel bags, and start following her."

"Ethan, I agree with the idea of the bugs and tracking devices, but I can't see how we can leave Tozlu out of it. If he's not at the meeting tomorrow, we're running a real risk of setting off an alarm bell for Dragut. The problem is Tozlu can't go back to Germany, they're probably waiting for him and might already have requested the Austrians' help to locate him."

"O-k-a-y, but how are you going to set that up?"

"Hang on," said Stevens. "Are you saying you're planning to let Tozlu meet with this woman?"

"Yes, that's the plan the four of us here in Vienna are

thinking could work. Digger hasn't given me his opinion yet. I suspect he will go with whatever we decide."

A protracted silence descended upon the group.

"So, you want to partner with Tozlu the terrorist to help you catch his friend, one of the worst terrorist masterminds in history?" Stevens was sarcastic.

"Precisely."

"And precisely how do you plan to do that?"

"It's going to be a red light for Martina and Dragut if Tozlu remains unreachable for another day or more. We need to keep everything as normal as possible.

"Our plan is to get Tozlu to call Martina to come to Vienna to meet with him. He's got this fantastic business opportunity, and he can't let it slip through his fingers. He wants to tell her about it and, of course, spent the night in her bed, or she in his."

"But that means you have to trust Tozlu to not give away anything?" said Richardson.

Rex shook his head. "No, I'll never trust him. But I'm willing to take the chance that he will do exactly what Josh and I are going to tell him to do."

For the next ten minutes, Rex let them debate the idea. It was not as crazy as it sounded, Josh tried to explain under many protests from Stevens, Julian, Brooke, and Thomson —everyone who had not worked with Rex and his team before.

Richardson was on the fence, but only temporarily. He still remembered very well how, on the last mission, Rex and his team smuggled a senior Chinese general out of China from right under the noses of the Chinese security services. Spencer had no issues. He told them he supported Rex's plan, and if Brandt were there, he would have given the go-ahead as well.

After a bit more back and forth, even the skeptics agreed, there were no real alternatives. They had this one opportunity and limited time to do it.

Eventually, Rex said, "Okay, Martin, the choice is ultimately yours. CRC works for you. You can end our contract, we'll step away, you can take over and do it your way, or you can look the other way and let us get on with it."

Martin thought about it for a moment, smiled, picked up his mobile phone, and turned his back to the TV camera. He held his cellphone to his ear for a long while, as if he were listening to someone, but he didn't say anything.

Everyone was waiting for him.

After more than a minute, he turned back and looked at everyone in feigned surprise. "You've been waiting for me?"

"Yes!" shouted almost everyone in chorus.

"My apologies. What's the topic under discussion now?"

Stevens grinned. "We were talking about Rex's plan with the weapons in the warehouse. Maybe it's best if he explains what he has in mind."

Rex said, "My suggestion is we don't barge into the warehouse and start arresting people and confiscating the weapons; Dragut would know about that very quickly. Rather, we should send in a team to replace the explosives with something like putty or playdough, take the firing pins out of the handguns and assault rifles, disable the detonators and put GPS tracking devices on as much of it as we can."

"Now there's a plan I can support," said Stevens with a big grin on his face.

"Same here," said Richardson. "Myles and I will work out the details and get it done."

Chapter Forty-Eight

A NEW BUSINESS OPPORTUNITY

Vienna, Austria

Day 15

One of the executive suites at the Ritz-Carlton, a five-star hotel on Schubertring, Innere Stadt, Vienna, Austria, was the meeting place.

Chuck Evans was a natural. His business card, which he gave to Ms. Streicher, proclaimed him to be Dallas Shaw, the vice president of sales and marketing of TBJ Inc, Texas Beef Jerky Incorporated. His company was the biggest jerky producer in America and had been exporting their products to Asia for many years. They recently set up a halal facility and were looking to break into the Muslim markets of Europe and the Middle East.

The company name, address, telephone numbers, and email address on the card were real. TBJ did indeed exist, Dallas Shaw was their vice president of sales and marketing, and there was a picture of a tall blond man with tortoise-shell glasses on their website which said that was Dallas Shaw. This legend was one that Evans created years ago and regularly used during covert missions, with the help of the CEO of TBJ, a patriot and former CIA analyst who had established the company when he went on early retirement.

Özdemir Tozlu was not so natural. But it was expected. After all, it couldn't have been comforting to know that his mobile phone was a listening device, and every word he said and every move he made was being recorded and streamed to an unknown location by unseen video cameras. On top of that, the lumps under his armpits, covered by duct tape, were constant reminders of how close to death he was throughout the meeting. According to the two men who had ruined his life and turned it into a nightmare the past thirty-six hours, those half-inch lumps were miniature remote-controlled bombs. One of them had the remote control in his hands. One wrong move, they told him, and he would experience a searing pain in his chest immediately before his torso and heart would be ripped to pieces. The same would happen if he tried to remove the bombs or if he strayed more than two hundred yards from the remote control.

Tozlu was not going to take any chances; he had gained more than enough experience with the two men in the past two days to believe them without any reservations. And there was the knowledge that the man known as Dallas Shaw was not a real businessman but a friend of the men holding the remote control, and he was armed.

If Tozlu was brave enough, which he was not, and examined the lumps under his arms, he would have discovered they were not bombs, only two headache capsules wrapped in plastic.

Tozlu was sweating, but fortunately not too much. He stuttered a little from time to time which was a little irritating but not overly so, and his voice sounded a little off. His explanation that he was coming down with the flu corresponded with his symptoms and seemed to waylay the concerns Martina Streicher had about her boss's well-being.

It did, however, ruin their plans about the frolic between the sheets at her hotel that night when Tozlu said that he had to return to Berlin as soon as the meeting was over as he had some pressing matters requiring his urgent attention back home.

The meeting lasted for a little over two hours. It was enough time for Evan's agents to get into Ms. Streicher's hotel room to bug it and hide a number of miniature GPS tracking devices in the seams of her luggage. It was a bit disappointing that they couldn't get their hands on her laptop and mobile phone; she took them with her to the meeting.

The meeting ended shortly before mid-day. They shook hands with Mr. Shaw and left. Outside the hotel, Tozlu apologized to Martina that he had to leave immediately and handed her a password-protected flash drive. It was a message for Ozmert; her job was to deliver it to him. Tozlu kissed her on the cheek and got into a taxi to take him to the airport. She shouldered her laptop bag and headed for a nearby café in search of lunch.

From across the globe, sighs of relief could be heard from the audience dialed into the video conference.

"Good show, I'd say. What do you think, Myles?" said Richardson.

Stevens said, "I owe you and your team an apology, Rex. That show turned me into a believer."

Rex acknowledged the compliment and said, "Declan, I think it's time for you to stock up and prepare the *TOMATS* for another voyage. Let's see where the GPS trackers take us. I'd like to have some of the crew available to help us if the situation arises."

"On it. The crew would welcome it. There's nothing exciting left for us to see or do here in Malta anymore."

Chapter Forty-Nine

LET'S NOT COUNT OUR CHICKENS

Vienna, Austria

Day 15

The taxi dropped Tozlu off four blocks further. He entered the black Mercedes SUV with tinted windows driven by Josh, with Rex in the passenger seat and Digger in the back to keep an eye on Tozlu.

Evans's agents reported an hour later that they had followed Martina. She was unaware of them. She had coffee and pastries at a café, and she had been on her phone almost the entire time.

They could not establish to whom she was talking or what was said. Nonetheless, the question was resolved soon after when she returned to her hotel. She immediately phoned Ryanair and booked the first flight out to Athens, after which she checked out of the hotel and made her way to the airport where her flight was scheduled to take off in three hours.

Rex and the team had to get everything organized and get to the airport to get on the CIA jet and to Athens before Martina's plane landed. The flight time was two hours and ten minutes. Thomson had to assign and brief agents to be at the Athens International Airport when Streicher arrived. They had to keep at a safe distance while watching her to see who she meets and where she goes.

What to do with Tozlu? They could not let him go or hand him over to the BND as yet. Evans offered to babysit him, but Richardson was worried about the international repercussions if Tozlu were found in CIA custody in a foreign country.

After a few minutes of brainstorming, Catia suggested that Yaron Aderet of the Mossad might be able to help. She called him and explained their predicament.

"No problem, Catia," Aderet said. "I'll get my agents at the safehouse to take him off your hands and keep him out of sight until you want him back."

While Catia was talking to Aderet, Richardson tasked Thomson to brief the US ambassador to Greece. Richardson said he would brief the DCIA and POTUS so that the latter could get the cooperation of the Greek PM and EYP and Hellenic Police.

Centuries of Ottoman rule over the Greeks left Greece and Turkey with tense relations, to put it mildly. Since the fall of Constantinople on Tuesday, May 29, 1452, the Greeks regarded Tuesday as an 'unlucky day' for Greeks. In 1922, Turkish troops drove Greek troops and the centuries-old Greek society, from Anatolia. During Ottoman occupation, some of the most horrific atrocities were committed by both sides.

In 1974, Turkey invaded Cyprus and established the Turkish Federative State of Cyprus, later the Turkish Republic of Northern Cyprus, unleashing an ongoing dispute about the sovereignty of several islands. Border zones between Greece and Turkey, a frontier between culture and religion, were hotbeds of conflict and confrontation. To the chagrin of Turkey, Greece was a member of the EU, and they were not.

In short, the Greeks and Turks hated each other with a passion, and there was no indication that the situation would improve anytime soon.

Richardson explained that it was highly unlikely that the Greek Prime Minister would agree to give the CIA carte blanche on Greek soil. He would more than likely insist that his security agencies take over and run the operation—he would see it as an opportunity to kick the hated Turks in the gut. The best outcome they could hope for was to negotiate with the Greeks to embed Rex's team in a Greek task force and that they would want to claim all the credit, not mentioning America's involvement.

Rex et al. didn't care one hoot about who got credit, they wanted Dragut, that was it. And that led them to another problem; if they got Dragut, they wouldn't want to leave him in the hands of the Greek authorities—at least not until he answered their questions. But they soon concluded it was POTUS's decision and his job to negotiate what would happen with Dragut.

"Let's not count our chickens before they're hatched," Rex said. "There's a lot that can still go wrong. We don't know if Streicher is going directly to Dragut; it's even possible that there's another go-between, maybe more than one. Dragut might not even be in Greece at all. Let's prepare for the worst and hope for the best."

Just then, Greg interrupted. "Boss, I think we've got something that might be useful. We saw regular monthly payments going through on Streicher's corporate credit card for parking in Athens. We took a wild guess and checked the long-term parking records at the Athens airport. She's got permanent long-term parking there. We got the car's license plate numbers and the number of the lockup garage." He smiled. "Sorry about the interruption, I thought you might want to know."

"For that kind of news, Greg, you're welcome to interrupt me at any time," Rex said. "Excellent work."

Rex turned to Ethan to ask him to send someone to put powerful GPS trackers on Martina's car. But before Rex could say anything, Ethan said, "Trackers on her car?"

"Yep."

"Already on it. One of my agents is on his way to my office."

"If everyone agrees, I'd like to send the *TOMATS* to Athens," said Rex.

Everyone agreed, and Spencer was happy to set sail for new shores.

"Martin, I think it might be a good idea if you could start pulling strings to get surveillance drones and satellite time so that we can deploy them as soon as we have an idea where Dragut is," said Rex.

Richardson nodded. "Will do."

Chapter Fifty

A BAD FEELING

Athens, Greece

Day 15

The CIA jet delivered the Daltons and Farleys to Athens one hour ahead of Martina Streicher. They were tempted to form a welcoming committee for her, but she knew what Rex, Catia, and Digger looked like and, presumably, also Josh and Marissa.

Thomson had a team of four agents in two vehicles following Streicher from the airport. The GPS tracking devices on her luggage and car were working perfectly; they were able to follow her from more than two miles away. There was no way she would know she was being followed.

Rex and team were following the procession to the west side of Athens into the Attica region toward the Megara Gulf, a bay on the Saronic Gulf. About twenty-one miles out of Athens, in the northern part of the Isthmus of

Corinth, opposite the island of Salamis, was the historic town of Megara. It was one of the four districts of Attica, embodied in the four mythic sons of King Pandion II. The town had two harbors, Pagae to the west on the Corinthian Gulf, and Nisaea to the east on the Saronic Gulf of the Aegean Sea. Megara was part of the Athens metropolitan area and had a population of about twenty-three thousand.

There was still enough daylight left for Rex and his companions to see the arid landscape, which reminded them of parts of Arizona and the Middle East.

About two miles out of Megara, Streicher turned off the main road onto a two-track dirt road and entered through rusty gates that, by the looks of them, hadn't been in operation for a very long time. She headed for a cluster of ancient, poorly maintained stone buildings surrounded by very old olive trees.

"Dragut Manor, I presume?" Josh quipped when they passed.

"I certainly hope so," said Rex.

Rex contacted Thomson's agents, thanked them, and said he and his team would take over from here. The agents returned to the city.

As promised, Richardson had done his bit and secured a HALE (high altitude, long-endurance) drone known as Orion UAS (Unmanned Aircraft System), operating out of the US Naval base at Souda Bay on the Island of Crete, a little over two hundred miles away.

The Orion was able to loiter in the air for up to five days, one hundred and twenty hours, with a payload of a thousand pounds and operated at altitudes of up to thirty thousand feet. The drone was equipped with a full-motion video electro-optic infrared sensor, communication relay equipment, ground penetrating radars, signal intelligence

(SIGINT), and wide-area airborne surveillance (WAAS) equipment. The wings of the Orion could also be mounted with munitions.

Even though they hadn't received authorization from the Greek Prime Minister to operate in their airspace, upon getting the GPS coordinates from Rex, Richardson asked the drone operators in Souda Bay to dispatch the Orion. It would take more than two hours to get into place, by which time he hoped to have the necessary approval.

Rex and company couldn't hang around the property for too long without risking detection. They drove past the turnoff, continued for a few miles, made a U-turn, and went back to the town of Megara to find a restaurant where they could have something to eat and wait for the arrival of the Orion drone.

Catia and Marissa went online in search of suitable accommodation.

And then the waiting started.

Rex and Josh were itching to go on an onsite reconnaissance mission but knew it could place the entire mission in jeopardy. Once the drone with its state-of-the-art surveillance equipment was in place, they would soon know how many people were on the farm, their locations, and a wealth of information they would be hard pushed to get if they were trying to collect it in-person.

The only thing that the drone wouldn't be able to tell them is if Dragut were there or not. Unless, of course, he would come out of the buildings, and the Orion could get a good 'look' at him.

There was nothing else to do but wait for the diplomatic process to take its course and the Orion to arrive and start streaming information—things over which they had no control.

Three hours later, the drone was in place and started broadcasting.

In the meantime, POTUS had a video meeting with the Greek Prime Minister.

Richardson was in the meeting and reported that it went more or less as expected. The Prime Minister was pleased to be informed of the operation, but he wanted Greek security forces in control of it.

Paratroopers and Marines were considered Special Forces in Greece. Their Raider Forces, officially known as the 1st Raider/Paratrooper Brigade, was a group of elite Greek light infantry and special operations forces under the command of Brigadier Michalis Zervopoulos.

The American and Greek Special Forces had been working together for decades, mostly by way of training events and the participation of Greek commandos in American military training schools. The US Navy SEALs had close relationships with the Hellenic Coast Guard's Underwater Demolition Teams, often participating in joint antipiracy and anti-drug operations in the eastern Mediterranean. The US Naval Support Activity (NSA) Souda Bay, on Crete, had often been the location of joint exercises.

The Raider Forces operated under the command of the Hellenic Army's Special Forces Command and were tasked with executing airborne operations, unconventional warfare, reconnaissance, amphibious assaults, and guerilla warfare but little in the form of hostage rescue and high-value-target raids. They had seen action during World War II, the Greek Civil War, the Turkish invasion of Cyprus, and the War on Terror in Afghanistan.

The Greeks liked to refer to them as the 'Spartans of our time.'

People often asked which Special Forces unit was the

best in the world. It was impossible to answer. There were too many factors, training, terrain, the operation, and many more. But whatever measures were used, the Greek Special Forces didn't feature in the top ten. The Greek military was ranked twenty-eighth in the world, holding a military power index rating of 0.4955 (0.0000 being perfect) with the USA rating at 0.062, Russia at 0.064, and China at 0.067. Turkey ranked at number nine, with a rating of 0.209.

Brigadier Zervopoulos was put in charge of the operation to capture Ushan Ozmert. He selected twenty of his best men from the Epsilon Raider Squadron, *E MK* - *Epsilon Mira Katadromon*.

Rex and Josh soon learned that Brigadier Zervopoulos was a bit of a bombastic character who didn't really listen to others, especially not foreigners. He immediately insisted on putting Greek manufactured military drones in the air. The HAI Pegasus deployed for the first time in 1982, was redesigned and upgraded with advanced electronics in 2005 and became known as the Pegasus II. Its technical features made it suitable for surveillance, target acquisition, and damage assessment. But it was no match for the Orion's capabilities. Even so, Brigadier Zervopoulos preferred to study the intelligence gathered by the Pegasus rather than the Orion's.

Athens, Greece

Day 16

The American Special Forces operators aboard the *TOMATS* were still twelve hours away when Zervopoulos started planning the raid. He had made it very clear that he would not be using any foreign forces for this operation.

The information gathered by the drones showed there were eight people in the target house. Some of them had been out of the buildings during the day; the face of Martina Streicher had been recognized, and so were the faces of two others. The latter was on the wanted lists of the Hellenic Police and the EYP, the Greek National Intelligence Service, for various matters related to the undermining of Greece's national security.

And that was enough for the Greek Prime Minister to authorize the launch of the operation even though they couldn't confirm Ushan Ozmert's presence.

Zervopoulos started by telling them the raid was scheduled for the next morning at 00:45. The task force consisting of four five-man teams of Raiders would fly in with four helicopters from all directions, rappel down, breach the doors and windows at the same time, and capture everyone inside.

"Short and sweet," Zervopoulos said. "Five minutes tops."

Rex and Josh were allowed to sit in on the planning but were not asked for their input until the end when the Brigadier had laid out his plan and everyone had received their orders. As if the brigadier only expected their stamp of approval.

Zervopoulos, in his battle fatigues, rank insignia, and rows of medals on his chest struck an imposing figure, but it didn't take long after he started talking for Josh to mumble, "Since light travels faster than sound, some people appear bright until you hear them speak."

Rex and Josh were not impressed. Rex tried his best to explain that they would've preferred a much more clandestine approach. "Don't give them notice, surprise them."

Zervopoulos roared with laughter. "You don't think this will surprise them?"

"No, sir, I don't. I would strongly recommend that you consider using gas to put them out before moving in."

"Our motto is Who Dares Wins."

Rex didn't bother to mention it was the motto made popular by the British SAS and also the name of a very popular Australian TV adventure game show from the late 1990s.

Rex warned them that their targets could be zealots. Without telling them all the details, he described how Destiny Parker committed suicide rather than be captured and that it might be wise to expect and plan for a fight-to-the-bitter-end scenario.

Zervopoulos laughed again. "That's, how do you Americans call it? —an oxymoron. Turks are not zealots, they're cowards. They'll be shitting themselves when my men come through the doors and windows. I doubt that any of them would have the guts to raise a weapon against my men."

Rex pointed out that they didn't know if the people were Turks or not. For all they knew they could be hired former Special Forces operators, maybe even OKK, *Özel Kuvvetler Komutanlığı*, the Turkish Special Forces.

"Our Special Forces are far superior to those Turkish rapists and baby-killers."

"What about the tunnels? They could escape through them."

"I'm well aware of the tunnels." He played the light of the laser pointer over the tunnels on the map. "They won't get there. We'll have them in hand before they can get into the tunnels."

He didn't explain how, when making such a big noise with four helicopters, which would be heard from miles away, they would not alert the occupants and give them time to ready themselves for a shootout and attempt to escape through the tunnels.

Rex, Josh, Catia, and Marissa had studied the two tunnels in detail. One entry was from one of the bedrooms and one from the family room. The two tunnels converged about ten yards beyond the walls and ran for more than two hundred yards, ten feet below ground, exiting inside the barn on the neighboring property. An indication that Dragut could get help from his neighbors, who were five in total according to the Orion's surveillance.

Mentioning this to Zervopoulos made him grin. "Do you really think the neighbors would want to get involved once they've seen how many men I have on-site?"

"I wouldn't know, but I think it's prudent to at least assign some of your men to make sure they don't get involved."

"Okay," he sighed. 'I'll assign two men to it." He was getting irritated.

Digger had been quiet all the time, but Rex could see he didn't take much of a liking in the pompous brigadier.

Eventually, Rex and Josh gave up trying to talk sense into the man's head.

Rex whispered sideways to Josh, "I've got a bad feeling about this one."

"Uh-huh, my bet is there's going to be a shootout at the O.K. Corral, and many of these starry-eyed youngsters are going to get dead or wounded."

Josh had no idea how prophetic his words would turn out to be. But even if he did, there was not much he or Rex could do to change Zervopoulos's mind. They could make a scene of it, try and bring POTUS and other heavyweights into the argument, but in the end, it would only muddy the diplomatic waters and even get them kicked out of it altogether.

They got Richardson and Stevens on the video after the planning session and told them what they thought of the operation's chances of success. Richardson said he would inform the DCIA and POTUS but said there was not much they could do without causing a diplomatic ruckus.

"And I don't think it's a good idea to withdraw from the operation and let them do whatever they want," said Richardson.

"No, absolutely not," said Rex. "We'll be there with them. But we were told we have observer status only and told in no uncertain terms to keep out of their way. Exactly what Josh and I intend to do."

Richardson nodded slowly. "Fools rush in where angels fear to tread."

Chapter Fifty-One

CONTACT WITH THE ENEMY

Megara, Greece

Day 17

Catia and Marissa were not invited to observe the raid in person. They were not happy, but there was nothing they could do about it. It was a consolation to know they would be in their hotel room dialed into a video conference with the rest. Greg had tapped into the feed from the Orion, which would give them a good view of what was happening on the ground. They would also be in contact with Rex and Josh through the comms system of the Orion to provide them with information as the Orion 'saw' it.

The *TOMATS* anchored at Athens Marina at a quarter past midnight.

At 00:45 a.m., the four choppers took off from KEED, the Special Forces Training Center on the outskirts of Megara, less than nine miles from their target.

Rex had Digger fitted out with his operational harness, which was equipped with a night vision video camera mounted between his shoulder blades Everything Digger would see would also be visible to Rex. Mini earphones were fitted in Digger's ears, completely invisible, and a mini microphone, not much bigger than a pinhead, was fitted on the harness between his front legs. All of it was wirelessly connected to an iPad mini, which Rex had strapped to his left forearm.

He and Josh were wearing black cargo pants, tactical vests, body armor, and night vision goggles but were not allowed to carry weapons, not even knives.

They were hoping that helicopters flying around the area that time of night was a common occurrence to the residents of the areas but didn't really believe it.

A few minutes later, the four choppers arrived on site, one at each corner of the house. Rex and Josh thought they landed too far away, more than a hundred yards for the team to run to get to the house. Critical seconds would be ticking away while they covered the distance; precious time they could have had to get inside the house.

The choppers hovered about twenty feet off the ground, and the operators fast-roped out. Rex, with Digger strapped to a harness on his back, and Josh were last to get out of their chopper. Two men scurried to the barn of the neighbors while four two-men teams rushed the front and back doors and two side windows.

Rex, Digger, and Josh were in the chopper coming in closest to the neighbor's barn. Catia told them the eight in the house were still there, so were the five in the neighbors' house.

The four teams smashed the doors and windows, hurled flashbangs in, blocked their eyes and ears from the blinding flashes and earsplitting explosions, waited four seconds, and rushed in, the remaining ten formed a security perimeter around the house.

Rex and Josh realized the men were too close to the house and yelled at them to move further away and take cover. Four of them listened and did it, the others ignored them and sidled up to the outer walls of the house.

Seconds later, the Raiders were in a firefight inside the house, and the traffic on the two-way radios sounded like the confusion at the Biblical Tower of Babble. All of it in Greek of which Rex and Josh understood nothing, although it was clear things were not going as planned.

Not surprising. Battle plans seldom survived contact with the enemy.

Rex and Josh had taken cover behind a big olive tree, about twenty yards from the back of the house and about the same distance from the neighbor's barn. Digger was getting impatient; he probably couldn't understand why he and his pack were not getting involved. The look on his face told Rex he might as well have said, "So why the hell did you bother to kit me up then?"

The next moment Digger spun around and looked at the barn. He started growling.

Rex and Josh looked at each other.

"Let's have a look," Rex said.

"Might as well. We've got nothing better to do," said Josh.

Rex clicked the Bluetooth earpiece and asked Catia for an update on what was going on at the barn and neighbors' house.

"Two of the five moved to the barn a minute or so ago. At the moment, the thermal images show there are four bodies inside the barn. Two standing and two lying on the ground."

Rex pointed to the barn and said to Digger, "Scout and hide." He opened the flap on his forearm revealing the iPad screen and tracked Digger.

Digger got to the barn, stayed in the shadows, and remained quiet. He sneaked around the corner; the double doors were open. He looked inside, and Rex said, "Stop. Keep still."

Digger went down on his belly and remained still, the night vision camera on his back pointing into the barn. Within seconds Rex saw two men with silenced Glock 19 pistols in their hands, standing over the bodies of two unmoving Raiders.

Rex said, "Digger stay and hide." He did so by crawling under the tractor inside and kept the camera on his back facing the two men.

Rex and Josh switched off the noisy radios. The gunfire and commotion in the house helped to mute the sounds of their approach to the barn, but they remained careful and approached slowly. Unarmed. Damn.

The sounds of the gun battle were still coming loudly from the house, though it was rapidly becoming more sporadic—the fight was about to end. Who was still standing would have been anyone's guess.

Rex and Josh had two threats to deal with: the armed men inside the barn and the three remaining occupants in the neighbor's house. There were two ways into the barn, through the double door facing the house or through the side door, hidden from the neighbor's house. The side door was open. They looked around, desperately trying to locate anything that could be used as weapons. Rex found a pickaxe handle, and Josh settled for a crowbar. Now they were armed but still thinking about how they would get in without being noticed.

Rex clicked the on-off switch on his earpiece three times.

Catia reported that the situation was unchanged, two in the barn, three in the neighbor's house. He checked the screen on his arm again. Digger's camera showed the men inside had their backs turned to the side door, focusing on the stairwell exit of the tunnel, as if expecting someone to come through it momentarily.

Rex and Josh were getting ready to sneak in through the side door when a man's upper body emerged from the opening in the floor. He was covered in a monk's robe and had a backpack on his back.

And then things took a dramatic turn.

The two men grabbed the man by the arms and pulled him to his feet, one of them raised his gun and shot the newcomer at point-blank range in the side of the head. The man fell sideways. One of the men removed the backpack, the other closed the lid to the tunnel opening and secured the bolt lock. They turned toward the double door and hadn't taken three steps when everything went deathly quiet for a nanosecond before they were thrown off their feet by the shockwave of a gigantic explosion coming from the house under attack. The barn shuddered, windows got blown out, and roof tiles got ripped off. It was a miracle the entire barn had not collapsed or blown away.

Rex's first thought was an airstrike.

The men inside the barn were on their backs, hands over their ears and screaming.

The ramshackle barn had been enough protection for Rex and Josh to still be on their feet and able to act. This was their one and only opportunity to take the two men down. They rushed in. Rex got to his target first and hit him over the head from behind. The man went limp. Josh got to his target at almost the same time and hit him in the back of the neck. The man let out a soft groan and went quiet, unmoving.

In silence, working quickly, they relieved the men of their guns and knives and took the backpack.

Rex called Digger and pointed to the double door. "Watch. Hide." Underneath the tractor, Digger turned around so that the camera on his back pointed to the neighbor's house. Rex studied the feed coming from Digger's camera while Josh ziptied the men's hands and feet and gagged them with duct tape.

"What was that explosion?" Rex asked Catia.

"A bomb in the house," said Catia. "The entire building has been turned into rubble. At the moment, it's impossible to distinguish between the thermal images of humans and things that have caught fire. But one thing is certain, the fight is over."

Rex couldn't help but remember the ambush in Afghanistan in 2014 when he and his men entered a house that was rigged with explosives. He and Digger were the only survivors.

Rex said, "In the barn, we have three dead and two unconscious and tied up. But before we do anything else, we need to take care of the three neighbors. Are they still in the house?"

"Only one inside now, in what I think is the kitchen. There's one under the tree at the front door and one on the verandah on the side of the house. The two outside are armed."

Rex looked at Josh and said, "Looks like it's you and me, buddy. No help from the Raiders."

"Story of our lives," replied Josh while checking his Glock. "Ready when you are."

From the door of the barn to the neighbors' house was about thirty yards, but there was no cover. The house was dark.

"We need to create some kind of distraction," said Josh.

Rex nodded.

The effective range of a 9mm round was about two thousand yards, but that only meant that if one got hit by a 9mm bullet within that range, it would kill them. Accuracy was a different story altogether. Hitting a target with a pistol at any distance beyond thirty yards required steady hands and outstanding marksmanship. Rex and Josh were trained and regularly practiced at distances of up to sixty yards, but at those distances, they were deemed to be crack shots if they could hit a human-size target anywhere in the body.

Rex said, "We crawl to the double door, see if we can spot the two outside, and take them out with the Glocks. It's about thirty yards to the house. We probably won't get kill-shots, but a hit anywhere on the body would be enough distraction."

Josh grinned. "So, we're going to shoot and call whatever we hit the target?"

"Exactly."

"Let's do it," said Josh.

They leopard-crawled to the double door, donned their night vision goggles, and studied the house. Within seconds they had eyes on the targets.

"I'll take the one at the front door," said Rex. "On the count of three."

Josh started counting softly into the lip mic. "One Mississippi, two Mississippi, three Mississippi."

The two silenced shots sounded like one. Rex's target

took the round in the chest and dropped to the ground, screaming. Josh's target also took it to the chest, but the round went through his heart. He was dead by the time his body reached the ground.

"Come Digger," Rex said. They were on their feet running at full speed toward the house in a zigzag pattern. There was no return fire. Rex and Digger headed for his target under the tree at the front door. Digger arrived first and grabbed the man by the back of the neck but didn't sink his teeth into him. Rex arrived and checked the man. He was alive but unconscious and bleeding profusely. He would be dead in minutes. He took the man's Glock 19.

Josh was about to kick the backdoor in when a woman started screaming hysterically inside. He turned and ran to the kitchen window and saw a woman, unarmed, sitting on a chair and screaming in the dark.

Rex and Digger went through the side door leading into the kitchen while Josh kept his gun trained on the screaming woman through the window. Rex entered the kitchen, very cautiously, the woman could have a weapon or could be rigged with explosives. He flicked the switch on his flashlight in his left hand and kept his gun pointed at her. In English, he told her to get to her feet and raise her arms. Whether she understood, he didn't know, but she did as she was ordered.

Her hands were empty. She had no explosives strapped to her body, and she was shaking violently. Mumbling incoherently.

Rex saw a cellphone on the floor, or rather, pieces of a cellphone.

Josh moved quickly, grabbed her hands, and ziptied them behind her back, then gagged her with duct tape, pushed her to the floor, and ziptied her feet.

Rex reported to Catia that the neighbor's house was secured. Two dead and one captured.

When Josh got back to his feet, Rex said, "Let's go back to the barn and see what we can make out of what happened there."

In the distance, the thumping sound of approaching helicopters could be heard.

Chapter Fifty-Two

THE MOST IMPORTANT BACKPACK

Megara, Greece

Day 17

While Rex and Josh walked back to the barn, Rex switched the two-way radio on and heard that chaos was reigning supreme on the airwaves. Brigadier Zervopoulos's voice was booming over everyone else's. The conversations, or rather, screaming, were all in Greek. Rex was waiting for a lull so he could cut in and make a report. It took a while before he managed to get Zervopoulos's attention and give him a sitrep (situation report) about the barn and the neighbor's house.

By now, they were back in the barn. Josh checked the two captives; they were still unconscious. Rex and Digger went to the body of the man who came through the tunnel. Rex removed the hood and shined a light on the face.

"Damn you!" Rex shouted.

"What's wrong?" Josh asked.

"This is Dragut."

Of all the possible scenarios Rex had thought of the past few weeks when he tried to envisage what would happen when he finally caught up with this man, this scenario never entered his mind. It was an anticlimax.

He shook his head in frustration and kicked Dragut in the side but got no response. More frustration. He shook his head slowly while getting control of his emotions.

Josh was staring at Rex and then at the body on the floor in silence. Then he said, "What the hell? How... I mean why..."

Rex said, "Here's what I think. Obviously, the house had been rigged with explosives. I guess it was one of the safety measures set up a long time ago for a situation like this. So were the construction of these tunnels. In the event of an attack on the house, they would escape through the tunnels, get out here and detonate the explosives, probably by a delayed trigger mechanism or something to that effect."

"Okay, but why did the men who were there to protect him and help him escape shoot him?" Asked Josh.

"Maybe *that* was their job, not to protect Dragut but to make sure all evidence was destroyed in case this site was compromised."

"The woman in the house... she set off the bombs with that cellphone."

"You're right, I think."

Rex picked up Dragut's backpack; it was surprisingly heavy. He checked it very carefully for wires and explosives, had Digger sniff it. And when he was sure there was no bomb inside, he opened it and looked inside. There was a laptop, stacks of thumb drives, and six external hard drives.

Rex closed the bag and shouldered it as they walked

away from the barn to the main house. The four helicopters that dropped them off earlier were now sitting on the ground in the open spaces around the house, and Brigadier Zervopoulos was roaring orders to everyone in sight.

It would take hours and an army of rescuers to go through the ruins of the house and retrieve the bodies of the dead and wounded and learn that nine Raiders had lost their lives: seven inside the house and two in the barn. The eighth Raider in the house only lived for an hour after he was pulled out of the rubble. Of the remaining ten Raiders, six were next to the house when the bombs went off: four of them were in critical condition, the remaining two had broken bones, damaged eardrums, internal bleeding, and severe concussions. The four who had heeded Rex's and Josh's advice to move further away from the house were in slightly better shape, they had lost their hearing and were totally disorientated.

Eight more bodies belonged to the occupants of the house, among them Martina Streicher, aka Sarah Sulzer, and Ushan Ozmert, aka Dragut. The remaining six would later be identified as members of the Greek mafia. The four men from the neighbor's house were former OKK, Turkish Special Forces. Under a bit of questioning, the woman admitted that she was a former employee of MİT, *Millî İstihbarat Teşkilatı*, the Turkish National Intelligence Organization. And she told them she was responsible for setting off the bombs remotely with her cellphone. Dragut, and for that matter, no one in the house, ever knew that the house was one big bomb waiting to explode.

Zervopoulos shot a fleeting glance at Rex, Digger, and Josh when they arrived but turned away immediately and kept on shouting orders. He clearly had no interest in talking to them. In fact, he avoided them like the plague.

Not surprising. He knew this disaster was his making. And was probably not in the mood to admit it to anyone, least of all the men who warned him about his lack of proper planning. In the post-mission review, his surviving men were going to rip him apart. Undoubtedly, he was thinking about early retirement, with or without a pension—most likely without.

Rex's satphone rang. It was Martin Richardson.

"What a mess," Richardson started. "But you warned them, and they ignored you."

Rex said, "A mess indeed, and Dragut is dead." Rex told him what had happened and his theory about why Dragut was killed. Then he told Richardson about the backpack.

Richardson went quiet for a beat and said, "Rex, that's possibly the most important backpack in history. And after the balls-up, they've made..."

"Don't worry, we will get it out."

Rex remained in contact with Catia and waited for the place to get really crowded. When there were almost fifty people and what seemed like the same number of vehicles with flashing lights, ambulances, police vehicles, and rescue unit vehicles, he told Catia it was time to make the move.

She and Marissa were in the rented Mercedes SUV parked at the entrance to the farm about a hundred yards away. Rex and Digger stayed behind at the main scene while Josh walked casually over to the SUV and handed the backpack over to Catia and Marissa, who left immediately. Within twenty minutes, Ethan Thomson took delivery of the bag at their hotel in Megara.

Rex phoned Richardson and told him the backpack was secured. "We'd appreciate it if you could help us get out of here as quickly as possible. We can't assume that Dragut and his President buddy won't have fail-safe measures in place."

Richardson said, "Leave it to me, I'll see if I can pull a few strings. I'll let them know you and Josh will make yourselves available whenever they want you."

"Thanks, Martin. I think it will take a little while before they get to the mission retrospective and lessons learned. But, in my unsolicited opinion, the most important lesson they should've learned must be to get rid of that bonehead Zervopoulos."

Eighteen hours after the disastrous raid to capture Dragut, after securing Richardson's assurances that they would make themselves available for questioning and testimony when called upon to do so, Rex and Josh were free to leave Greece.

Chapter Fifty-Three

A PROLIFIC WRITER

Video conference

Day 18

Dragut's backpack had been rushed to one of the CIA jets in Athens and flown directly to CIA headquarters in Langley in a nonstop twelve-hour flight across the Atlantic. Thirteen and a half hours after the raid in Greece, analysts started poring over the treasure trove of information.

Catia and Marissa checked out of their hotel that morning, returned the rental vehicle, and took a taxi to the *TOMATS* in Athens Marina.

Rex, Digger, and Josh, bone-tired and famished, arrived on the *TOMATS* after 9:00 p.m. They took showers, changed clothes, had something to eat, fed Digger, and went to the comms room. Catia, Digger, Marissa, and Spencer, as well as Thomson, who had joined them on the *TOMATS*, were present for the video conference with Richardson, Stevens, and McArdle.

Digger got his kong filled to the brim with peanut butter, retreated to his favorite spot in the corner, and went to work on the delicacy with gusto.

Richardson started. "We are extremely fortunate, Ushan Ozmert was a prolific writer. In his own words, 'geniuses write things down.' He kept a diary his entire life, from the age of about fourteen until yesterday. The last entry was made a few hours before he entered the tunnel to escape. The diary, strange enough, was not encrypted and was kept on one of the external hard drives. It's going to take the analysts a few days, maybe a week, to extract all the information from the laptop and remaining hard drives. But here's what we have so far."

As they listened to Richardson and looked at the documents on-screen. Slowly but surely, they all came to a conclusion; over the years, hatred had turned Ushan Ozmert into a person with a personality disorder manifesting itself in extreme antisocial attitudes and behavior and a lack of conscience.

"He was a certifiably insane sociopath," said Richardson. "Geniuses can often be neurotic."

It was clear that Ushan Ozmert's life changed after he met Destiny Parker. He was bedeviled by her, although he earnestly believed it was love. It was apparent, she controlled him and shaped his thoughts. It was weird and difficult to understand how such an intelligent man could be so hypnotized by a woman who was not nearly as smart as he was. Nevertheless, the two of them had laid their plans for the future since university days.

"Did he say anything about turning Dimitris Rossas, the

guy who raped his sister and insulted them, into a cement statue?" Spencer asked.

"Oh yes, he spent quite a few pages on that one. And his friend, Özdemir Tozlu, was indeed the one who helped him. They drugged the man, cut off his privates, and then drowned him in the concrete."

"Why didn't he take up that posh job in Switzerland?" Thomson asked.

"According to his diary," said Richardson, "two days after his arrival in Geneva, a day before he was supposed to start his job at Roche, he got run over by a car driven by a Roman Catholic priest. He sustained no serious physical injuries, but it definitely damaged his psyche. In his words, 'It was a message from Allah that I should not mingle with, nor work for the infidels. It is Allah's will that, like my ancestor, Turgut Reis, Dragut, my sole purpose in life is to restore and serve the Ottoman Empire and nothing else.'"

There was quite a lot of information about his and Destiny's activities since they had decided to abandon home and hearth and set out on their personal crusade. For twenty-five years, they lived in Turkey, countries across Europe, Asia, and South America, even in Canada and the US. They studied, schemed, prepared, and recruited men and women for the day the Ottoman Empire would rise up like the mythical Phoenix from the ashes.

"Did Ozmert and the Turkish President ever meet?" Thomson asked.

Richardson nodded. "Yes, they did. One of Destiny's conquests, a professor of international politics at the Istanbul University, is a school friend of the Turkish President. He introduced them to each other in 1995. That was before the president entered politics. According to Ozmert, he and the future president got on like a house of fire. It was during that time that the foundations of the Delphi Group were laid. Ozmert and the President met at least once a year, in secret, to discuss strategy and progress."

"What about Almasi?" Rex asked.

Richardson said, "As Josh suspected, he and Destiny Parker had a fling during their university days. That was until Ozmert appeared on the scene. Ozmert, it seems, was extremely jealous of Almasi, even though Almasi and Parker had no contact anymore, at least not what Ozmert knew of. Even so, probably under Parker's influence, Almasi was recruited for the cause about five years ago.

"But Ozmert didn't trust him. He had Almasi's phone tapped, and his computer, and his apartments, and then he got the hint from Joanne Sanders that Almasi had a meeting with a CIA undercover agent in Rome. Then, a day or so later, he got the message from her about Reece Cole's trip to Rhodes Island, and, of course, when he discovered Almasi had booked a trip to the same place, he knew Almasi was about to betray the Delphi Group to the CIA.

"He didn't give any specifics, but he must have somehow convinced Destiny to kill Almasi and Cole and get the flash drive. He wanted to watch the executions. He thought the Palace of the Grandmaster, the former headquarters of the Ottoman Empire on Rhodes Island, to be a poetic location for the killings. The man was quixotic about anything related to the Ottomans.

"He and Martina Streicher, her real name was indeed Sarah Sulzer, took photos of you, Catia, and Digger that day. And since that day, Ozmert had an overpowering obsession with killing all three of you. Destiny Parker's death drove him to the edge of total insanity. There are pages and pages filled with incoherent odium about the three of you. The failed attempts to kill you in your hotel room on the island and Alexandroupolis only drove him further down the path of madness.

"He knew we were closing in rapidly on him. But it seems he was so preoccupied with hatred and paralyzed by it, he couldn't think straight anymore. And, of course, Destiny wasn't there to set him straight: He mentioned a few times that it was probably time to pack up and find a new place to live, but fortunately for us, he didn't."

"What about Tony Parker?" Stevens asked.

"Another bizarre story," said Richardson. "Apparently, Tony and Emily were on a secret dirty weekend on the French Riviera, which turned out to be not so secret because his sister had bugged their hotel room and video-taped them in flagrante. That was about fifteen years ago. Tony had begged her to keep it quiet, she agreed, but it cost him. He had to bankroll their bohemian lifestyle and supplied the money to buy the property in Megara, where she and Ozmert had been living for the past ten years under the assumed name of Jensen Davies, a crippled and retired businessman from London, and his wife, Cathy. Tony Parker, in other words, knew full well Ozmert and Destiny were alive and living together. Tony had regular contact with Destiny, but Tony didn't know what she and Ozmert were up to. At least that's what the diary says. There is no indication that Emily knew anything about all of this."

Stevens said with a big smile, "But don't forget my newfound friend Digger over there in the corner. He knew about Tony Parker's lies all along."

Digger was too busy with the kong to acknowledge the compliment.

"So, the story Tozlu told Rex and Josh about Ozmert making a ton of money from the sale of Bitcoins seems to be a lie from one or the other?" Chris McArdle asked.

"So far, we haven't found anything to prove it either way," said Richardson. "But keep in mind we've only scratched the surface. We haven't gotten to the laptop or remaining hard drives yet. I suspect we'll get insight into their financial matters when we get into those devices."

Richardson continued and told them about the people who Ozmert and Parker had recruited to work for them over the years, including Almasi and Tozlu. The diary revealed the names of no less than ten prominent academics, politicians, business people, and others in Turkey and Europe who were part of the Delphi Group's brain trust.

The targets which Ozmert still had in mind were also disclosed. The most spine-chilling, the grand finale, was the attack he had planned on the Vatican. No date was set, the strategy was to build up support and sympathy across Europe for the idea of the new Ottoman Empire and then use the Vatican attack as the final motivator. The plan was to use drones loaded with anthrax to dive into Saint Peter's square on a Wednesday when up to 80,000 people usually gathered in the square for the weekly Papal Audience.

Richardson told them that the shipment of weapons and explosives earmarked for the attack in Brussels had been duly tampered with and bugged. Europol had been following the shipment, and arrests were in the offing.

At the three-hour mark, Rex and Josh put their hands up in surrender. They could barely keep their eyes open, and no amount of coffee could keep them awake anymore.

Richardson adjourned the meeting to the next morning after breakfast.

Within days the CIA analysts and four MI6 analysts who had joined the Cousins in Langley had gathered enough dooming information for POTUS and the President of the EU to confront the Turkish President.

But to call it a hairy situation would have been a gross understatement. Turkey's, or rather their president's dream to establish a new Ottoman Empire, was in tatters, to be sure. And the president, no doubt, knew he was going to be called to account. The heads of state who were kept in the loop were not inclined to let the Turkish President and cronies get away with it. But Turkey was an important NATO member, a bulwark against Islamic extremists. The second-largest military power in NATO. The EU and the US would not go to war against them. Yet, the President knew his hourglass had run empty. Western Europe and the United States and NATO would want to keep Turkey in place but under different leadership.

Two weeks after the attack on Ozmert's compound outside Megara in Greece, the President of Turkey suffered a massive stroke. He was incapable of continuing his duties. Two days later, his entire government was ousted in a coup d'état led by the secret service. Within six weeks, democratic elections were held and won in a landslide by the opposition party who had been campaigning for the return to the policies of the famous Kemal Atatürk, the founding father of the Republic of Turkey.

Rex and the team followed the news, and they received bits of insider information. They could only shake their heads; the art of politics would remain a mystery to them. They couldn't help but agree with Sir Ernest John Pickstone Benn, who said, "Politics is the art of looking for trouble, finding it whether it exists or not, diagnosing it incorrectly, and applying the wrong remedies."

Epilogue

The Ranch, CRC Headquarters, Arizona

Fourteen days after his brain surgery, Brandt was discharged from the hospital in Phoenix and flown back to The Ranch, CRC's headquarters.

When he and Christelle arrived back on the ranch, Rex, Catia, Digger, Josh, Marissa, and Declan Spencer were there to surprise and welcome him back. Under many protests telling everyone that he was fit enough to walk from the car to the house, Christelle all but shoved him down into the wheelchair and pushed him into the house, straight to his bedroom, and put him into his bed. "Doctors orders," she explained to the visitors who were having a hard time not laughing at the sight of the fearsome John Brandt like putty in the hands of Madame Christelle Proll.

In John's spacious bedroom, they soon found places to sit around his bed, and then they started talking. Christelle told them they had an hour before John would have to take his medication and get more rest.

Catia got up, asked to be excused, and called Digger to follow her. A few minutes later, Digger walked back into the room with one end of a leash in his mouth. On the other end was a nine-week-old, short-haired, brindle-colored Dutch Shepherd pup.

Catia pointed to John in his bed. Digger walked to John and dropped the leash in his hand.

John's jaw dropped. Everyone had gone quiet.

"Cupcake," said Catia with a big smile. "Your first grandchild." She stooped, picked Cupcake up, and put her down next to John on the bed.

Christelle wiped a tear from her eye.

It was love at first sight for John, Christelle, and Cupcake. And to demonstrate how much she liked the new members of her pack, the first chance Cupcake got, she went straight for John's leather slippers underneath the bed.

Christelle was enamored by the little bundle of playfulness and absolutely loved the name Cupcake. John had no issues with the name either, or so he told Christelle.

Not long after, the conversation drifted to the wedding. Christelle told them that they had decided on a date and they wanted to get married on the *TOMATS* but hadn't yet decided in which harbor they would like to tie the knot. John said that he thought Vietnam to be a potential venue. It was an exotic country and a former French colony.

Christelle immediately liked the idea.

Fact and Fiction

To the best of my knowledge, Crisis Response Consultancy, CRC, does not exist, neither do they have headquarters on a ranch in Arizona or anywhere else.

All the characters in the story come from my imagination. As I have said in the foreword, any likeness to actual people, alive or dead, businesses, companies, events, or places is entirely coincidental.

There are quite a few hotels and guesthouses in Lindos harbor on Rhodes Island, Greece, but none of them have ever been visited by the Dalton family.

The Palace of the Grandmaster on the island is real, and I have tried my best to reflect the history of it as accurately as possible. I do, however, apologize to the management for letting my fictitious characters create so much mayhem in such a historical place.

The Delphi Technique, from which the title of this book is derived, is indeed a problem-solving technique, as described in Chapter 10.

The Grand Hotel Egnatia and the seafood restaurant

Elies & Dafnes in Alexandroupolis, Greece, are real but, as far as I could establish, have never been visited by either the Dalton or Farley families.

The same goes for the Park Plaza Riverbank Hotel and The Black Dog pub in London. The establishments are real, but one would search the visitors' registers in vain for evidence that the Daltons and Farleys had set foot in them.

The BND Headquarters building in Chausseestrasse in the Mitte district in the center of Berlin is real. But as far I know, they never had a vice president by the name of Tilmann Wieser or a senior analyst by the name of Andrea Degen.

The Turkish Quarters in Kreutzberg, Berlin, Adalbert-strasse, and the popular Turkish market on Maybachufer-strasse are all real. But, thank God, the bomb explosions that happened there only happened within the pages of this book and my imagination. The same goes for the atrocities in The Netherlands and Paris, France.

Visitors to Vienna, Austria, would be able to find Phil-harmoniker-Strasse in the city center easily, but they would search in vain for the Hotel Kurt von Francois.

Megara, the town in Greece where the final chapters of this book played out, is real, but, to the best of my knowl-edge, Ushan Ozmert never lived there.

I did my best to be factually correct about the history of Turgut Reis, nickname, Dragut, and the Ottoman Empire.

In recent years, there have been widespread reporting in the media about Turkey's expansionist policies embedded in their concept of Neo Ottomanism. Much speculation exists that it's nothing but a precursor to the demand for the creation of a new Ottoman Empire. However, I have to confess, I gave my imagination free rein about the topic.

Next in the Rex Dalton K9 Thrillers Series

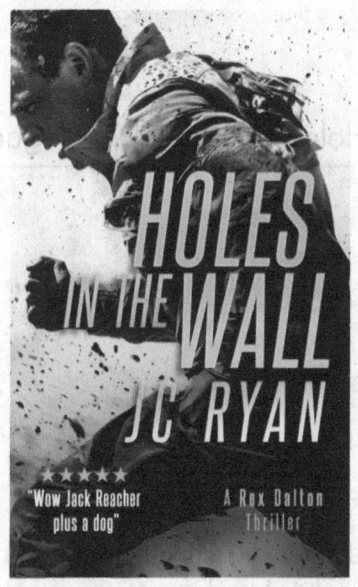

vinci-books.com/holes-in-the-wall

A petty theft. A world on the brink of war. Rex Dalton's most thrilling adventure yet.

When an office cleaner's petty theft in Beijing sets off a chain of events that threatens global stability, Rex Dalton finds himself in a race against time. As a CIA operative is murdered and Rex's friends are abducted, he must unravel a sinister conspiracy that reaches the highest levels of power.

Turn the page for a free preview…

Holes In The Wall: Prologue

Beijing, China

Present time

Every weeknight at 10:00 p.m., the buzzer on the door from the rear alley sounded, and one of the guards would let the cleaner in. They called her *Lǎo fù rén*; it meant old woman. Her real name was Sun Jia. She wasn't old; she was in her early fifties, 54 to be exact. But the privations of life had manifested in her features: dull eyes, deep lines on her face, hunching shoulders, and silver-gray hair. When she laughed, which was not often, gaps could be seen where teeth used to be when she was younger. In China, dental problems were considered a minor health concern, and dental care education all but non-existent.

Pushing a trolley with cloths, bottles with liquid cleaner, a bucket, dusters, brooms, and a vacuum cleaner, she reached the office of General Lang Jianhong, Commander of the People's Liberation Army (PLA) Ground Force. His was one of seven offices she cleaned every weeknight. General Lang's office was the most prestigious of them all; that's why she always started with his.

She had no husband; he left her thirty-four years ago when she told him she was pregnant. Her son worked for the government—something to do with computers. She didn't understand anything about computers, but Sun Yan was the pride of her life. He was married and had one child, a four-year-old girl, Lei, Jia's only grandchild, and the delight of her life. Once a month, on a Sunday morning early, she would make the one-hour train ride to visit her family and spend the day with them. On the other Sundays, she attended church in the morning.

She had always taken pride in her proletarian job, which was the best she could get with her basic education. Serving one of the top generals in the PLA and his staff, even if it was only to clean their offices five times a week, late at night when they'd all gone home, was an honor not bestowed on many.

That was until she met General Lang, once, about seven months ago, when he came into the office late one night to get some documents from his wall safe. He was extremely rude to her, ordering her to wait outside with a barrage of invectives. And when he came out of the office, he told her to spray air freshener in there when she was done to get rid of her disgusting body odor lingering inside.

His words were humiliating, degrading. Jia was dirt poor and uneducated, but she had dignity. She never neglected personal hygiene. Her mother would not have used the words 'cleanliness is next to godliness', but she definitely understood the principle and taught it to Jia from an early age.

That was the day when Jia's respect for the revered general and the joy of her job took a nosedive. But, she didn't have another job to go to. She needed the money; the little financial support her son could afford to give her was not enough to keep body and soul together if she didn't earn an income of her own. Even then, she had barely enough.

Though the joy of her job was gone, there was one thing she still relished: sitting in General Lang's luscious leather swivel chair behind his desk every night and eating one candy from the big hand-painted ceramic bowl sitting on top of the general's impossibly large desk. She knew what she was doing was not only a sin; she was also living dangerously—the general could have counted the candy. But this was her payback for his incivility.

She always took two candies; one she ate, and one she kept for her granddaughter. Tonight, she studied the variety of candy bars and noticed one she had never seen before. It was red, rectangular, about half an inch wide by two inches long, and a quarter of an inch thick. She took it out of the bowl. It had no wrapping. It felt like plastic. She turned it around carefully; she had never seen any candy like that. She licked it—no sweet taste. *Maybe Lei would like it.*

She put it in the top pocket of her overall jacket and retrieved her favorite, a *pinyin*, white rabbit, milk candy wrapped in printed waxed paper. She removed the wrapper and put it in the same pocket as the plastic candy. She put the *pinyin* in her mouth, leaned back in the chair, closed her eyes, and allowed the sweet sensation to fill her mouth and thoughts.

Manhattan, New York, USA

Present time

Josh and Marissa Farley arrived in New York shortly after midday in their rental car. They had a dinner date with Marissa's best friend from university and her husband that night. The next day they'd visit the Statue of Liberty and a few other sites around the city, and on Sunday morning, they would be off to Martha's Vineyard, Massachusetts, for seven days. They'd never been to Martha's Vineyard and wanted to see for themselves what all the fuss was about.

The Farleys had reservations at the four-star One Tree Hill hotel in Manhattan, less than half a mile from Wall Street. They checked in, dropped their luggage in their room, and went out for lunch. Afterward, they returned to the hotel and had a nap, then showered and got ready to meet Marissa's friend and her husband for dinner at their home on Long Island.

Josh fastened his seatbelt, looked at Marissa to see if she was ready, and turned the key in the ignition. His head started spinning. He looked at Marissa; her mouth was open as if she was taking a deep breath. Her image blurred, and then, darkness.

Unknown location

Present time

The pounding headache was the first sign that he was alive. Next was the thundering disconsonant noises filling his ears and then the filthy smell that filled his nostrils, roiling his stomach.

Josh remained still and tried to reconstruct, but all he remembered was starting the car, feeling dizzy, seeing Marissa gasping for air, and then, darkness. He was on a bed, his hands and feet tied to the frame. He was completely naked. His mouth was covered with duct tape, his head covered in a hood—the source of the nauseating odor threatening to rid his stomach of his lunch. *They must have dipped the hood in a cesspool.*

Over the hood was a set of earphones strapped tightly over his ears blasting the sounds of fire alarms, police sirens, breaking glass, crying babies, and screaming people into his brain. With no amount of shaking and wiggling of his head, was he able to get rid of the earphones pumping out the cacophonous sounds.

He pulled on the restraints holding his arms and legs down, but they wouldn't budge.

"Marissa!"

No answer.

He had no idea where he was or what time it was. What he did know was that he and Marissa had been abducted. And both of them were going to die—after they'd been tortured for information. Who their abductors were, what information they wanted, he didn't know, not yet. For now, the abductors were softening him up with the age-old